The A MISH
CANDY
MAKER

a novel by
LAURA V. HILTON

The *AMISH* *CANDY MAKER*

Love Is Better with Chocolate
The Amish of Mackinac County

WHITAKER
HOUSE

All Scripture quotations are taken from the *New King James Version*, © 1979, 1980, 1982, 1984 by Thomas Nelson, Inc. Used by permission. All rights reserved.

THE AMISH CANDYMAKER

Laura V. Hilton
http://lighthouse-academy.blogspot.com

ISBN: 978-1-64123-119-0
eBook ISBN: 978-1-64123-120-6
Printed in the United States of America
© 2019 by Laura V. Hilton

Whitaker House
1030 Hunt Valley Circle
New Kensington, PA 15068
www.whitakerhouse.com

Library of Congress Cataloging-in-Publication Data
Names: Hilton, Laura V., 1963- author.
Title: The Amish candymaker / by Laura V. Hilton.
Description: New Kensington, PA : Whitaker House, [2019] |
Identifiers: LCCN 2018054075 (print) | LCCN 2018056393 (ebook) | ISBN 9781641231206 (e-book) | ISBN 9781641231190 (paperback)
Subjects: LCSH: Romance fiction. | BISAC: FICTION / Christian / Romance. | GSAFD: Christian fiction. | Love stories.
Classification: LCC PS3608.I4665 (ebook) | LCC PS3608.I4665 A7 2019 (print) | DDC 813/.6—dc23
LC record available at https://lccn.loc.gov/2018054075

1 2 3 4 5 6 7 8 9 10 11 **LU** 26 25 24 23 22 21 20 19

DEDICATION

To the God that hears me, saves me, loves me.

ACKNOWLEDGEMENTS

Thanks to Michael (USCG and volunteer firefighter) for information about the Upper Peninsula of Michigan Amish, for buggy snapshots taken with his cell phone, for actually driving out to the area where the Amish live, and for bringing home Mackinac Island fudge. Yum. I love you, son. Also, thanks for housing us when we came up to visit and do research in person. And thank you for making rock candy so we could watch it grow.

Thank you to Marilyn Ridgway for auction insights and for the recipes you shared. I value your friendship.

Thanks to Garrett for your help with describing Sam's burn recovery experience, and especially for actually living through the pain, surgery, and recovery time.

Thank You, God, for knowing what I needed and providing firsthand experience.

Also thanks to Craig for comments made in a sermon that I used in the story, and for Amish wisdom for providing me with memorable quotes.

Thank you, Steve, for helping me get the ending the way I wanted it when I couldn't think. Thanks to Jenna, Steve, Candee, Lynne, Linda, Heidi, Marie, Christy, Kathy, Julie, and Marilyn for your critiques, advice, and/or brainstorming. Also thanks to my street team for promoting and brainstorming.

Thanks to Jenna and Kristin for taking on the bulk of the cooking while I'm working toward a deadline.

Thanks to Whitaker House for taking a chance on me, and to Tamela Hancock Murray for representing me.

GLOSSARY OF AMISH TERMS AND PHRASES

ach:	oh
aent/aenti:	aunt/auntie
"ain't so?":	a phrase commonly used at the end of a sentence to invite agreement
boppli:	baby/babies
bu:	boy
buwe:	boys
daadi:	grandfather
daed:	dad
"Danki":	"Thank you"
der Herr:	the Lord
dawdi-haus:	a home constructed for the grandparents to live in once they retire
dochter:	daughter
dummchen:	a silly person
ehemann:	husband
Englisch:	non-Amish
Englischer:	a non-Amish person
frau:	wife
Gott:	God
grossdaadi:	grandfather
großeltern:	grandparents
grosskinner:	grandchildren

grossmammi:	grandmother
gut:	good
haus:	house
"Ich liebe dich":	"I love you"
jah:	yes
kapp:	prayer covering or cap
kinner:	children
koffee:	coffee
kum:	come
maidal:	young woman
mamm:	mom
mammi:	grandmother
maud:	an older unmarried woman (old maid/spinster)
morgen:	morning
nacht:	night
nein:	no
"off in den kopf"	"off in the head"; crazy
onkel:	uncle
Ordnung:	the rules by which an Amish community lives
ser gut:	very good
sohn:	son
süße:	sweetie/sweetness
verboden:	forbidden
welkum:	welcome
wunderbaar:	wonderful
youngies:	young unmarried individuals in the Amish community

1

Mackinac County, Michigan

S o then I got all confused." Agnes Zook waved her hands through the air as she tried to describe to her captive, green audience what had happened. Why should she merely talk with just her mouth when she could use her whole body? "He said, 'Television interview,' and my mind went blank. Like, stressed blank, not regular blank. I'm sure you've never had that happen to you."

The lush row of plants she nursed on the southern windowsill of her new candy shop never got flustered. Even now, the plants sat there quietly, listening to her. Except for the odd "hmmm" that followed.

"Do you think it'd work if I asked someone to tell him I was abducted by aliens?"

"Are you on drugs?" The answer-in-a-question was spoken by a male voice. Deep, rumbly. Sexy. She'd never thought of her plants as having a gender.

She spun around, liquid sloshing out of the small watering can in her hands, and surveyed her empty shop.

Except that it wasn't empty.

A stranger—a very handsome, very male, very Amish stranger— stood inside the doorway, a frown on his clean-shaven face. Wisps of sandy blond hair peeked from beneath his hat.

"Sorry, I didn't hear the chimes." She glanced past him to the door, and the marked-down strand of sleigh bells hanging from the knob. The treasure she'd bought at a steep discount from the thrift store was still there, but it must have been wowed into silence by the man's unexpected appearance, too. Otherwise, she would've known.

She should've seen his approach from her position by the window. But she hadn't. He'd just appeared. From nowhere. A handsome Amish man who appeared without warning.

Maybe she was losing her ever-loving mind. Nobody would blame her if that was true, considering all she'd been through. But she wasn't ready to give up. She would survive.

The man set a suitcase on the floor by the door but stayed where he stood, as if he doubted her sanity and questioned his safety in the presence of a half-crazed Amish woman.

A valid assumption, especially after she'd mentioned aliens.

She groaned. Way to make a gut impression.

Agnes blew out a breath, then carried her watering can behind the counter and into the kitchen. Of course, if the man wasn't real, he'd vanish as quickly as he'd appeared. She set the can on the counter, then washed her hands in the too-big, evil sink that hurt her back. Her muscles twinged just thinking about it. After drying her hands on a towel, she peeked back into the other room.

He was still there. He'd dared to move closer to the glass case, where an assortment of fudge and other candies were displayed on trays lined with paper doilies. So, he was a customer? One of only a hundred since she'd opened her store at the beginning of the month.

She took a deep breath, wiped her suddenly sweaty palms on her apron, and stepped behind the counter. "May I help you?" Hopefully, she sounded professional this time, rather than like a raving lunatic.

He leaned closer to the glass case—close enough for her to see the vibrant blue of his eyes, framed by the thickest lashes she'd ever seen on anyone, let alone a man. "Sure. I—"

"Ach, my word. Your eyes are gorgeous." Agnes's heart beat triple-time. Her face heated. So much for sounding professional. Hopefully, she'd managed to disguise the more-than-a-touch of envy that worked through her.

His blue eyes narrowed, a flicker of some indiscernible emotion in their depths. "I, uh, danki." He shook his head. "I need to pick up some treats for my nieces and nephew. Something to ease the transition my appearance will cause. They don't know me, you see. But my brother and sister-in-law need my help."

She didn't "see." "How could your own family not know you?" She leaned forward on the counter.

His face darkened, the blue eyes turning stormy gray. She stared, fascinated.

"Sam and Jenny Mast," he mumbled.

Ach. That was all the explanation she needed. He must be Sam's long-lost brother, the one who traveled the United States to work in various communities as an auctioneer in such high demand that he never visited home. She searched for a family resemblance but didn't see any, perhaps because Sam's face had long been covered with a beard, while this man's wasn't. What was his name? Agnes shook her head. Nothing came to mind. Sam and Jenny did need him, though. Sam had been badly burned in a wildfire earlier that year and had been sent to some big hospital in Minnesota for skin grafts. Jenny needed to be with her husband, so their very young, very adorable *kinner* were currently staying with Bishop Miah and his *frau*, Katherine. With Agnes, too, since she lived with the bishop. For now. Someone went to Sam's twice daily to care for the animals.

Agnes firmed her shoulders and did a little wiggle to get a kink out of her back.

His gaze lowered, then shot back up. His lips tightened. "You know them, ain't so?"

She pictured the sweet, but sad, *kinner*. Sometimes she took home treats for them, just to ease the grief for a while. She knew what it was like to lose one's family. "*Jah.* The *kinner* love my rock candy. Their favorite flavors are cherry, green apple, and blueberry."

A semblance of a smile appeared on his face. "Then that's what I'll get. And the family they're staying with? What should I get them?" He scanned the display case again.

Bishop Miah would enjoy a slice of fudge with his *koffee*. This man would be offered the same hospitality, and the *koffee* might send him running far away before he could help his brother's family. "*Ach,* before you go there, there's something else you need." Agnes grabbed a to-go cup and filled it at the carafe, then turned to hand it to him. "It's hot. And free. Katherine doesn't make *gut koffee.*" She punctuated her comment with a shudder. "Trust me, you don't want to drink her *koffee.*"

His brows drew together in a frown. He accepted the cup but stared at her as if questioning her sanity again. "Who is Katherine?"

"The bishop's frau. She's the one caring for the kinner. There's sugar on the table"—she flapped a hand toward the small table in front of the counter—"and I can get you cream, if you like."

"Black is fine." He took a sip as if to prove it.

Right. "Bishop Miah is especially fond of peanut butter fudge." She reached for a folded box and started assembling it.

"Miah. I was told his name was Nehemiah…oh. Of course. Miah. That makes sense." He blew out a breath. "I'll take a half pound of peanut butter fudge, too."

Agnes cut a slab and put it into the white box labeled with the name of her shop, Sweet Treats. She put the box in a white bag and then filled a small paper sack with five sticks of each of the kinner's favorite flavors of rock candy. "Katherine loves white chocolate fudge." She pointed to it.

He glanced at it. "It's pink. And heart-shaped."

"I think it adds a special something, don't you?" She grinned at him.

He blinked, that spark of something lighting his eyes again. "That it does. Half a pound of that, too, please. I'm Isaac Mast, by the way."

"Agnes Zook." She boxed up some white chocolate fudge and then tallied his total.

Her candy wasn't cheap, and she was happy for the sale, but guilt ate at her for charging him full price for treats he was purchasing to take to the home where she lived.

He pulled out his wallet and handed her a twenty-dollar bill. "You'll have to tell me about the television interview sometime, but I have a long walk to where my nieces and nephew are staying, and then we'll need to find a way to my brother's haus. I don't know what I'll need to do there to get it ready to move back into. Sam and Jenny have been gone a while."

At least he had a pleasant day for the walk. The late-summer sunshine, blue sky, and light breeze hardly warned of the hard winter that was sure to arrive in a few months.

He sighed, and a muscle jumped in his jaw. His eyes darkened even more, with…dread? Anger? Or maybe it was weariness. He did look tired.

"Sam has had quite an extended hospital stay, and Jenny has hardly left his side." Agnes handed him his change, then glanced at the battery-operated clock on the kitchen wall. "Tell you what. I'll be closing the shop in about an hour. I've got a buggy, and I'm happy to take you where you need to go. I'm gut at operating a broom and a mop, too, if you need help clearing the cobwebs at your brother's haus."

Isaac considered her a moment as he tucked the change into his wallet. "Danki, Agnes Zook. And while I wait, you can tell me about that stressful television interview. Is it even permitted? Amish aren't allowed to be photographed."

His words brought the knots back to her stomach.

"And do you always talk to your plants?"

⁓

Isaac took another sip of his delicious koffee and studied the fascinating Amish woman in front of him. Something about her had made his heart sit up and take notice. Her dress was a drab brown that matched the shade of her eyes, only her eyes sparkled with life. Her hair was the color of espresso. Then she shifted, and he noticed some auburn strands amid the dark brown, depending on how and where the light hit. The touches of caramel seemed to match her personality. He tried to soak up her energy as he prepared to face his family. Her joy was refreshing after the rough weeks of being ridden by guilt since finding out about his brother and trying to make plans to kum home without shirking his work responsibilities.

"Talking to plants is gut for them. It's a scientific fact. It helps them thrive." Agnes put her hands on her hips and did a quick twist, first one way, then the other, as if attempting to loosen a tight muscle. Second time she'd done that while he was in the shop. Was her back out of place?

The movement drew his attention to her lovely curves—the curves he knew he shouldn't be noticing. He turned away to survey her shop, taking in the scattered tables and simple layout instead of ogling her.

"Is that so?" He glanced once more at the greenery filling the bay window, then looked at her. "Do you make a habit of personifying things?"

Agnes hesitated. Frowned. "I suppose I do."

"Interesting." He took another sip of his koffee and looked back at her. "That television interview?"

Her face paled, and she spun away. "I've got a ton of things to do if I'm going to get out of here in an hour. Have a seat. Help yourself to more koffee if you want a refill." She disappeared behind a swinging door.

Immediately the door swung back and she reappeared. "Call me if another customer suddenly appears out of nowhere." Then she disappeared again.

Hmm. Curious. Isaac sat at a table near the silent plants and looked outside. Old buildings lined the street, with stone steps leading up from the wide sidewalks to the doors of various shops. Evenly spaced pots and hanging baskets on either side displayed flowering geraniums. It felt almost chilly here, compared to his most recent whereabouts—Pinecraft, Florida, where he'd spent some time auctioning off a deceased Amish man's home and belongings. He'd gone swimming in the ocean after work in the evenings. According to the weather app on his smartphone, the current temperature here was 80 degrees. Not cold, really; but, compared to the 100-plus-degree temperatures he'd just left…well, he'd edit the "chilly" to "comfortable."

He pulled out the letter from Sam's frau, a fresh wave of guilt washing over him. His brother could've died, and he wouldn't have known about it unless Jenny had written.

> *Dearest Ike,*
>
> *As you know, Sam was badly burned in a terrible fire. We need you to care for your nieces, Mary and Martha; your nephew, Timothy; and our farm. The kinner are staying with Bishop Nehemiah and his frau.*
>
> *Can't wait to see you again!*
>
> *With all my love,*
> *Jenny*

It was sad that know his twin brother had three kinner Isaac had never met. But he supposed it'd been a while. The last time they'd seen each other was three years ago, at a livestock auction in Iowa. The auctions were held in different places every year, and Amish came from all over. Sam had never mentioned his kinner. But then, what right did Isaac have to know? He brutally shoved the thought away.

When news of the wildfire in Mackinac County started arriving in bits and pieces via *The Budget* and the Amish gossip line, Isaac had called a local phone shanty and left a message inquiring after Sam. Someone called him back and told him that Sam's home and farm had been preserved, but Sam had suffered third-degree burns and was hospitalized. Isaac had called the hospital, twice, before finally reaching Jenny. Her letter had arrived by then.

Jenny cried. Isaac had a hard time hearing it. Memory lane took him to a painful spot when he'd imagined himself in love with her. And if he hadn't been teasing his married sister-in-law.... Isaac yanked his mind back to the hot topic of the kinner. She hadn't mentioned them—not then, nor when Isaac had called a second time. All she'd had to say, between her tears and gushes of gratitude, was the phone number for Bishop Nehemiah and a request that Isaac call to inform him of his estimated day of arrival.

Isaac swallowed a lump in his throat. That call was easy. All he did was leave a message on the answering machine.

Bangs and clatters came from behind the swinging door, followed by "I'm in a hurry, you know. A little cooperation would be nice." Another clatter followed.

Was someone else in the kitchen with Agnes?

Isaac drained his koffee and got up to refill the cup for the energy it might provide. He took the opportunity to peek into the kitchen. Agnes stood, with her back to him, bent over a deep basin sink, scrubbing something. He watched her body move with the motion.

Intriguing.

But the way she leaned over the sink probably explained her sore back.

Even though he knew better, Isaac entered the kitchen and glanced around to see who she might have been talking to. As far as he could tell, the room was empty, except for Agnes. "Anything I can do to help?"

She squealed, jumped, and turned at once, her hands dripping soapy water on the floor. "Ach, you startled me. Do you always sneak up on people?"

He hadn't thought he was being particularly sneaky.

"I didn't mean to scare you. I heard a sound and came to investigate. I can wash dishes, if you'd like. Free you up to do other things." He eyed the splatters of melted chocolate on the counters and floor. Agnes was *not* a neat cook. Hopefully, this fact wasn't reflected in the flavor or quality of her candy.

"I suppose that would get us out of here earlier. You must be anxious to see your nieces and nephew."

Isaac made a noncommittal grunt. It was actually rather daunting to realize he was the only family available to care for—and be solely responsible for—three kinner he didn't know, for an undetermined amount of time. How was he to maintain his client base? He had to support himself and couldn't just drop off the auction radar. Right now, he was in high demand. He wanted to keep it that way. After receiving Jenny's letter, however, he couldn't ignore his family's existence. Or their need for help.

But farming? It'd been a dozen years or more since he walked behind a plow.

And his last attempt at….

Bile rose in his throat.

He wasn't sure Jenny understood what she asked of him.

He was even less sure that it could actually be done.

But for his only brother? He had to try.

⌒

Agnes handed Isaac the dishcloth. "This sink is such a pain. I wanted an industrial-sized one, so that's what Gabe ordered, but I can barely reach the bottom. I'm eternally dropping stuff in here, and it's hard to retrieve smaller utensils like knives and spatulas."

"Gabe your ehemann? Beau?"

Agnes sighed. "I would've married him in a heartbeat. He's a dream. But, nein. He's my sister's ehemann. Well, she isn't technically my sister, but we both lost our families in one way or another after that fire that so badly burned your brother, and we decided to claim each other as family. Bridget's family moved back to Ohio, somewhere." Sudden, burning pangs of sorrow had her blinking. She was orphaned and made homeless in the fire, and she tried to brush the pain aside with busy activity and chatter. "Gabe owns a construction company. He was contracted to renovate the candy shop." A project paid for by the sale of her parents' land and charred shell of a home.

She turned away. She was talking too much. This man didn't need to know about her unreciprocated crush on Gabe Lapp, and yet she'd blabbered on about it.

Isaac made the same odd hmming sound he'd made when he'd heard her talking to the plants. Then he rolled up his sleeves, exposing tanned and muscular forearms. Water sloshed as he plunged his hands into the hot, soapy water.

Her heart sped up at the sight of his arms. Or maybe from the embarrassing mention of the man she had made a fool of herself over not too long ago.

She inhaled a deep, shuddery breath and pressed her lips together to keep from saying something foolish, such as: *You'd do quite nicely, though.* That'd scare him out of her shop and out of her life in nein time.

She got out the spray bottle containing her homemade cleaning solution with essential oils and misted the countertops. Isaac was in her peripheral vision—a gut place to keep him so she could gawk without him noticing. *Wow.* What a gorgeous man. And to think he'd be around for a while.

"I could probably locate an old farm sink, if you want to replace this one. They're auctioned off frequently." Isaac rinsed a mixing bowl.

"Would you? That'd be lovely." Agnes wiped away the chocolatey, sugary mess she'd left. "But how could you bid if you're the one behind the, um, pulpit...podium...stand...whatever it's called?"

"Auction block." He grinned. "And I'd ask someone else to bid for you. Just let me know how much you're willing to spend. Farm sinks generally don't go for too much, though. Not too many people looking for those." He rinsed a pan.

The idea appealed. Could she sell this monstrosity of an industrial sink and kum out ahead? "Danki." Somehow she'd managed to keep her answer to one word, not an avalanche. She'd thought she'd been doing better lately at controlling her verbal vomit, but something about this man unhinged her tongue.

With the counters cleaned, she opened the closet and fetched the mop and bucket. Isaac reached for them. "I'll do the floors. I'm sure you need to take care of things out front. And I think I heard sleigh bells."

Agnes hadn't heard anything. But she had been making a racket getting the bulky pail out of the back closet. "Danki."

In the front room, an Englisch man pointed to a basket of chocolates. "I'll take that."

"Excellent choice." She leaned down to remove the basket from the display case, excited about the sale. It was a pricey item and the profit would help to defray her start-up costs.

She straightened her posture and stared into the barrel of a gun.

2

Isaac grabbed the bucket Agnes had loudly wrestled out of the closet and filled it with water. He glanced around, looking for a bottle of cleaning solution Agnes might use on the floor, but didn't see anything. He didn't want to interrupt her while she was taking care of a customer. He listened but didn't hear any conversation.

He barely knew her, yet her suddenly quiet demeanor struck him as odd. She seemed to be a talker. Maybe the person who'd entered the store had left already. Isaac walked over to the door and pushed it open a narrow crack.

The breath caught in Isaac's throat at the sight of a man aiming a gun, shakily, at Agnes. Agnes needed help. Now. Isaac eased the door shut and hurried to the back of the shop while dialing 9-1-1 on his phone.

"Nine-one-one, what's your emergency?"

"Robbery in progress at Sweet Treats." Isaac gave the location and hung up, ignoring the directive to stay on the line. He needed to help Agnes in whatever way he could. He didn't know how, but he'd figure something out. Adrenaline pumped in his veins. His heart thudded, and his fingers itched to do more than call the police. Maybe he could distract the thief and redirect the aim of the gun.

He returned to the front of the store and pushed open the swinging door to see Agnes shoving money into a cloth bag on the counter. Bills fluttered to the floor in her rush. Wow, she had that much money on hand at the end of the day? It bothered Isaac that she seemed about to lose the proceeds of much hard work. Surprising how much he cared what happened to her.

The thief hadn't disguised himself at all. Stupid mistake. He'd be easy to identify. Maybe Isaac should take a picture with his phone. The guy was clearly high on drugs. Isaac had a flashback of his first words to Agnes: *"Are you on drugs?"* Nein. Someone who talked to plants was immeasurably preferable to a gun-waving crook.

Isaac swallowed and snapped a picture.

"Hurry it up, there," the man muttered. His grip on the gun tightened.

No one in his right mind would shoot his victim in a robbery—not until he had the money in hand, that is. But this thief wasn't in his right mind, if his bloodshot eyes, dilated pupils, and shaky demeanor were any indication. Isaac wouldn't take any chances. He lunged forward and pushed Agnes to the floor as the roar of the firearm echoed in the shop. The breeze of the bullet stirred the hairs on his head as he fell.

Agnes trembled beneath him, but other than the grunting noise she'd made as they landed, she didn't utter a sound.

A hand slapped the counter above their heads. Bills rained down around them as the thief made a grab for the bag. Instead, he knocked it off the counter. It landed with a thunk on Isaac's head.

The thief cursed. Another shot rang out. Glass shattered overhead.

Sirens wailed in the distance.

The man cursed again. Steps pounded. Sleigh bells rang.

Isaac rose to his knees and cautiously glanced over the counter. Through the front window, he saw the thug dart past.

Isaac stood and looked down at Agnes. "Are you all right?"

Agnes rolled over and sat up. She gathered the money scattered around her. "He left his bag." Her voice shook as she reached for it.

"Don't touch it. The police will want it for evidence." At least, Isaac assumed they would, based on the crime dramas he'd seen on hotel televisions.

She jerked her hand away. "You called the police? How'd you know what was going on?"

"I came to ask you where you kept your cleaning supplies, and I saw the guy with the gun." His chest had constricted the second he'd realized Agnes was in danger, and he still felt the tightness in his lungs. How was it that he already cared so much about this woman he hardly knew?

Shrugging off his annoyance with this realization, he strode to the door, flipped the sign so that the "Closed" side faced outward, and peered outside. A police car squealed to a stop in front of the shop. Too late to catch the would-be thief. He was long gone. Except for the picture on Isaac's phone and the fact he and Agnes were alive to testify and provide a description.

"The money. He left the money. Danki, Lord." Her voice caught. "I can touch that, right?"

"I think so." He wasn't sure, though. "Maybe not until we ask the police." He opened the glass door to let in a tall, thin officer. Another officer peeked in through the front window. "Do you need help standing?"

The tall officer gave him an odd look.

"I think I can manage." There were some bumping sounds and a grunt, and then Agnes popped up behind the counter.

The officer looked around. "Someone reported a robbery here…?"

"An attempted robbery, at least. Not sure if he took any money. He left the bag. It's back here." With a shudder, Agnes glanced over her shoulder, her hand closing around the edge of the display case. "He shot twice."

Isaac followed her gaze. Something silver glinted in the wall.

He sucked in a breath. A bullet. She'd seen it. He lamented her pain and wished he could go back and do something different. Like close and lock the shop before going into the kitchen. Regret was the story of his life.

"Ach, nein. So much candy, wasted." Agnes leaned over the ruined display case, her shoulders slumping.

The tall officer pulled out a notepad. "Can you tell me what happened?" He looked to Isaac.

Isaac nodded toward Agnes. "Talk to her about how it started. But here's a picture of the guy. He was high on something." He showed the photo to the officer.

The officer took the phone and tapped the screen. "Is it okay if I send this to myself? It'll be helpful."

"Of course."

"You took a picture?" Agnes's voice sounded strangled.

Isaac glanced at Agnes, then looked back at the police officer. "You need to talk to her. I just noticed what was happening and made the call."

"And saved my life. My hero." Agnes glanced once more at the bullet hole in the wall. Then she turned grateful, hero-worship eyes in Isaac's direction.

Unworthiness filled him. If she knew what he'd done....

He shook it off. Maybe he had saved her life. If he hadn't tackled her out of the way, the bullet might've struck her. And, for some reason, he desperately wanted her to stay safe...just not necessarily safe from him.

Agnes's gaze roved around her shop. What a mess. Shattered glass, smeared panels, fingerprint powder everywhere, and mud tracked in from one of the officer's shoes. At least the police had left. Their questions and nosing around her shop made her uncomfortable. She bit her lip and stared out the window. The would-be thief still lurked out there somewhere. Had he taken anything? She wouldn't know until she counted the money and compared it with her sales report, but she would do the math later. Right now, it seemed more important to take Isaac to meet his young relatives and then drop him off at Sam's haus. Tomorrow, she would clean the shop, talk to Gabe about ordering and installing a new display case, and handle the financial matters. She also needed to restock her supply with ingredients she couldn't afford right now. Hopefully, she wouldn't be out of business for long. She needed to pay her looming bills and somehow support herself. For the rest of her life.

She turned off the lights and opened the door.

Isaac picked up his suitcase and backpack. "Where's your buggy?"

"Around the side of the building."

Isaac nodded and disappeared out the door.

As Agnes returned to the kitchen to lock away her cash, she tried to still her quivering body. She'd had way too much drama for one day. To-nacht, she would brew some chamomile tea and take a bath with lavender salts to calm down before bed. Selfishly, she was glad Isaac was here, so the kinner could return to their own home.

Agnes double-checked the lock on the back door, then glanced at the clock. Almost six. She would arrive home an hour late. Katherine would need help getting dinner on the table right away.

She wouldn't suggest it to Isaac yet, but it might be prudent if he were to spend the nacht at the bishop's home and then tackle cleaning his brother's haus tomorrow. Of course, she wouldn't be able to help him then. Not with all she had to do at her shop.

"Man makes plans, and Gott laughs," Agnes muttered, echoing one of Bishop Miah's endless proverbs. But He probably had gut reason for stalling her ideas at the get-go instead of allowing her to race blindly on. Hadn't she learned her lessons with Gabe? She'd tried to make herself indispensable to him, and he'd chosen another. She wouldn't play the fool twice.

She firmed her shoulders in resolve, then marched across the floor of her shop and out onto the street. Her confidence wilted a little, and she double-checked the lock. By the time she'd reached her buggy, Isaac had loaded his bags into the back and untied her horse from the hitching post. Wildfire had been appropriately named, considering the natural disaster that had led to the necessity of Agnes's owning this horse.

The twinge of loss hit hard, and she blinked away the tears that sprang to her eyes at the thought of the animals that had been lost in the burning of her family's barn. Especially Cherry Blossom, which Daed had bought for her and Gabe as a wedding gift—before Gabe came, back when hope for a happily-ever-after was in the forecast.

The name Wildfire was a perpetual reminder of her pain, as if she didn't already live with regret. After all, if she hadn't been chasing after Gabe, she would have been home to help her family escape the blaze… or would have perished with them rather than be doomed to live on the charity of others.

She opened the door of the buggy and climbed in next to Isaac. "I thought I'd best take you to the bishop's haus first. It's almost dinnertime."

The man's face lost all color. Odd. After a moment's hesitation, Isaac set his jaw and nodded. Was he afraid of the bishop? Afraid of the kinner? Or what? Surely, he wasn't terrified to be alone with Agnes for the duration of a couple miles' drive?

Or maybe he was. She had been a bit forward with her comment about his gorgeous eyes. Her face heated again.

Except, he'd taken her up on her offer of a ride *after* hearing the crazy comment, so that couldn't be it.

Once they were outside the city limits, he cleared his throat. "You're shaking."

She glanced at her trembling left hand. "Stress. It was rather terrifying, ain't so?"

"Jah. I know." There was a grim element to his voice, as if he'd faced something similar before.

"Why'd you call the police? And take a picture of the robber? You're Amish. You know we usually don't get the law involved. Besides, graven images are verboden."

He snorted at the same time as Wildfire. Apparently, man and beast held the same opinion, whatever it was.

"I'm not your typical Amish man, Agnes. Some might say I'm not Amish at all." There was a bit of a challenge in his tone. "I'm here because my brother needs me. That's all."

Of course. He certainly wasn't here to offer to marry and take care of her for the rest of her life.

She pursed her lips. "So, you never joined the church?" Well, he was still young enough that she could hold out hope that he might actually change, join the church, and her crazy daydream of a rescue might kum true, after all. "How'd you know to kum here?"

"Jenny wrote me."

Agnes shook her head. "You didn't answer my question." Several questions, actually.

His brow furrowed. "I called the police because it was the right thing to do. Nein man should prey on young maidals and steal from them. And I took a picture to help the police find the guy and make an arrest. Certainly not so I could look upon his image. If I never see him again, I'll be happy."

She could agree with that.

"And I actually did join the church—in a different community, more like a galaxy far, far away—I just don't particularly care about the rules. I can think for myself. Plus, I find myself in so many different communities with so many different unwritten laws, it's easier to do what I feel is right. I don't have time to memorize all the various Ordnungs."

Agnes coughed to smother a gasp at his approach to life. But then, who was she to judge? She wasn't the typical submissive Amish woman. Daed had warned her that she would never marry if Gabe didn't choose her. And he hadn't. But, according to the bishop, Gott made her an individual for a reason. She wanted to cling to Bishop Miah's heavily disguised hope that maybe there was someone for her, but Daed's pessimism—or, more accurately, his realism—was stronger. Nobody had ever wanted to court her. Not here, and not in Pennsylvania, where they used to live.

Daed had taken Gabe into their home when he'd arrived in hopes of having him fall in love with Agnes. He had fallen in love only with her fudge and other confections. In fact, it was his fondness for her sweet treats that had encouraged her to open a candy shop—something Daed had strongly discouraged until it became plain Gabe had chosen another. Only then had he acquiesced. Gut thing, since, with her family home in ashes, she was alone now, with the shop as her sole means of support.

Agnes shook off the melancholy and tried to think of something to say. But silence ruled.

Isaac leaned back with a sigh and closed his eyes. Shutting out Agnes, shutting out the world, shutting off all avenues to conversation. He ran his hand over his smooth-shaven jaw, a tiny smile on his well-shaped lips.

Agnes whipped her attention away. She would *not* make another blunder like she had in Sweet Treats when she'd thoughtlessly blurted out that he had gorgeous eyes. It was true, but she shouldn't have said it. Making a comment about his kissable lips would definitely be over-the-top. She clamped her mouth shut to keep the words that danced on the tip of her tongue at bay.

On the side of the road, a man walked in the opposite direction of the buggy.

Her heart pounded as she studied him. Something about him reminded her of the man who'd tried to rob her. The clothes, the height, the hair color. It probably wasn't him, but she'd play it safe and not offer him a ride in case he decided to relieve her of her transportation and leave her stranded. She tried to dismiss her twitchy fears. Maybe she was seeing things that weren't there. She'd probably jump at every shadow and shy away from men for a while. As she drove past him, the man kept his face averted, gazing off into the woods. Just as well. Now she couldn't be certain.

A soft snore beside her drew her attention back to Isaac. Poor man must be exhausted. She should've thought of that instead of allowing him to help her in the shop. At least he didn't have to lug his belongings to Bishop Brunstetter's haus on foot.

Silence prevailed for the rest of the three-mile journey. Agnes drove into the circular driveway at the bishop's haus and parked in front of the barn.

Two of the three Mast kinner raced toward the buggy. "Martha felled in the mud, so she's in the tub!" Timothy announced loudly. "And we're hungry!" Yelling was his normal volume. Agnes winced. Chamomile tea was definitely in her evening plans.

The shouting woke Isaac. He straightened, a muscle working in his jaw.

The bishop emerged from the barn. His mouth moved, but his words were lost in the shouting. Just like always.

Agnes climbed out of the buggy and handed the reins to Bishop Miah.

Isaac started to get out but stopped as Timothy clambered into the buggy. "Daed! You're home! We missed you. Where's Mamm?" He flung himself into Isaac's arms. "Where's your beard?"

"Daed?" Mary was right behind Timothy, crying. "Daed!"

Isaac's eyes were wide as he glanced at Agnes. He returned Timothy's hug, patted Mary's arm, and gulped. "I'm not your daed. I'm your onkel Isaac."

~

Isaac hadn't expected to be mistaken for his brother, since they were fraternal twins rather than identical twins, but he should've planned for it. They did resemble each other enough to confuse casual acquaintances. At least, they had until Sam married and grew a beard, the mandatory sign of a married man. Up close, Isaac was an inch taller. Their eyes were different colors, too; Sam's were more hazel. But the brothers' appearances were probably close enough to make them easily mistaken for each other by two kinner who had never met their daed's twin.

The bishop murmured something to Agnes that Isaac didn't catch, but she shot a startled glance toward the haus before heading that way at a quick pace. Probably had something to do with whoever had gotten in the mud and now needed a bath. Someone Isaac would soon be responsible for. His stomach knotted.

"Kinner, let your onkel get out so I can take care of the horse and buggy. Gut to see you, Isaac. I was surprised to hear your phone message saying you were coming. Especially with your busy schedule."

Isaac climbed out as the kinner ran after Agnes to the haus. "I'm still not sure how it'll all work out. I have engagements I need to keep. I'm hoping you and Katherine will mind the kinner in my absences."

The bishop tugged at his beard, his gaze moving to the haus. "The spirit is willing, but the flesh is weak."

Isaac frowned. "Is that a nein?"

"With Agnes working, it falls on Katherine to watch the kinner, and she's not as young as she once was. Our grosskinner are in their early teens now. She has a hard time keeping up with an active eighteen-month-old. Martha has already had four baths today. It's not so bad when Agnes is home to watch them."

Agnes lived here with the bishop? Why hadn't she mentioned that? Isaac was surprised, considering the way she liked to chatter in general. Nein wonder she knew everyone's favorite treat—and that Katherine's koffee tasted bad.

Isaac shifted. "I'll find someone else, then. Might as well leave the buggy out. I'll need a way of driving the kinner home after Martha's bath." Though how he would manage that remained to be seen.

"They're hungry. Agnes went in to put a quick supper together. Besides, I'm not sure what kind of food you'd find at Sam's. Their pantry was raided to feed others since they were gone due to Sam's hospitalization."

"After we eat, then." Isaac rubbed the horse's nose.

"Katherine and Agnes will insist on scrubbing the haus down before you move in. It's been empty for six months. The kinner are usually asleep by seven. They can stay here to-nacht. You, too, of course."

"Of course." Isaac was only half-tempted to stand his ground. Truthfully, he wasn't looking forward to playing temporary daed to three young kinner. His career as an auctioneer hardly qualified him for such a task.

Not that he was worthy of caring for his brother's kinner anyway.

"Gut. That's settled. I'll take care of the horse. You can either kum out to the barn with me, and we'll chat, or go to the haus, wash up, and wait while Agnes fixes supper." The bishop raised his graying eyebrows, whether in challenge or in question, Isaac didn't know.

Isaac stood a moment in indecision. Both options entailed conversation, and he was exhausted. "I'll help with the horse. There's something I—"

"Those who do not cross rivers before they get there have few rivers to cross," the bishop murmured.

Isaac blinked. Twice. "Okay...?"

The screen door flew open, and a naked, dripping-wet toddler ran across the porch, Agnes in hot pursuit of her.

Bishop Miah chuckled. "That one is a handful. A blessing, but a handful just the same."

"Martha?" Isaac assumed aloud.

Agnes scooped up the child and headed back inside.

Isaac watched her go.

Another chuckle from the bishop. "Martha, too. But I meant Agnes."

3

Agnes removed the pan of biscuits from the oven as Katherine shuffled into the kitchen carrying a now-dried-and-dressed Martha on her hip. The older woman sat the child on a stepladder masquerading as a toddler seat and pushed it up to the table. "Stay here, Martha. I need to help Agnes with supper."

"Rough day?" Agnes gave Katherine a sympathetic smile.

"I never thought I'd be so glad to have their onkel arrive. Please, tell me I correctly guessed the identity of the strange man standing in the driveway with Miah."

Agnes grinned. "He's here." Larger than life, and twice as dangerous for her heart.

Katherine sighed. "Ach, gut. I chased Martha around all day long. Didn't get a lick of work done. Except four baths, ham sandwiches for lunch, and dishes while she napped. I sat on the porch and attempted to mend while keeping an eye on the older two, since I couldn't talk them into resting. They'll probably fall asleep at the table."

At least they had a big, strong man to carry them to bed. What would it be like if he were to scoop up Agnes and carry her off to her bedroom?

Agnes jerked the wooden spoon out of the white sauce. Splatters flew, burning her palm. She dropped the spoon on the counter and rubbed the sting. Her face flamed hotter. *Stop, stop, stop.* With her luck, he'd fall for someone else, and she didn't want to suffer another broken heart.

"Supper is almost ready," she told Katherine. "I made creamed asparagus and biscuits." Hopefully, Isaac liked asparagus. "I also brewed some chamomile tea."

"I'm sure that'll be fine, with koffee and whatever leftover treats you brought home." Katherine poured herself a mug of the foul-tasting brew and sank into a chair with another sigh.

Agnes forced a smile. "Nein leftover treats today, I'm afraid." Except for the sweets Isaac had bought as gifts for the family. Agnes wouldn't tell them about the attempted robbery. Or about the ruined fudge imbedded with shards of glass that she'd left in the case. There wasn't any need to mention it, lest they worry excessively and possibly overreact, forcing her to close her business and resigning her to wait for that glorious someday when a man would take notice of her.

That would likely be on the twelfth of never, if Daed's dire predictions carried any prophetic value.

Agnes set the table, then set out pickled eggs, sliced ham, leftover potato salad, chow-chow, cabbage salad, and raw vegetables they'd recently harvested but hadn't canned yet. There was nein telling when she'd have time for canning, with all that'd been added to her busy schedule. She shouldn't have volunteered to help ready Sam's haus for Isaac and the kinner. Her offer probably smacked of desperation; in light of the attention her shop now needed, she should withdraw it. Isaac would manage. After all, the kinner were his relatives. Not hers.

She'd tell him after dinner. He'd understand, due to the circumstances.

Agnes drained the asparagus. "Dinner is ready."

Katherine moved her koffee cup out of Martha's reach and pushed to her feet. "I'll ring the dinner bell. I'm so looking forward to having a break from the kinner. Not very Christian of me, I know, but it's been six months, and I'm exhausted."

Agnes nodded. "I'm sorry I haven't been here for you for the last month."

"Ach, child. We discussed it before you opened your shop. You need a source of income. I'd figured you'd move into a room there, too. Miah said you would. But I'm in nein hurry. You've made yourself irreplaceable to us." Katherine hobbled over to the door, rubbing her hip, and opened the screen wide enough to give the bell a couple of clangs.

Moments later, Timothy and Mary dashed inside, pushing each other in their haste to be first.

"Wash up." Agnes pointed a spoon at them, splattering more sauce on the floor and counter.

The kinner splashed water in their haste, but they were finished and seated when the two men finally made their way in.

Katherine smiled. "You must be Isaac. Or do you go by Ike? So glad to finally meet you."

"I answer to both Isaac and Ike. Generally prefer Isaac, though." He followed Bishop Miah to the sink. He skimmed the room, likely noticing the splattered counters and wet floor where Agnes had accidentally sloshed the cooking water for the asparagus.

She should be more careful. Especially in the presence of small kinner and older individuals who might slip and fall. She avoided glancing at Isaac.

She didn't care if he didn't like her. Didn't care and wasn't attracted. She gave a tiny nod to emphasize it.

"Ach, and by the way, Isaac will be spending the nacht here, since Sam's haus will need some attention before being lived in again." Bishop Miah rinsed his hands and reached for a towel.

Agnes had figured that would be the case. She glanced over at Isaac. A mistake.

His gaze was focused on her. For one heart-stopping moment, he stared into her eyes. She almost forgot to breathe. Her lips parted. Tingled.

His gaze turned knowing, and he winked.

Her face burned.

⌒

Isaac laid his silverware across his empty plate and leaned back in his chair. "That was ser gut. I don't get to enjoy asparagus very often. Danki, Agnes, for putting dinner together. And danki, Katherine, for watching the kinner."

Both Timothy and Mary were asleep, one cheek pressed against the tabletop, and Martha's little head bobbed as she fought to keep her eyes open.

"I'll do the dishes." Katherine rose. "Ike, you can help Agnes put the kinner to bed."

He wasn't ready for tackling the childcare duties so soon. At least he had Agnes.

Agnes picked up Martha, motioning for Isaac to grab a child. He lifted Mary gently from her chair and carried her upstairs, to a bedroom where Agnes lay Martha in a crib. "Where does Timmy sleep?" Isaac whispered as he lowered the girl onto the nearby bed.

"In here, with his sisters." Agnes nodded toward the double bed. "The Brunstetters have only three bedrooms, and since I'm in one, the kinner have to share."

Isaac raised an eyebrow at her. "Where will they put me, then?"

"There's a sleeper sofa on the first floor. That's where Gabe slept after he had surgery."

"Ah. Gabe again." Isaac suppressed a smile. "I'll bring Timmy up, and you can get them ready for bed. Then perhaps we should talk. Should I be jealous of this Gabe who married your not-exactly-a-sister and put the industrial-sized sink in your shop?"

Agnes spluttered. "Jealous? Why? I'm nobody to you."

He grinned. "Ah, but you *could* be someone." Especially after that moment in the candy shop when their gazes had locked, and a feeling he'd never experienced had washed over him. As if his heart knew her...or something. And then again in the kitchen, when, for a second, they were the only two people in the world.

Even though her face flamed red, she eyed him with an expression that seemed hopeful. A look that reminded him of when their eyes met earlier. Jah, she felt it, too. Her yearning gaze brought him a foreign twinge of hope, as well. Hope that, just maybe, his future promised a time of being at peace instead of always on the run. Or maybe hope that his "duty" time here would at least provide a lovely distraction to make things better. But her look, whatever it was, quickly died, and she made a dismissive noise.

"You are a flirt."

He shrugged. "Of course, I am. But we need to talk. I'll get Timmy."

"Timothy," she muttered.

Ignoring her, Isaac strode down the hall and descended the stairs, silently cursing himself for flirting with a sheltered Amish woman who probably thought he was serious when he should be anything but.

He did enjoy casually dating women in the different communities he visited, but, so far, nobody had caught his attention enough for him to desire courtship.

Yet something about Agnes appealed to him. She'd be a gut girlfriend while he was here. Nein strings attached.

Except for the never-before-felt, completely inexplicable tug on his heart.

⟜

Once the kinner were tucked in bed, Agnes went downstairs. Katherine had finished the dishes and was hanging the damp dishcloth to dry when Agnes entered the kitchen. The older woman smiled wearily. "I'm going to rest a bit and do the mending before bed, but the onkel is waiting for you outside. He said he needs to talk to you about something. Miah is out there with him now. They had some things to discuss, too."

Fear coursed through Agnes. This Isaac wouldn't be so quick to take away her dreams and her source of income by reporting what had happened today, would he? But then, why not? She hadn't asked him not to tell the Brunstetters about the attempted robbery, and it was the Amish way for men to want to protect their women as much as possible. Some women weren't even allowed to drive themselves into town to shop.

Of course, she wasn't Isaac's woman, or anyone's. Bishop Miah was technically her guardian, however, since her parents had died.

Agnes cringed. If the bishop decided to take away her shop, she'd have to argue for her continued employment. However, he, of all people, should understand her need.

She swallowed the lump in her throat and forced a smile. "Maybe I should let them talk, and Isaac can call me when they're finished. I could help you with the mending. I'm adept with a needle and thread, you know."

"Jah, you are. But Ike said to tell you to go on out when you were finished with the kinner."

She supposed she may as well get this over with. If the men were discussing her and her business, she'd need to defend herself. The sooner, the better.

She managed a curt nod. "I'll do that, then. Danki, Katherine." She stepped into her flip-flops, sprayed herself liberally with insect repellant to ward off the mosquitos that swarmed in the evenings, and went outside.

The bishop sat on an antique metal porch chair that his gross-sohn had painted a muted red with leftover barn paint. Isaac leaned against the porch rail, his legs crossed at the ankles. Their faces reflected the glow of several citronella candles arranged on the table between them.

"Katherine said to kum on out," she explained when both men looked at her with identically grim expressions. "And he didn't take any money. I don't think it'll happen again. He seemed pretty scared when he ran off, and…."

Bishop Miah squinted. "Agnes, what are you talking about?"

"Ach." He hadn't told. And she'd had to bring it up.

She grimaced. "Someone attempted to rob the candy shop today, but Isaac called the police, and he ran away."

The bishop's brow furrowed. "Why would anyone rob a candy store? Granted, your candy is second to none, but…." He glanced at Isaac. "Did she give you any samples?"

"Nein, but I didn't ask. I just bought some. It's in my suitcase, still in the back of the buggy. I purchased some candy for the kinner, too. I'll get it on the way back inside after our walk." Isaac looked at her in a way that made her stomach flutter and her nonromantic resolve falter.

"I'll leave you two alone." Bishop Miah rose to his feet. "Please extinguish the candles when you kum inside."

Isaac straightened. "You might want to spray yourself with repellant. The mosquitoes are terrible here."

"I already did." Was the attempted robbery so easily forgotten? Or was she so unimportant? She shook off the negativity. More than likely, Bishop Miah needed to take some time to think and pray over his response.

She followed Isaac as he strode toward the road. "Where does your Gabe live? Within walking distance?"

Agnes hesitated. "Will I need better shoes for this?"

He turned around and glanced down at her feet. Smirked. "Pink flip-flops. Cute. Jah, probably."

If only her tennis shoes were pink, too. That would really shock him. But Daed had said a very firm "nein" when she'd made that request.

She went back inside and put on her very plain, black tennis shoes. They matched the equally plain socks balled inside the shoes, which she left discarded on the shoe mat, to be retrieved upon her return.

She found Isaac waiting by the mailbox, flipping the faded red plastic flag up-down, up-down.

"Gabe and his frau live about a mile in that direction." She pointed west. Why did he want to see Gabe? Did he want to size up the competition for her heart? To stake a public claim? Or, more realistically, enlist Gabe's help with fixing up the shop?

"His frau is your make-believe sister, ain't so? Why not refer to her by her name?" His upper lip curled.

She wanted to smack him. Instead, she pressed her own lips together and silently counted to ten. Twenty. Thirty. "You called him 'my Gabe.' He has never been mine. And her name is Bridget."

His mouth quirked, but he nodded. "And you're still a bit sore. Jealous."

Was she? Agnes frowned. "Nein. Just upset by the prophecies that prequelled his decision."

"'Prequelled.' Is that even a word? Prequel is a noun, not a verb."

She glared at him. "I'm using it as a verb."

"I think the verb you're looking for is 'preceded.'"

"I wasn't looking," she muttered.

He laughed. Then, with a smile still in place, he headed west. "I was thinking, and I've reached the conclusion that we need to get your shop up and running again. We can take the kinner to the shop tomorrow, they can play while we get your business back in order. Then, once we get to a gut stopping point for the day, we'll go to Sam's haus and do some cleaning. I'll stay at the bishop's haus until Sam's place is habitable."

"Did the bishop suggest that?" It was an appealing plan, and she was glad he'd suggested it rather than her having to pursue his help. Should she put up a fight for appearance's sake? Or, worse, was there an ulterior motive brewing somewhere, either for Isaac or for Bishop Miah?

Isaac shrugged. "Not about the shop. He didn't know about that until you mentioned it, in the very vaguest of ways."

"I *need* my job."

"And I *need* mine. Which is why I will do all repairs in your shop—including buying the supplies—in exchange for your watching the kinner when I have to leave town for an auction. You'd be kind of a surrogate aenti."

"You aren't going to stay?" Her voice rose. She couldn't help it.

"I'll be around. Some. But you could watch the kinner when I'm not, ain't so? I do have several commitments I need to keep. A playpen in the kitchen would work for Martha. And the other two—"

"What if there are laws against this?" Her voice shook. He was threatening her livelihood so he could rush off to who knows where and leave her with two exhausting tasks to juggle all by herself. Not only that, but, at his request, her hope for a permanent solution surged to the top. She had to bite her tongue to keep it contained.

"What if there's not? I need you, Agnes. And in return, you get free supplies and labor from me."

"People will think we're courting." Her cheeks heated. So what if she secretly hoped the ruse turned into something real? After it was over, her reputation, with the prequelled prophecy from her daed, would be even worse.

He chuckled. "Let them. Maybe they'll think you finally moved on from your Gabe. Only we will know the truth. You haven't. But it's time, ain't so? Time to let go of the past and embrace the future."

Never mind "heated"—her cheeks flamed at the mental picture of an embrace with Isaac. Her mouth worked, but she couldn't make any words form. She ended her silent tirade with a huff.

He turned to face her, a teasing glint in his eyes. But there was something else there. Something deeper that'd caught her attention earlier in the kitchen.

"I am your destiny. Resistance is futile."

4

Isaac sidestepped around a rut in the two-tire-track road. They'd followed it a short distance through the woods when a small cabin appeared.

He studied the nondescript building, having expected a fancier haus, since Gabe owned a construction company. This structure looked more like a hunting cabin than a home.

A man sat on the front porch, whittling. Wood shavings fell at his feet. He looked up as they neared, and slowly folded his pocket knife. He stood, surveying Isaac.

Nein beard. Had Agnes been lying when she told him where her Gabe lived? Isaac couldn't think of a reason why she might have done so. Or maybe her Gabe had trouble growing facial hair.

"Hello…?" His gaze shifted to Agnes, and he grinned. "Hey, Agnes."

The easy greeting irritated Isaac, though he couldn't say why. It was friendly, welcoming, and everything it should be…if Agnes's feelings weren't what Isaac knew them to be.

"Gabe, I presume?" The statement came out sounding a bit harsher than he'd intended. How had Agnes gotten under his skin so fast?

The man's green eyes widened. "Nein, I'm Noah. Noah Behr. Gabe is in the barn, talking on the phone." His gaze returned to Agnes, and his eyebrows rose. "What brings you and your friend by to-nacht?"

"I…there…this is Isaac Mast. Sam's brother, from…." She glanced at Isaac.

He shrugged and tried to help her out. "From anywhere and every-where. I travel a lot. I thought I probably should meet this infamous Gabe."

Agnes caught her breath, blushed, and looked down. He probably shouldn't tease her.

Noah looked from her to Isaac and back again. "I see." Except, his furrowed forehead and slight frown said the opposite. "Gabe's married to my sister Bridget. I...I live here. With them."

"I expected more of a haus than a hunting cabin." Isaac frowned at the primitive steps leading up to the porch, which had nein rail. Then he grimaced, realizing how rude he must sound. His usual manners that helped him make fast friends of strangers in every community he visited had picked a poor time to fail him. And all because of the lovely woman beside him and the strange, new, uncomfortable feelings she'd awakened within him in the past four hours, since they'd met.

Noah nodded. "Well, the community is still recovering from the fire that put your brother in the hospital. Gabe needed a home, and this hunt-ing cabin was available. He's been putting everybody else's needs before his own. So much loss. But we're beginning to find our footing. I went to California to fight fires there instead of staying here to help him, and the ones who evacuated are returning in spurts. Makes it hard to plan ahead." He shrugged. "Kum on in. Bridget is working on a boppli blanket she's crocheting for an auction."

Isaac glanced at Agnes. "Go on in and visit, if you want. I'll wait for Gabe."

Noah's frown deepened, and he scratched his neck. "Is there some-thing I can help you with? I am co-owner of the business, you know."

"I'll wait for Gabe. Got a question for him about specific measure-ments in the candy shop. Unless you know?" Isaac hitched a brow. He knew he shouldn't needle the other man.

"I was in California when he ordered the supplies for it." Noah tilted his head toward the barn.

Isaac glanced that way, expecting to see a building that was equally run-down as the cabin. He did a double take. The building appeared to be brand-new. Of course, for housing horses and other livestock, barns were absolute necessities for the Amish. Another building, maybe a shed, protruded from one side of the barn.

"He should have the answers you need. He's in the office, in that shed. If you want to give me a moment, please take a seat, and I'll be right back. Or you can go on out to the barn, and I'll be there directly." He turned to Agnes. "Kum on in, Agnes. I'll get you a couple of cookies and a cup of koffee, so Bridget won't have to untangle all that yarn she's got wrapped around her fingers. She'll be glad to see you."

Agnes glanced at Isaac with an apparent mixture of irritation and fear. As if she were afraid of what would happen when he met her Gabe. Scared of what Isaac might say to him. Or maybe Isaac had misread her expression, and she really wanted to see Gabe instead of Bridget.

The possibility hurt him more than it should, especially since he was not interested in anything more than a temporary flirtation while he was here. Except, he couldn't forget that moment in the kitchen...or earlier, in the candy shop.

Agnes finally nodded and, without a word, went up the steps and disappeared inside.

Noah hesitated in the open doorway. "Would you like a few cookies and some koffee? I know Gabe wouldn't mind."

"Maybe later, after I get some answers."

"You're letting the mosquitoes in," shouted an unfamiliar female voice from inside.

Noah laughed and pulled the door shut behind him.

Left alone to make his decision, Isaac glanced toward the barn. After another moment's hesitation, he strode in that direction. As he neared the attached shed, he heard a male voice speaking inside.

Isaac tapped on the open door and peeked inside. A blond man with the beginnings of a beard looked away from the laptop screen in front of him, held up his index finger in an unspoken "Just a minute," and muttered "mmm-hmm" into the phone that was clamped between his shoulder and his ear. He tapped away on the keyboard. "Tracking report says they should be here tomorrow by eight p.m. I'll give you a call when they arrive, and we'll set up a time...talk to you then. Bye." He tapped the phone, set it on the table next to the laptop, and glanced back at Isaac. "May I help you?"

"Isaac Mast," Isaac said as Gabe stood. "I need some specs for the candy shop in town."

"The candy sh...." Gabe's eyebrows rose as he surveyed Isaac, as if trying to assess whether he was worthy of Agnes. "Did Agnes find a new contractor?" He didn't sound peeved.

"More like, I found her. The sink you installed is so deep, it's been causing her some back pain."

Gabe frowned. "I'm not going to ask how you know that. She never said anything to me."

Of course not. It was plain that Agnes basically believed Gabe walked on water. Not that Isaac would tell the guy. None of his business.

Isaac cleared his throat. "She needs a shallower sink. I work as an auctioneer, and the big farm sinks go up for sale routinely. I think one of those would work well. I also need to find out who supplied the glass display case, since a would-be robber shot out the current one." Isaac leaned his hip against the nearby worktable.

"A would-be robber?" Gabe's eyes widened. "Wow. Is she all right? Bridget will be so worried when she hears." Concern shadowed his expression.

Isaac nodded toward the cabin. "She's here."

Gabe frowned. "Bridg—ach, you mean Agnes. Gut. That means she's fine, then."

The speed with which his concern was resolved told Isaac he didn't care about Agnes in that way at all. But the fact that he was so concerned in the first place proved Agnes was right to admire him. What a conundrum.

Gabe turned to a file cabinet, pulled open a drawer, and thumbed through it. He pulled out a folder and plopped it on the table near Isaac's hip.

Isaac straightened and looked at the folder. It was labeled "Samuel Zook" in big, bold, black letters. Who was Samuel Zook? Another man to be envious of? Nein, Zook was Agnes's last name. Was Samuel her daed? Brother? Cousin?

"Okay, let's see what we can find out. How badly was the display case damaged? Do we need a whole new one, or could it be a matter of having new glass installed?"

"Only the side facing the shop was damaged, so new glass should be sufficient. The police took the bullet out of the case as evidence." They'd also taken the one lodged in the wall, but nein need to mention that.

Gabe wrote something on a pad of paper as Noah came in, carrying a plastic bag full of cookies. "Bridget said to take your time. They've lots of news to catch up on."

"Mmmm." Gabe ripped the note off the pad and handed it to Isaac. "Here you go. That's the phone number for the local glass repairman. He'll answer the phone saying something about auto glass repair, but he really replaces any kind of glass. Gut man. And I wrote the measurements of the sink I ordered for her. I'm sorry it's giving her problems. You can auction it off once you find a replacement, or I'll buy it back. I might be able to find a new home for it easily enough." He started to reach for a cookie, then hesitated and held the bag out to Isaac. "Help yourself. And have a seat. They're going to want to talk a while."

Gabe was definitely a competent contractor.

"Danki." Isaac pulled a peanut butter cookie out of the bag and glanced at the clock. "We'll need to be back at the bishop's in about an hour, I'd guess." He snagged a nearby chair and straddled it with the back between his legs.

Noah did the same with another chair.

Gabe replaced the file folder before he pulled a chair over and sat on it normally. "So, you're staying with Bishop Brunstetter?"

Isaac shrugged. "Unplanned. I'm here to take care of my brother's kinner, and Agnes and the Brunstetters think the haus needs to be deep-cleaned before it's fit for human inhabitation."

"Sounds about right. They scrubbed this place from top to bottom." Gabe chuckled. "So, your brother...Mast. You're Sam's brother? I shared a hospital room with him for a while after the fire. How's he doing?"

It hurt to know St. Gabe was actually friendly with the brother Isaac hadn't spoken to or seen in years. He was glad his twin had friends, of course, but his own twin should have been his closest friend.

It was Isaac's fault. All his fault. He swallowed the cookie that'd turned to sawdust in his mouth.

"I don't know how he's doing, exactly. I've gotten most of my news from Jenny, and she's not much of a writer. I called the hospital twice to talk to him. The first time, he couldn't talk because they had something in his throat. A respirator, I think. The second time, he said a few words, but it hurt his throat. He's healing, but they're going to do some reconstructive surgery if they can, so they're still in Minnesota. Not sure how long they'll be there. You were injured in the fire?" Isaac scanned Gabe's face and hands for any visible damage.

"I wasn't burned, if that's what you mean. But I was recovering from other injuries sustained before the fire and ended up doing a lot more damage to myself. Had to have surgery and do physical therapy. I imagine your brother will need physical therapy, too."

"He's already had some." At least, Jenny had mentioned something about it.

Gabe took a bite of his cookie and rocked back in his chair. "How well do you know Agnes?"

Both men scrutinized Isaac. Probably judging him and finding him not worthy.

"Just met her today. Got off the bus in St. Ignace, hitchhiked to town, and...." *Walked in on Agnes talking to her plants about a television interview.* Something he was still curious about. "Long story short, she offered to give me a ride to the bishop's haus, so I offered to help clean up her shop for the day." Which still wasn't clean.

Noah waved his half-eaten cookie in the air. "Agnes makes the best fudge."

Gabe nodded. "But be wary of any tea she may offer you. I'm not sure what kind it was, but it tasted like freshly mowed grass." He shuddered.

Isaac chuckled. If only Agnes could see her precious Gabe right now. "I've been warned away from Katherine Brunstetter's koffee and Agnes's tea. Anything else?"

"The well water has a strong sulfur taste," Noah said.

Isaac grinned. "That so?"

He liked Gabe and Noah. If he spent much time here, they might become friends.

"So...." He leaned forward. "Tell me about the area. About the people." Including Agnes. "And who's this Samuel Zook listed on the candy shop file?"

⌒

"And that was my day." Agnes shifted on the cushion covering the straight-backed chair. She tried not to look around Bridget's one-room cabin, but it was hard not to notice the bed in one corner of the room and the cot against the opposite wall. Both areas were visible now, but two clotheslines strung with king-sized bedsheets offered a measure of privacy when needed. There was a small kitchenette against the back wall, with a square folding table and four mismatched dining-room chairs Bridget and Gabe had picked up somewhere. The only other place to sit was the rocking chair Bridget now occupied.

Such was the home of two newlyweds who had lost everything in the wildfire.

Bridget's hands had frozen in crocheting position, colorful strands of variegated green and yellow yarn wrapped around the fingers of one hand and dangling from the crochet hook she held in the other. Granny squares? Must be for a boppli blanket. She'd said she planned to contribute one to the fundraising auction that was coming up. Or maybe it was Noah who'd mentioned it out on the porch. She'd been so embarrassed by Isaac's behavior, she couldn't remember. He definitely unsettled her.

Agnes hadn't paid much attention to the details when the auction was announced on church Sunday—such as when it would be and what it would benefit—because she hadn't planned to go. Or to donate any items. But what if Isaac were the auctioneer?

It wouldn't change anything if he was. She still couldn't go. She had to work. But she would also need to babysit. And she shouldn't feel so interested in him. She'd be accused of making cow-eyes and throwing herself at him. Quite frankly, once was enough for those shameful—but true—accusations.

Bridget leaned forward, her eyes wide. "An attempted robbery by a man with a gun? That's so scary. And also kind of exciting. To think this auctioneer walked in and saved you from certain death…."

Agnes might've accidentally exaggerated. Though, she didn't remember using the phrase "certain death."

"And he's drop-dead gorgeous?"

She might've said that, except using different language. She was pretty sure her exact words were "gut-looking," because she wanted to downplay her interest.

Apparently, she'd failed. Of course, the breathlessness of her voice might've given her away.

Agnes forced a smile but didn't know what to say.

"You lead the most exciting life." Bridget sighed. "You own your own business, you do what you love, handsome strangers wander in and save the day.... Your diary must read like an adventure novel."

Not even close, even if she kept a diary. Kum to think of it, her day-dreams were much more exciting than reality. Usually. Today might have been an exception....

"Maybe, if I grossly exaggerated things. Which I don't. At least, not often. Or on purpose. When is the auction you're crocheting for, again? I forget." Not that she'd ever stored it in her memory bank.

Bridget frowned at her project, then resumed crocheting. "Sometime this fall. I don't remember, exactly. I want to have a gut supply of items to offer, because the proceeds support the community's fund for the needy. Englischers are supposed to kum, too. Christmas shopping, I suppose. Do you think I should make pink and blue blankets?"

"Maybe a whole bunch of different colors. People won't necessarily want them for boppli. If you make them a little bigger, they'd be gut for adults to cuddle beneath on chilly days. You could make pillows to match, too. I'd buy one in pink, if I had a home."

"Ach, that's a great idea." Bridget smiled. "Have another cookie."

Agnes glanced at the full plate Noah had set beside her. Overkill, really. They'd eaten supper right before walking over here, and with all that had happened, she wasn't really hungry. She shook her head. "Danki, but I'm full."

"Are you going to donate fudge for the auction? I know that would draw lots of interest."

She still didn't plan on it. Her expenses still exceeded her profits, even though the gap narrowed every day. Of course, the damage from the attempted robbery would increase the difference again. She couldn't expect Isaac to repair the candy shop for free. Even if he did the labor pro bono, she would probably need to purchase the necessary supplies. Though, he might sell them to her at cost. She swallowed. Shook her head. "I really can't afford to donate anything."

Bridget's crochet hook paused a moment. "I think you really can't afford not to. You're bound to get more customers as a result."

Something to consider. But a lump akin to a heavy rock had taken up residence in Agnes's stomach. She swallowed. "I'll think about it."

"You mean, pray about it?" Bridget asked gently.

Agnes took a deep breath. "Jah. That, too." Conviction ate at her. But it was easier to accept the reminder from her friend than from her preacher daed's stern pronouncements.

Bridget ripped out a few stitches, then continued to crochet. "How long will Isaac be in town?"

The change in topic threw Agnes for a moment. She blinked. "I don't think he said."

"Probably not long enough for anything to develop, relationship-wise." Bridget frowned.

"Probably not." Agnes forced a cheerful note into her voice to add, "I'm not interested anyway." Okay, that might've been a lie, but she didn't need Bridget—or anyone else—following that buggy down a rabbit trail, and she certainly didn't need anyone or anything fueling any unrealistic expectations. It was enough to know Isaac was a flirt, and that, if she was going to be anything to him, it'd be a summer fling. Nothing more.

She didn't want to be a summer fling. Not his, not anyone's. She wanted forever.

But that was impossible.

The rock in her stomach grew larger and threatened to evict the cookie she'd eaten.

"I probably should see if Isaac is ready to head back to the Brunstetters'. They go to bed early, and we need to get the sofa bed made up for him." Agnes pushed to her feet.

Bridget glanced outside at the darkening sky. "I'll stop by the shop and help with cleanup sometime tomorrow. In fact, I'll talk to my friend Arie and a few other girls in the morgen and see if we can have a work frolic."

"That'd be greatly appreciated." Agnes put her tennis shoes back on and opened the door. "See you soon."

"Jah. It was real gut to see you," Bridget said as the door shut behind Agnes.

Agnes trudged across the yard to the shed where Gabe had set up the office for his and Noah's construction company. She was almost there when a man stepped out of the shadows and into her path. He seemed huge, silhouetted in the light of the barn. She stumbled to a stop, pressing her hand against her mouth so she wouldn't scream.

A hand closed around her upper arm, warm against the fabric of her dress. Heat spread from the source of contact to the tips of her fingers and toes.

She jerked away. The scream pushing past her hand emerged as a squeak not anywhere near mouse-worthy.

Isaac cleared his throat. "I was just coming to find you."

Isaac shook his tingling hand in the cool evening air, disturbing a swarm of mosquitoes but not erasing the sizzle of Agnes's touch. "You're ready to go?" His voice was still gruff, even though he'd cleared his throat.

"Jah," she said breathlessly. She made another noise, as if starting to say something else and then cutting herself off. Odd. Self-restraint in the verbal department, just when he was beginning to wish she would babble on and on.

He turned toward the road, and both of them remained quiet for maybe three or four steps. But he wasn't in the mood to walk back to the Brunstetters' in companionable silence. If that were the case, he'd be reaching for her hand, entwining their fingers, and thinking romantic thoughts. Maybe even considering spiriting her into the darkness under a big tree and stealing a kiss or two. It was much too soon to do more than think about that, though. Far better to be sparring with this attractive, attention-grabbing, curvy bundle of womanhood.

He searched for something to say. "Did you have a gut visit?"

"Jah. I told Bridget about the attempted robbery, and we talked about an upcoming auction she's crocheting some items for. She tried to talk me into donating fudge."

"And?"

Her body jerked. "And you. Okay? We talked about you." The words tumbled out, tripping over each other, and landing hard on the two-tire-track road they trod along.

Isaac barked out a short laugh. He'd wanted to know whether she'd decided to donate any fudge, not find out if she and Bridget had gossiped about him. He swiped a hand over his jaw, feeling a day's worth of stubble. "What about me?"

She made a sort of strangled sound. "How long you might be around."

That strangled sound indicated a lot more than her words. As if they'd speculated about him and discussed more personal stuff. How much had Sam and Jenny shared about him? But he wouldn't press. "Ah. How long is rather hard to say. I need to give my brother a call, I suppose." He glanced off into the darkness. "So, you're running your daed's business? I saw the name Samuel Zook on the file Gabe pulled out, and he mentioned he's your daed. *Was.*"

"Jah, he's gone now, but the business was never his. It's always been mine." Defensiveness had entered her voice. "A single woman alone, who has nein prospects of marriage, has to have some way of supporting herself, ain't so?"

Hmm. Had these harsh, self-critical thoughts kum from herself? Or from her daed?

"I could live in the room in the back of the shop, but it's unfurnished, and I was needed to help Katherine with your nieces and nephew." She stubbed her toe on something on the road and stumbled, flailing her arms.

He grabbed her elbow to steady her. The same sparks from before worked through him anew.

And again, she jerked away. "But they won't need me now, so I guess as soon as I get the shop cleaned up, I'll move in." There was a curious mix of determination and brokenness in her voice.

"Do you have furnishings that would need to be moved there?" He wasn't sure why he'd asked.

"Nein, but I don't need anything. There are chairs in the shop, and I can sleep on the floor."

"You shouldn't have to sleep on the floor. I'll look for some furniture for you at my upcoming auctions." He wanted to take care of her as best as he could while he was around.

She snorted. "Nobody asked you to be my guardian, Isaac. I can take care of myself."

"Ach, to be sure, and I'll expect payment from you—in the form of childcare." He winked, but she didn't look his way. A perfectly gut wink, gone to waste.

A few kisses down the line might also be an acceptable form of payment....

He cringed. He shouldn't think like that.

They reached the main road and moved to the other side of the street so they'd be walking against traffic. Isaac positioned himself closer to the road, to protect Agnes.

"Did you get what you needed from Gabe?" She slowed a little.

Isaac matched her pace. "Jah. Name and phone number for the glass repairman and the measurements of the current sink. I'll call the glass guy tomorrow. But I didn't find out a single thing about a television interview." He cocked his head. Jah, he was baiting her. He hadn't mentioned a thing to the other men about the interview.

She startled, stumbling again.

He wrapped his fingers around her elbow.

More sparks.

He could get used to this.

Almost belatedly, she pulled away. Maybe he'd begun to wear down her defenses a little.

Except, she moved further from him, so he couldn't touch her as easily as before.

Too bad.

Shame filled him, and he grimaced. He should've stopped teasing when she called him a flirt. Instead, the label had spurred him on. If he wasn't careful, she'd refuse to watch his nieces and nephew when he traveled to auctions, and then he'd be in a fine fix.

Probably time to back off.

But she was so adorably cute when she became flustered.

And, gut or bad, he wanted—needed—craved—her attention.

He swallowed. "I really ought to know about the television thing. Sam and Jenny might have issues with their kinner being on TV. And I really can't see Bishop Miah agreeing with the idea."

"Neither can I." She sounded almost cheerful, as if happy for an excuse to decline doing the interview.

"And, being without a daed, you probably should have a man to watch over you." He glanced at her.

She stiffened. Probably gearing up to repeat her retort from earlier about being able to take care of herself.

He rushed on to get the rest of his words out before she had a chance to erupt. "I'll be the hero and take care of you while I'm here."

"While you're here," she repeated with a sarcastic tone.

"Well, of course. I—"

"Listen up, Isaac Mast. I *can* take care of myself. It's going to happen, whether I want it to or not. Nein drop-dead-gorgeous, clean-cut hero is going to kum rescue me near a live Christmas tree while the snow crunches pleasantly under my feet."

Isaac blinked. Wow, she was specific in her dreaming. He looked up at the star-studded sky, then around at the leafy summer forest surrounding them. Not a snowflake in sight. It was August, after all. And any Christmas trees around here were of the natural variety, growing wild in the woods. He opened his mouth to repeat the first question he'd asked upon entering her candy shop that afternoon and catching her talking to her plants. *Are you on drugs?*

Except, she wasn't.

The words hovered, unsaid, on the edge of his tongue as her words replayed in his mind. *Nein drop-dead-gorgeous, clean-cut hero is going to kum rescue me near a live Christmas tree while the snow crunches pleasantly under my feet.*

She brushed at something on her cheek.

Isaac swallowed hard. "I'll be that hero."

He desperately wanted to be that hero. Finally. For her.

Except, with his past mistakes....

5

Agnes swiped at another tear. Hopefully, Isaac hadn't noticed she was crying. She didn't want him thinking she was desperate for an ehemann, because she wasn't. She had simply resigned herself to her fate.

Sort of.

Okay, not at all.

But that changed nothing.

I'll be that hero.

Right. Another tear made an escape. She blinked at the burn and looked away. "You do that, Isaac." She tried for an appropriate measure of sarcasm.

He didn't comment. His only response was the same odd hmming sound he'd made twice at her shop.

They strolled along the side of the road in silence for maybe ten minutes—with her staring off into the dark woods, trying to get her emotions under control—before he finally spoke again. "Tell me about the television interview."

She huffed and looked at him. "You aren't going to let it go, are you?" At least she wouldn't cry over this topic.

He arched an eyebrow. "Were you serious about it? If you were, then, nein, I won't let it go."

She kicked at a tuft of weeds in her path. "Okay. I've been approached by a television station doing a feature on Amish businesses, and one of their reporters got wind of my candy shop. So, the station informed me they would kum by one day next week with him—or her, the name is BJ—cameras rolling, to film a segment on my business."

As scary as the prospect was, it constituted another reason why she needed to get her shop back in shape. This news feature could be her chance to boost sales and increase her profit margin.

"They 'informed' you?"

"Jah. In the note they sent, it didn't read like a request. Apparently, they are featuring other Amish-owned businesses, too, but I haven't heard anyone else in town talking about it."

"The bishop needs to know," Isaac stated flatly. "And you'll need to make it clear they can film or photograph you only from behind."

"Have you ever been interviewed on television?" She glanced at him.

"Nein. But I might've been on TV or video before. I've seen cameramen filming at some auctions." He hesitated, then reached for her hand.

She skittered away. Nein need to fuel the sparks his touch ignited.

He sighed. "Would you like me to be there when they kum?"

Jah, she would. "How can you be if they don't schedule a specific date and time? All they said was 'sometime next week.'"

He grunted.

Big help there. Irritating man. She looked away. "Exactly." She probably could've used a little less bitterness in her tone.

"I could plan on hanging out at the candy shop all week."

Jah, please. Except, she would need to work extra hard to keep her crazy dreams and emotions and verbal vomit under control.

They stopped by the mailbox at the end of the bishop's driveway. She glanced at him. "And what would you do? All the repairs would need to be done already, so we're prepared for the camera crew."

He chuckled. Winked. "Getting underfoot, of course. I've been told I'm quite gut at it."

Her face burned. "I bet you are."

Another chuckle.

Then he leaned closer as if about to share a delicious secret. "We could heat up the candy thermometer together."

Isaac flipped the mailbox flag up and down a couple more times, enjoying the shocked look on Agnes's face probably a little too much. And after he'd told himself at least twice to tone it down.

Apparently, with this woman, that was impossible.

He should be ashamed of himself, but he wasn't. It was too much fun. Maybe she'd learn to loosen up and give it out as glibly as he did.

He wasn't sure he liked that idea, though, especially if she used her newfound skills to flirt with one of the single men around these parts. Noah Behr, or...well, he didn't know who else. Of course, it'd be worse if she flirted with a married man. *Gabe.*

Shoot, Isaac liked the guy. Another time, they could be friends. Gabe seemed fun, smart, hardworking, and a bunch of other positive adjectives. But he was married. Agnes needed to get over him and move on.

And if she set her affections on Isaac for a time, all the better. They'd have fun while he was around, and then....

Then.

Isaac sighed.

She'd be left nursing a broken heart—again—while he moved on to the next district, the next state, the next woman who made him look twice but had nein chance of capturing his heart.

He flipped the mailbox flag down and nodded toward the haus. "Shall we?" They'd lingered by the mailbox long enough. Bishop Miah would suspect Isaac of being interested in courting the lovely Agnes, when, in reality, he....

What?

Okay, he was interested. But he needed her. Period. The strong attraction was a positive surprise, but secondary.

Somehow, he'd need to find a way to tell...ask...nein, warn.... Ugh. He couldn't think of the right word. Not when she brushed past him, the temptingly delicious aroma of chocolate teasing his senses, and headed toward the haus.

Without him.

Would her kisses taste of fudge?

He caught his breath, sucking in another delicious scent of lingering sweetness, and rushed to catch up with her. "I need to get my bags from the buggy. I suppose I should plan on passing out the candy in the morgen, since the kinner are in bed."

"There's a lantern burning in the living room." Agnes pointed. "The bishop and Katherine might enjoy a taste of fudge before bed. But I'd suggest saving the kinner's rock candy until we get to your brother's haus after working in my shop. It shouldn't take all day to clean it, especially if Bridget organizes a frolic like she promised. And I can't reopen until after the glass is repaired, ain't so?"

"Hopefully, the cleaning frolic will extend to helping with Sam's haus, too." The sooner he got out of the Brunstetters' home and into his own place, the better. Except, then he'd lose Agnes's help tucking the kinner into bed.

Unless she stayed to help.

Leaving the two of them alone together afterward....

Dangerous thoughts, those.

He would also worry about her going home alone after dark, especially if she ended up moving into that room behind her shop—her shop where a thief had shot at her.

He cleared his throat. "Maybe the glass repairman can kum out tomorrow. It shouldn't take long for him to fix. And getting your candy shop up and running needs to be our top priority. Do you think Katherine will watch the kinner while we work tomorrow?"

Agnes pursed her lips.

The silence said volumes. "They're mine from here on out, ain't so?"

"Pretty much. I suppose they could play inside at one of the tables while we clean. I could mix up a batch of homemade play dough to keep them entertained a while. If they're gut, we could reward them with the rock candy when we get to Sam's haus."

Isaac laughed. "Bribery. Works every time."

"And if Bridget gets a frolic organized, one of the girls could watch them while I clean and you make your phone call."

"Hey, I'm going to do more than talk on the phone. I intend to fix the drywall damage from the bullet, too, and I can clean if you need to count money, figure out sales, and make a run to the bank."

They reached the haus. "I'll go in and see if that sleeper sofa is ready for you." Agnes climbed the porch steps.

"I'll get my bags," Isaac said. But he stood there watching her as she crossed the porch to the door. He startled when a shadow moved nearby. Shouldn't have, because the citronella candles dimly illuminated the corner where the man sat. Isaac's attention had been too focused on Agnes.

His face burned.

"Wondered when you two would return." The bishop stood and snuffed out the candles. "Agnes, after you help Katherine with the bed, I think we all need to have a talk. We'll meet you in the kitchen."

Isaac moistened his lips and turned away. They did need to talk, but he had his own set of topics in mind. What did Bishop Miah want to discuss?

⌒

Agnes walked down the hall to the spare room. Katherine had taken the cushions off the sleeper sofa and was tugging ineffectually at the handle. Agnes touched her arm. "I've got it," she said quietly.

"I'll get the bedding." Katherine moved to the closet and reached up to the top shelf for sheets, a spare pillow, and blankets.

Agnes pulled the mattress out, took the sheets from Katherine, and tried not to think of the last time this bed had been used, or her foolish thoughts about Gabe. The painful knowledge that he cared for Bridget instead of her. A pain eclipsed by the loss of her family and the lost chance to prove her daed wrong.

Katherine laid the blanket and pillow on the dresser. "I'll go see if there's any koffee left. I made decaf earlier. Would you like some chamomile tea instead?"

"Sounds gut. Danki." Agnes doubted the tea would do much to calm her heart and mind before bed. She'd likely lay awake all nacht, replaying every flirtatious word and touch Isaac had given her in the few hours they'd known each other. And daydreaming about working together to make fudge, playing "mamm and daed" to those three precious kinner whose lives had been disrupted in such a terrible way, and worrying about how she would handle all the changes—positive and negative—in her life. Not to mention, having nacht-mares about the attempted robbery. She shuddered.

If Isaac hadn't pushed her to the floor, she might be dead. Or, at least, badly injured and in the hospital.

She had thanked him for saving her life, hadn't she?

She couldn't remember. She'd make sure to say "danki" sometime, either to-nacht or tomorrow.

Agnes finished making the bed, fluffed the pillow, and folded back the worn-out tumbling-block quilt invitingly, then went to join the others in the kitchen. Isaac's bag was beside the door, and he'd set the two packages of fudge on the table.

Katherine laid a knife beside the boxes. "This will be such a nice bedtime treat. Danki, Isaac, for thinking of us."

"Danki for taking care of the kinner until I could kum," Isaac said.

"Agnes handled the bulk of their care when she was home." Katherine gave him a look that said he should have bought another box of fudge to thank her.

Isaac grinned. "How do you thank the candymaker when candy is out of the question?" He eyed Agnes. "Never mind. I'll thank her later."

Her whole body warmed with the hint of a promise in his quiet words. But, nein. He couldn't—shouldn't—wouldn't mean it the way she'd interpreted it.

Then again, he might. He was a flirt.

She'd have to be very careful to avoid being alone with him. Which should be easy with three kinner underfoot. Especially when two of those kinner were loud and chatty and would tattle about whatever they saw at such a volume that the entire community would know her private business.

Agnes made herself a mug of chamomile tea and went to join the others at the table. Katherine had already poured each of them a mug of decaf koffee. Apparently, Isaac hadn't taken Agnes's warning seriously, though he had refused any koffee at supper. She dropped into the chair across from him and glanced away, meeting the bishop's steady gaze.

Bishop Miah cleared his throat. "About the robbery. Nein sugarcoating it. What happened?"

Agnes told him about it, then, with dread, pulled the crumpled letter from the television reporter out of her pocket and handed it to him. Maybe he'd put an end to it. "I found this at the post office when I went there this morgen. I check the mail once every couple of weeks, so it might've been there a while."

Bishop Miah took the letter with a heavy sigh. "They contacted Gabe and Noah, too, though they addressed the letter to Behr Construction, attention Hosea Behr, so clearly they hadn't gotten news of the change of ownership. Gideon Kaiser"—he glanced at Isaac—"the owner of the Amish salvage-grocery store...he got one, too. I gave permission, with the agreement that nein faces would be photographed." He looked back at Agnes. "The same goes for you. As far as I know, they aren't featuring any other Amish businesses, maybe because they deemed them not as newsworthy. You have to admit, your candy shop is doing better than anyone anticipated."

Maybe so, even if she had yet to turn a complete profit. She had nein choice but to make it work. She was responsible for herself.

And would be for eternity, if Daed's words proved true. And they would, surely, since he'd been a preacher.

She peeked from beneath her eyelashes at Isaac.

Handsome, blue-eyed auctioneer flirts wouldn't change a thing.

6

Isaac leaned back in the chair, kicking his legs out in front of him, and looked his fill at the attractive woman across from him as she talked with the bishop.

Katherine pulled a stack of plates from the cupboard and set them on the table. "For the fudge."

Isaac wouldn't have bothered with plates for a few thin slices of candy. Both the peanut butter fudge and the pink, heart-shaped kind—whatever it was—smelled delicious. He picked up his mug of hot koffee.

Agnes gave him a warning glance, looking pointedly at the mug. He frowned. The beverage couldn't possibly be as bad as she'd claimed. Who could ruin java? Still, he exercised caution as he took a sip. And almost gagged. He'd had strong koffee before, but this was awful. Somehow, he managed to swallow it. Then he set the mug down and pushed it away. He should've taken Agnes up on her offer to fill a mug for him at her shop.

Katherine set a plate in front of him with one sliver of each of the two kinds of fudge on it. He would've cut the treat into cubes, if he'd been in charge. The bishop's frau had somehow managed to slice it paper-thin.

His mouth watered. His fingers trembled to pick up his slivers and eat them, but he forced himself to be polite and wait.

"Would you like chamomile tea instead?" Katherine glanced at his mug.

Isaac frowned. He'd been warned away from Agnes's tea, too. This time, he would play it safe. "Water would be fine, danki."

Katherine filled a glass at the faucet and set it in front of him. "The water here has a bit of a taste, but you'll get used to it."

Right. Noah had warned him about that. Was anything safe to drink in these parts?

He blew out a frustrated breath as the bishop's gaze shifted from Agnes to him.

Isaac ignored the bishop's stare and took a bite of the peanut butter fudge. Amazing. As soon as Agnes's candy shop was back in business, he'd buy a slab for himself.

And then run a marathon to work off the calories and fat.

Agnes sipped her tea in silence, the table in front of her bare.

Isaac raised his eyebrows. Why hadn't Katherine served her any fudge? "Do you want some?" He gestured at the pink heart-shaped kind. It made him think of Agnes, which made him think of love. And the impossibility of that made his heart hurt.

She smiled and shook her head. "Danki, but nein. I sample enough at the candy shop."

Bishop Miah cleared his throat, drawing Isaac's unwilling attention. "The trouble with our past is that it refuses to stay past."

The remnant of peanut butter fudge coating Isaac's tongue turned into a congealed blob. He returned the bishop's stare, but he didn't know what to say, or whether an answer was even expected. He supposed there was a remote possibility Sam had spoken to this man about the events that had separated the twin brothers, making them more like strangers than family. But Isaac sort of doubted he had, since Sam's telling on Isaac would have implicated himself. Something Sam would never do.

Unless he'd blamed everything on Isaac.

Bishop Miah seemed to be waiting for a response, though, so Isaac muttered, "Mmm-hmm." When in doubt....

"The Bible says in Isaiah one, verse eighteen, 'Though your sins are like scarlet, they shall be as white as snow.'"

Was this turning into a not-so-private counseling session? His past wasn't up for discussion, even if Sam had blabbed or blamed. Not even with a bishop in a district Isaac had nein intention of staying in once his duty to his brother's kinner was fulfilled.

And especially not in front of a woman Isaac was strongly attracted to.

Isaac started to push the remaining sliver of pink fudge toward Agnes but changed his mind and passed it to Katherine. "Sweets for the sweet." He downed his strongly flavored-of-sulfur water and stood. "Gut nacht."

"We'll talk tomorrow," the bishop said.

Not if Isaac had anything to say about it.

He grabbed his bag and disappeared into the room they'd prepared for him, firmly shutting the door.

The next morgen, Agnes tiptoed downstairs early to get breakfast ready before she woke the kinner. Since they would be going with her to the shop, she would need time to get them fed and dressed before heading into town. And once they were up, her hands would be full.

Breakfast would be simple. Oatmeal bubbled on the stove, biscuits were fresh out of the oven, and she'd just finished stirring crumbled bits of sausage into milk gravy. She set out maple syrup, brown sugar, cinnamon, and a bowl of sliced apples and bananas. They could fix their cereal anyway they wanted.

The bishop had gone out to do the morgen chores, and Agnes hadn't seen either Katherine or Isaac yet. Whether they still slept, or if they were in the barn, she didn't know.

Agnes moved the pot of oatmeal to a cooler spot on the woodstove, wiped the sweat from her forehead, and opened the window a little wider in hopes of getting some cross ventilation going. On her way upstairs to wake the kinner, she opened the two living room windows as wide as they would go. The day would be a scorcher, for certain.

Behind her, the kitchen door opened, and someone entered, kicking off shoes with soft thuds into the plastic tray for that purpose. Agnes continued upstairs and opened the door to the bedroom where the kinner slept.

Martha reached out her pudgy little arms. "Mamamamama."

Katherine suspected Martha had some learning difficulties, since she claimed to remember her own kinner talking clearly by that age. Agnes had nein point of reference by which to judge the girl's speech, and it was sweet, being called "Mama," even though it meant nothing. Every female was mama to this child. And since this might be the only time any child called her by that name, she was determined to soak it up, along with every sweet sound and warm hug. Martha made a lot of babbling sounds, most of which neither Agnes nor Katherine understood.

Agnes lifted the little girl out of her crib, changed her diaper, and put her in a clean dress. She returned her to the crib, then shifted her attention to three-and-a-half-year-old Mary. Isaac would have his hands full taking care of the kinner. Especially since Katherine had recently started potty-training Martha. Katherine claimed that she'd trained her own kinner by the time they were six months old. That seemed a bit unrealistic to Agnes, too, but what did she know?

Timothy sat up, rubbed his eyes, and tumbled out of bed. He scrambled out of his pajamas and into his pants without a word from her.

"Is Onkel Daed still here?" He stuffed his arms into his shirtsleeves.

Agnes helped Mary into her dress. "Jah, your onkel Isaac is still here."

"Gut." Timothy ran from the room, shirt untucked and flapping open, suspenders dangling, and socks balled in one hand.

"Get dressed and brush your teeth," Agnes called after him. "You're coming to the candy shop with me today."

"Nein, I'm staying with Onkel Daed."

"Me, too." Mary struggled against Agnes as she tried to pin her dress shut.

"Hold still. Onkel Isaac is coming to the candy store, too."

"Ca-dee," Martha yelled.

Agnes sighed. "We'll have candy later, if you're gut. First we need to eat breakfast, so Onkel Isaac and I can get some work done. Put your socks on, Mary, and kum downstairs."

She hadn't fixed the girls' hair yet, but perhaps Katherine would do it. She was much quicker at it anyway. Agnes scooped up Martha, grabbed a comb and a brush, and went downstairs.

Surprisingly, Timothy was seated at the table, tugging his socks on, instead of running to find Isaac. Katherine must've caught him.

When Katherine took Martha from Agnes, Agnes laid the comb and brush on the table, then dished out food for the three kinner.

She'd just finished when the kitchen door opened, and Bishop Miah came in, alone. Agnes glanced toward the closed door of the room where Isaac had stayed last nacht.

The bishop took his boots off, washed up, and then pounded on the door. "Rise and shine."

There wasn't any answer.

He pounded again, then flung the door open.

Agnes glanced in that direction, expecting to see Isaac bolting out of bed to his feet. Instead, there was nothing. Not even a sound.

Bishop Miah turned and looked from her to Katherine. "He's gone."

Isaac had gotten up early and gone to Sam's, following the instructions Bishop Miah had given him. Finding the haus had been easy enough; he just cut through the woods at the back of the bishop's small farm and emerged at the rear of his brother's property. A lot shorter of a journey than if he'd taken the road.

Someone else's horse and buggy was parked in front of the barn, the doors of which were open when Isaac arrived. He went into the dimly lit interior and found a man milking the lone cow.

"Gut morgen." His voice was still a bit rusty from lack of use. He cleared his throat.

The man turned around with a slight smile, and Isaac recognized him as Noah Behr. "Gut morgen. It was our turn to help out today. I suppose you'll take over to-nacht?"

"I don't know yet." Isaac controlled a shudder at the realization that taking over the farm chores would imply being here alone with the kinner he'd be responsible for. How did Amish widowers handle the responsibility of farm, home, and family? He wasn't sure it could be done. "I just thought I'd see what things were like over here, so I'd have at least a vague idea of what I might need to pick up at the store."

"Nein food left here. It was taken to help the needy after the wildfire. But I'm sure the women will organize something to make sure you have meals brought in, and they might even donate some canned garden produce. And the fire station is having a chili cook-off next weekend for Labor Day, so you can count on a gut meal that day, at least. My, uh, girlfriend, Arie, is entering her recipe." Noah's face flamed red.

"Is Agnes entering?" Isaac probably should've asked about Katherine, not Agnes.

Noah frowned. "Katherine gave Arie the recipe she's using, so I doubt it." He turned his attention back to the cow. "But I imagine Agnes might bring some fudge to sell. Or maybe she's helping with the drinks. Everyone will be involved somehow, even if it's just eating." He grinned.

Isaac couldn't help but smile. "Sounds gut. Unfortunately, I need to be in Montana for an auction next weekend, so I'll have to miss it. Think I'll go inside and see what shape the haus is in. If someone could do chores to-nacht and tomorrow morgen, that would be great. I don't know if I'll be here or not. I snuck out while the Brunstetters were still asleep, so I'd best hurry back before I'm missed."

Noah nodded. "Do you want me to leave the milk here in the icebox?"

"Ah, nein. Not today." Isaac shook his head. "Danki, again."

He turned and hurried toward the haus. The unlocked door opened with a squeak. The gloomy interior smelled musty. Isaac wrinkled his nose, then sneezed. A gut scrubbing was in order. Someone had tracked mud across the floor, and cobwebs filled the corners.

He shoved several windows open to get some circulation going and in hopes of clearing out the worst of the odor. The pantry was as empty as he'd been warned, and it looked as if Jenny's cleaning and laundry supplies had been taken, too. He'd need to restock everything before bringing the kinner home.

Even though there was a great deal of work to be done, relief flooded him. He wouldn't be on his own to-nacht. Probably not for the rest of the week.

Then again, once word got out, the local women would descend, and they could probably have this place whipped into shape by bedtime. Maybe he should pray for some sort of delay.

He wasn't ready.

He'd never be ready.

He should've pretended Jenny's letter had never reached him and gone on to the next auction. He'd have to leave soon for that event anyway. He needed to check the bus schedule to find out when he would need to depart.

Instead, he'd kum here with a feeble hope of making amends.

Or maybe severing the family ties forever.

7

Agnes's breath shuddered. Her heart skipped a beat. She exchanged a look with Katherine, whose eyes were wide, her mouth gaping. Agnes probably wore an identical expression.

"Gone?" Agnes whispered. "How could he be gone?" Her heart shattered, and she hurried over to peer into the spare room. The mattress was neatly tucked back inside the sofa, the cushions replaced, and the bedding folded on one side. She didn't see any sign of his suitcase. "He can't be gone. What about the kinner? What about his brother? What about...." *Me?* She bit that word back. She didn't matter. Not to him.

"Onkel Daed!" Mary screamed.

Timothy pushed past Agnes into the bedroom. The sight of his tear-filled eyes almost broke Agnes's heart.

She forced herself to walk farther into the room and peek into the closet. Then she sagged with relief. Isaac's suitcase was on the floor, wide open, with one sock straddling the side. "He's still here. Somewhere."

Bishop Miah sighed. "Gut. The bu needs to face his fears and problems, not run from them."

Isaac was hardly a bu. He was a man. But Agnes wouldn't argue. Other than his brother's kinner and his job responsibilities, what problems did he have? And what of his fears? He hadn't given the impression of being afraid of anything in particular, except maybe her. Or the kinner. She wasn't sure which.

Maybe, since he'd pressed her for answers about the television interview, she could question him about the secrets he hid. The ones Bishop Miah had alluded to.

The kitchen door opened and shut. Timothy whirled around. "Onkel Daed?"

A chair hit the floor as Mary gave a delighted squeal.

"First thing we'll have to teach those kinner is his name," Bishop Miah muttered. "Followed by volume control."

Agnes nodded. She walked into the kitchen in time to see Isaac crouch down to hug the kinner.

Timothy flung himself into Isaac's arms. "You didn't leave us."

"Of course not. I'm here until your daed and mamm kum home. Except for when I have to travel for work, and then Agnes will take care of you." He looked over at her with a smile.

She couldn't quite find a return smile. Not when she wanted to throw herself in his arms and cry.

"Glad to hear you aren't abandoning your responsibilities." The bishop sat at the head of the table. "We'll eat as soon as you've washed up."

Isaac nodded, rose, and motioned the kinner back to the table. He slipped his shoes off, leaving them on the plastic tray, and padded across the floor to the sink. After washing up, he headed for the table. As he passed Agnes, she reached out toward his arm but then pulled back without touching him.

He stopped, and her gaze snagged his. "Danki for still being here."

Isaac nodded, but an emotion darkened his eyes. Pain? "I honor my responsibilities." He almost growled the words as his gaze moved from her to the bishop. "To everyone."

"It's impossible to drive in the wrong direction and end up in the right destination," Bishop Miah quipped.

"Not impossible," Isaac countered as he sat. "You might just take the scenic route instead."

The bishop chortled.

Agnes hid a smile. It was entertaining to hear someone turn the bishop's odd proverbs back on themselves. She sometimes preferred the scenic route, too. As she began ladling the oatmeal into bowls, she glanced at Isaac. Such an interesting man.

Katherine brought over the plate of biscuits and the bowl of sausage gravy.

"Let's pray." Bishop Miah bowed his head as the women took their seats.

Martha whammed her hands on the table and let out a stream of words Agnes couldn't understand.

Agnes looked at Martha, pressed her fingers against her lips, and closed her eyes. Then she peeked to make sure the toddler had obeyed. The child's eyes were open, but she had at least folded her hands.

Lord.… Agnes sighed. *Please heal Isaac's pain, whatever it is. Be with his brother and help him to be well enough to kum home soon. And my shop, Lord…please help it to be up and running again soon. And help me to ignore Isaac's flirting and to stand firm. I know my future and realize there's nein point in getting my hopes up. Not sure I want a flirt anyway.*

Gabe had been a considerable flirt, though he'd settled down quickly enough with Bridget and stopped flirting with any other girls. Maybe there was hope for Isaac. With the right woman.

She wasn't that woman.

"Amen," the bishop said, a bit too heartily, as if he was in agreement with her silent thoughts.

Agnes blinked at the sudden burn in her eyes. Did he *have* to agree?

Katherine hopped to her feet. "Koffee, anyone?"

"Ah, nein. Danki." Isaac tried to conceal his shudder, but Agnes caught it.

"Agnes made it." Katherine poured a mug of koffee and set it in front of him. "I've heard vicious rumors that her koffee is better than mine, but I don't know how that could possibly be true. Koffee is koffee."

Isaac chuckled. "Well, I've been warned away from her tea. And from the local water supply, which I tasted last nacht. I'm not sure anything liquid is safe at this point."

Agnes gasped. "Who warned you away from my tea?"

He tilted his head back, as if challenging her. "Gabe."

At least he didn't call him "your Gabe" this time.

"He compared it to the taste of freshly mowed grass." A dimple flashed at the corner of his mouth, as if he struggled to keep a smile at bay.

Agnes glared at him. "Of course, it did. It was medicinal, meant to speed the healing of his sprained muscles and torn ligaments. It's a proven fact that—"

Isaac laughed.

Agnes wanted to throw something at him. Like the kitchen table. Or even herself. And beat his strong, muscular chest with her fists....

Better kill that thought right there. In her imagination, the scene would end with his lips on hers. With laughter. And with declarations of love.

It wouldn't happen in real life.

"I assure you, Agnes's tea is very gut." Bishop Miah sprinkled brown sugar on his oatmeal. "Although, admittedly, I've never tasted any of her medicinal teas."

Agnes pursed her lips and held Isaac's twinkling blue gaze. "I'll make sure you get a double dose of medicinal tea."

His dimple flashed again. "Is that so?"

She waved her biscuit at him. Crumbs flaked off and scattered like confetti. "You are the most annoying man."

Another dimple appeared on the other side of his well-formed lips. Not that she noticed.

"I've only just begun, Agnes Zook." He lifted his brow.

A definite challenge.

Bishop Miah chuckled.

And Agnes stared at Isaac. Speechless.

⌒

Isaac took a bite of his banana-laden oatmeal as Katherine set a mug of koffee in front of Agnes. He wouldn't waste his breath telling himself not to tease her anymore. She was much too fun.

Cleaning her shop today promised to be more entertainment than drudgery, especially if they could somehow keep the banter going.

He eyed the kinner, because they were coming, too, and detected a hint of amusement in the boy's eyes that implied a similar penchant for troublemaking.

When breakfast was over, Katherine combed the girls' hair—another job he'd be worthless at—and Agnes fixed sandwiches out of the leftover biscuits and some cheese, tomatoes, and onions. It was a combination Isaac had never heard of but was willing to try. He decided to head outside to hitch up Agnes's horse to the buggy. He put on his shoes, with his shadow, Timmy, mirroring his every move.

"Can I help with Wildfire, Onkel Daed?" Timmy tugged on his hand.

The horse's name was equally appropriate for the personality of the woman who owned him.

Isaac smiled at the bu. "Sure. But my name is Isaac. Can you call me Onkel Isaac?"

"Onkel Isaac," the bu parroted.

"Gut. Now say my name three times in a row. When you repeat something three times, you're less likely to forget it. And I need you to teach your sisters."

Timmy trotted after him, repeating "Onkel Isaac" over and over and over. More than three times, but it didn't matter. Just so long as he stopped calling him "Onkel Daed."

Isaac wasn't worthy of that designation.

They'd just finished hitching the horse when Agnes came outside, carrying a tote bag in one hand, with Martha perched on her opposite hip.

Mary ran ahead of Agnes and flung her arms around Isaac's legs, giving him a tight hug. "Go with Onkel Daed," she stated firmly.

It really was too bad Katherine wanted a day off from watching the kinner. But Isaac supposed there was nothing like being immersed completely, all at once. Like jumping into the icy swimming hole in the spring-fed river when he was a child. If the initial shock didn't kill you, you got used to it in a hurry. This would be a huge initial shock.

Except, he'd have Agnes for help, so maybe the shock wouldn't be as huge as it would otherwise be.

Isaac also figured the bishop had matchmaking on his mind and wanted to make Isaac think about family, maybe with Agnes as the mamm and the three kinner, theirs.

It was working.

But there was nein reason to hope. If Agnes knew his secrets, she'd have nothing to do with him.

The bishop had nein idea what he meddled with. If he did, he was being beyond cruel.

Judging by Bishop Miah's sense of humor, Isaac figured he must be clueless. It was better than considering the older man might have an unkind motive.

Some chasms were impossible to bridge.

Sometimes, troubled waters weren't meant to be forded.

And, in many cases, the past needed to be laid to rest, not revisited.

The ride to Sweet Treats was uneventful. Agnes bounced Martha on her knee while Isaac drove; the other two kinner, seated between them, chattered back and forth after fighting over who'd get to sit next to Isaac. It was nice his nieces and nephew accepted him so readily. Probably due in large part to their perceived resemblance between him and their father.

Agnes knew they were twins, but she still didn't see it.

Once Isaac parked in front of the shop, Agnes helped the kinner out of the buggy, then carried Martha and the lunch tote up the uneven steps. She unlocked the door, stepped inside, and looked around.

She'd almost expected to arrive and find the windows smashed in and the money gone. Or maybe a creepy stalker-ish gift waiting on the counter. But everything seemed to be the same as the way she'd left it the nacht before. She'd probably been reading too many suspenseful romance novels lately.

"Don't touch the broken glass," she warned the kinner. They'd wandered over to peek in at the glass-sprinkled fudge in the display case. That'd be the first thing to do: throw away the ruined fudge, as painful as such wastefulness would be.

The sleigh bells on the door jingled as Isaac came in. He set the toolbox he'd borrowed from Bishop Miah on the floor. "I hitched Wildfire around the corner where you parked yesterday. Everything okay in here? As I was driving around the building, I thought I probably should've checked the place for intruders before you came in."

Agnes grinned. "You've been reading too many suspense novels, too."

"Watching. On hotel televisions."

Ach. She blinked at the reminder of his not-so-Amish lifestyle. "I'm going to make some play dough for the kinner to keep them occupied while I dispose of the ruined fudge."

"And I'm going to call the glass repairman and get the case ready for him. I also want to repair the drywall." He glanced at the bullet hole in the wall. "Then I'll be all yours. Whatever you need."

If only.

Timothy went outside with Isaac while he made his phone call while Agnes enlisted the girls' help preparing the play dough. While the mixture was heating in a big pan on the stove, she peeked outside to see what was taking Isaac so long.

Neither he nor Timothy were anywhere in sight.

She returned to the kitchen and set the dough aside. "Don't touch," she warned the girls. "Hot." She set them up with empty mixing bowls and wooden spoons to play with while the dough cooled.

Sleigh bells rang.

Isaac and Timothy?

Agnes whirled around and hurried out front.

Bridget, Arie, and several other girls came in, armed with mops, buckets, and other cleaning supplies. They wouldn't be the natural, homemade cleaners with essential oils that Agnes preferred, but gratefulness filled her.

She hugged Bridget. "Danki so much."

"Where's the drop-dead-gorgeous guy?" Bridget teased.

The door opened again, and an Englisch man came in, wearing a shirt embroidered with the phrase "John's Glass." "I'm here about the display case...?"

"Thank you for coming so quickly." Agnes indicated the display case. "Isaac hasn't removed the broken glass yet."

But obviously he'd made the phone call, so where was he? And where was Timothy? Had the bu run away, and had Isaac gone looking for him?

She cast a worried look out the front windows. Nothing. Nobody.

"It's okay, I can take it out. I'm John." He smiled and set his kit on the floor beside the case.

Agnes returned her attention to her friends. "I don't know where Isaac went. He said he was stepping outside to call John here." She waved her hand toward the repairman.

"There's a hottie and a bu coming up the stairs. You're open, right?" Sarah Fisher rushed to open the door. "Welkum to Sweet Treats."

"Danki." Isaac barely glanced at her. His hands were full with bags from the grocery store, and he had a square of drywall tucked under one arm. "I got the drywall. And everything we'll need for banana splits once the work is done."

"Banana splits," Arie breathed.

Bridget grinned. "He's a keeper," she whispered.

Agnes imagined mounds of vanilla, strawberry, and chocolate ice cream piled atop sliced bananas and covered in whipped cream and other goodies.

Isaac's gaze locked with hers, a crooked smile on his face. For one heart-stopping moment, the world paused.

Agnes sighed dreamily. "I think I love you."

8

She *loved* him?

Isaac stared at Agnes, shocked speechless for probably the first time in his life. The glass repairman chuckled and the room full of unknown girls—er, women—after the initial loud gasp, either stared wide-eyed at Agnes or giggled nervously behind their fingers.

Agnes turned beet red.

Isaac found his voice. "Well, that didn't take long. Just in case you ever wondered, John, the road to a girl's heart is paved with banana splits."

"I heard chocolate is a girl's best friend." John retrieved a tool from his case.

"I didn't…I…I don't…I mean, I…." Whimpering, Agnes spun on her heels and disappeared through the kitchen door.

Isaac felt like a class-A jerk. Flirting and teasing in private was one thing, but doing so in front of witnesses was another thing altogether. He should have remembered how horrified she'd been when he mentioned Gabe in front of Noah. And one of these women was probably Gabe's frau….

If only he could have a do-over. For his entire life.

Behind him, a few of the women snickered and whispered among themselves. The one who'd been standing next to Agnes glared in their direction, then swiveled and, with a swish of her skirt, followed Agnes through the swinging kitchen door. Two others followed. Leaving two in the front room with him.

Loud banging came from behind the closed door. It sounded like a hammer beating on metal, but it wasn't a solid, timed beat. It couldn't be a carpenter; and if someone back there was taking up the drums, he or she needed a lot more practice.

He knew he should probably go talk to Agnes, but he didn't know what to say. She didn't *love* love him. It was just a way of expressing her gratitude to him for thinking of ice cream on such a hot, muggy day.

Nothing to make a big deal about. And he'd had to go and make it a big deal.

The women who'd followed Agnes could handle her embarrassment. He turned to the glass repairman. "Glad you could kum so quickly, John. Is there anything I can do to help?" Despite his still-full hands, Isaac stopped beside the case, Timmy by his side, as John removed a broken piece of glass.

"Nope, I've got it."

"Then I'll get started on the drywall." Except, he needed to take care of the ice cream, which would mean invading the kitchen. Plus, he needed to put a stop to that annoying pounding.

He handed the piece of drywall to Timmy. "Stay here. I'll be right back." He took a deep breath for fortitude, pushed the door open, and stopped. Mary stared at a bowl of something on the counter, her hands clasped tightly behind her back as if she'd been told not to touch, and it was taking all her strength not to. Martha whammed a rolling pin on the upturned bottom of a metal mixing bowl, probably leaving dents. There was nein sign of Agnes or the other women.

Isaac stashed the ice cream in the freezer, set the bananas and the cones he'd picked up for the kinner on the counter, then turned and confiscated the rolling pin from Martha.

Her face screwed up as if she were about to start screaming.

Isaac shook his head and set the pin beside the sink. "That's enough." He said it as firmly as he could, then turned to Mary. "What are you doing?"

"Agnes said nein touch till it's cool. I wait."

Isaac noticed a box containing four small bottles of food coloring nearby, but nein color had been added to the dough. He poked a finger into it. "It's cool. Take it to the front room and sit at a table to play with it."

"Kum, Martha, we play this." Mary grabbed the bowl with both arms and trotted toward the front of the store, where, hopefully, one of the two snickering *maidals* out front would take over childcare.

The back door was chained shut, so Agnes couldn't have gone outside. There were three closed doors along the left side of the kitchen, and Isaac finally heard chatter coming from one of them; it was unclear which one, however. One of the doors, he knew from the previous day, led to the supply room and the bathroom. The second door had also been open the day before, and Isaac had spied a folding table stacked high with messy piles of papers and a set of chairs—probably the closest thing Agnes had to an office. Isaac should look for a desk for her at an auction, too.

So, the third door…Agnes's eventual bedroom. He exhaled. Inhaled. Then mustered the courage to tap.

The chatter didn't stop. It didn't even pause.

He would talk to her later. Maybe by then he'd figure out what to say.

Isaac blew out a breath and returned to the front room. John had already removed all the glass from the display case. Talk about a fast worker. Gabe's recommendation had paid off.

Timmy stood where Isaac had left him. His face lit up when Isaac smiled at him. One of the snickering women—how dare she laugh at Agnes?—sat at a table with the younger girls, showing them how to fashion shapes out of play dough.

The woman who'd opened the door for him approached, batting her eyelashes. "Hi. I'm Sarah Fisher."

"I'm *not* available." He pressed his lips together. "Agnes could use help washing dishes. You appear tall enough to reach the bottom of the sink."

Sarah Fisher scowled at him. "You're rude."

Isaac smirked. "Whatever works."

She huffed and stalked off into the kitchen, while the woman with the *kinner* giggled at the exchange.

Isaac couldn't afford to make enemies here, but he also didn't need female manhunters prowling around him. Not here, not now. He had enough to keep him busy with the *kinner*, Sam's small farm, and helping Agnes, in addition to the auctions he'd already booked.

Isaac retrieved the small toolbox he'd borrowed from Bishop Miah that *morgen* and took the drywall from Timmy. "Let's get this repaired."

The kitchen door swished open, and a honey-blonde woman strode toward him. She stopped before him and folded her arms across her chest. "Agnes wears her heart on her sleeve, and she tends to talk without filtering her words. But she didn't mean it the way it came out. She's mortified."

Isaac nodded. "I understood what she meant. I shouldn't have teased. I'll be sure to apologize later."

The woman smiled. "I'm Bridget Lapp. Gabe's frau."

"Ah. Agnes's pretend sister. Nice to meet you." He held out his hand. "Isaac Mast. Sam's brother."

She shook hands with him. "She told you about me. I'll tell Agnes you understand and start assigning jobs."

The glass repairman shook his head and gathered his tools as Bridget went back into the kitchen. "You've got your work cut out for you."

Isaac nodded, even though he wasn't quite sure what John meant. He pulled out his wallet and counted out the cash for the amount John had quoted him over the phone. "Thanks again for coming so quickly. I know Agnes is eager to get her business back up and running."

"Not a problem. We all love her candy and appreciate her free cups of coffee. Let me know if there's anything else I can do. I'm greatly disturbed that the would-be robber is still on the loose."

"That makes two of us." Isaac turned his attention back to Timmy, who still held the piece of drywall.

Isaac appreciated that Bridget had assembled some women to help clean, but he would rather it be just him and Agnes and the kinner. Working side by side toward a common goal as if they were a married couple, or a family. Teasing, playing, having fun together. Instead, he and Timmy worked solo to the sounds of women gabbing.

Would he have the option of sending them home so he could work alone with Agnes on Sam's haus?

Probably not. He'd get a reputation for being an unfriendly hermit, and the untrue rumor would spread quickly to other communities, undoing everything he'd worked for. He probably shouldn't have rebuffed Sarah Fisher so harshly.

And working without extra help at the haus would mean that Agnes would carry the bulk of the load, and it'd be unfair to ask that of her.

It would also mean prolonging the time he'd be staying at the bishop's, giving the older man too many opportunities to pry Isaac's secrets out of him.

Nothing gut could come from opening those old wounds.

He sighed. Far better to get out, remove himself from the bishop's constant watch, and find alternative methods of spending time alone with Agnes.

Somehow.

He glanced at the little girls. The younger one had play dough smeared in her hair. Probably a wise decision to omit the food coloring. Even so, she would need another bath in the near future.

He sighed. He couldn't spend time alone with Agnes unless he survived taking care of the kinner.

⌒

If only Agnes could just hide out in the back room of her shop for the rest of the day. Her face still burned from the words she'd so thoughtlessly blurted out, though Bridget had assured her Isaac understood what she'd meant. She couldn't begin to imagine what Bridget had told him. Hopefully not that she was desperate and had blatantly chased Gabe, even after his gentle explanation that he wasn't interested. She wasn't that same girl. At least, she didn't want to be.

Another tear escaped, and Paris Kaufman pulled her into a hug. "There, there. We know you didn't mean anything by it."

Agnes swiped at the tear, stiffened her shoulders, and pulled away. She didn't want to be a big boppli about the whole thing.

"I think we ought to pray," Arie Zimmerman said.

She didn't specify what it was they ought to pray for, but she was right. Agnes bowed her head, while her friends fell silent.

Agnes's mind was a messed-up jumble, and so her prayer was more steam-of-consciousness, following her meandering train of thought, rather than focusing on any one thing. Kind of like her real life, darting here and there, from one subject to the next. Multitasking.

She took a deep breath and tried to focus. *Lord Gott, help Isaac to truly realize I'm not chasing him. Help me to follow Your will for my life and not my own selfish agenda. Help me to be Isaac's friend. I'm not sure what's going on with him, but there's a reason he hasn't been involved in Sam's life, and he needs to fix their relationship. Maybe that is the reason You brought him here. Danki, Gott, that I can trust You with these things. Amen.*

There, not too selfish. She hadn't prayed that her business would succeed, or that Gott would drop a handsome, kind man like Isaac into her life with a beautifully decorated, glittery pink card signed "To Agnes, with love from Gott. Treat him well."

Stuff like that didn't happen to outspoken Amish women who didn't fit the mold.

Of course, stuff like that probably didn't happen to anyone. But a girl could dream.

She pulled in a deep breath as Bridget rubbed her shoulders. "Gott has this, Agnes."

Jah, He did. Just like He had everything else related to her. She forced a smile and nodded.

"I need to go assign jobs," Bridget told her. "Gwen seems to have taken over the childcare responsibilities. She was playing with the two girls when I was out there. Sarah was scowling and muttering to herself in the kitchen. Maybe she'd be willing to scrub dishes. Or I could ask her to clean out the display case. It would put her closer to Isaac, and she seems to have set her eyes on him." Bridget turned slightly, looking at Agnes as if trying to assess whether there'd been any truth behind Agnes's thoughtless outburst.

Agnes flinched and tried to mask her reaction. She avoided Bridget's pointed gaze. Pretending it didn't matter might throw Bridget and the other girls off the scent of this juicy story.

Sarah's boyfriend, Peter, had recently left town. With him gone, Sarah was probably moving on to the next eligible catch. She always seemed to have more success in the romance department than Agnes.

That bothered Agnes. She couldn't bear to watch Isaac turn his charms on Sarah. It'd only serve to prove he was a flirt.

Of course, it might help Agnes be stronger around him and not take his flirting seriously. It might be better to see it firsthand with someone else so she could convince her foolish, daydreaming heart not to pine after him.

Or give her hope if he rebuffed the manhunter Sarah again.

"I'll do the dishes," Paris said. "Unless someone else wants to."

"I'll scrub the counters and the floors." Arie reached for Agnes's hands. "You do what you do best: make fudge. If you have the ingredients you need."

Agnes nodded. She was pretty certain she had all the ingredients she'd need for several batches.

"And don't worry a bit," Bridget added. "We've got this under control. We sent a separate crew over to Sam Mast's haus to get it scrubbed and ready. And someone will take a meal over there to-nacht—and probably every nacht for the next week. That ought to give him time to shop for groceries."

"Danki for everything, Bridget. I'd be lost without you." Agnes smiled. Then, inhaling a deep, fortifying breath, she opened the door and stepped out of the room—right into a solid wall.

She reared back. Stumbled over something behind her. And lost her balance.

The wall reached out and grabbed her arms, stopping her before she could fall on her backside.

Isaac steadied Agnes by the arms, barely resisting the urge to pull her tightly against his chest. That would be completely inappropriate. Not that it would've stopped him if he hadn't been surrounded by a trio of wide-eyed witnesses. It would've been beyond fun to fluster her that way.

Of course, it would've been a major temptation for him to steal that kiss he'd been thinking of way too often since their walk home the previous nacht.

Her face turned a lovely shade of pink, and she kept her eyes averted, focused on something over his shoulder, as she stepped away from him. "Danki," she murmured.

He cleared his throat. "Timmy and I patched the wall. Do you have any leftover paint stored here? Or I can buy more if you know the name or the code from the label."

"It's called 'eggshell.' I think there's a small can in the storage room. Let me check."

He stepped away, allowing her to pass, and followed her to the doorway of the bathroom. He kept his gaze focused on her kapp, which covered hair of a fascinating mix of colors. He'd love to see it hanging down some-day, but he wouldn't count on that happening. He wouldn't push it either.

She stepped into the storage room, turned on the gaslight, and scanned the shelf installed to the right of the door. Then she reached for a paint can and lifted it down. "Here's the leftover paint. Do you need a brush?" She grabbed one and held it out to him.

It wouldn't be ideal—it was more of a touch-up brush—but it would work. The job would just take a little extra time. "Perfect."

And it was, until he discovered Sarah Fisher scrubbing the glass dis-play case. While she might not have been fluttering her lashes at him any-more, she was trying out a variety of poses as she cleaned, frequently look-ing his way to see if he was watching her. And how could he not notice?

If they'd been in any other community, he would have started a tem-porary fling with her. But not here, where his brother lived, and with a bishop who'd already made major efforts to get to know him and even tried to reach into the darkness to wrestle out his long-guarded secret. Not to mention, Agnes....

Agnes. Ah, Agnes.

He sighed, turned his back on Sarah Fisher, and focused on the painting job, with Timmy supervising.

Nein temporary fling would be on the agenda in this town. Not even with the lovely, curvy, entertaining Agnes. He might flirt; he definitely teased; but she was the type of woman a man wanted to spend forever with. Not just a few days or weeks.

And if things were different—if he were free, if he could stick around—he would court her.

But they weren't. He wasn't. And he wouldn't. Therefore, he couldn't.

Agnes bustled out of the kitchen and stopped beside him. She put her hand on Timmy's shoulder and studied the repair work Isaac had done. "Beautiful work. Timothy, I'm going to make some fudge. Do you want to help? I need someone to stir and also be a taste-tester."

Timmy beamed at her. "Jah, I can help."

"I can, too, as soon as I finish here." Isaac turned to face her. "I'd love to be a taste-tester." He had nein control over the huskiness in his voice. In spite of himself, his gaze lowered to her lips. Oh, jah, he'd gladly be a taste-tester.

She blushed. Fidgeted. Then glanced pointedly at Sarah Fisher, who'd moved to stand too close beside him, as if staking her claim.

With Agnes on the scene, Sarah Fisher wasn't even in the picture. Couldn't Agnes understand that?

He'd have to work to make Agnes see her value. Not just as a candy-maker but as a woman.

And to take her thoughts of what might have been with the married St. Gabe, and transfer them to...

Isaac.

Nein drop-dead-gorgeous, clean-cut hero is going to kum rescue me near a live Christmas tree while the snow crunches pleasantly under my feet.

Gott willing, someday, he would return; and, if she was still available, he'd be the hero who would make her very specific dreams kum true.

9

The candy shop was cleaner than Agnes could remember ever seeing it. Paris, Arie, and Bridget had put church-Sunday precision into their cleaning, as if the health inspector himself would make an appearance at any moment and check for dust on the doorframes or cobwebs in the corners. Or as if the biggest gossip in the community would be performing the inspection. The building smelled of lemon-scented cleaner and chocolate.

The glass display case and the front windows shone in the late-morgen sunlight. It was almost noon, and her friends would soon leave for their homes. She would break out the sandwiches she'd brought for a quick lunch before resuming the candymaking. Unless Isaac wanted to leave right away for Sam's haus and continue working there with the cleaning crew Bridget had dispatched.

They probably had things well under control, maybe even finished by now.

Agnes scanned the printouts of the fudge recipes she'd lined up on her worktable. Three different flavors—peanut butter, rocky road, and maple nut—cooled on racks, while the fourth batch was nearing the "softball" stage. She checked the candy thermometer. Almost there.

She moved to the end of the line for the banana splits. Isaac had sliced the bananas down the middle, both length-wise and width-wise, and stood with three open cartons of ice cream in front of him. He had already filled three cones for the kinner, and now he scooped massive quantities of ice cream on top of the banana in Gwen's bowl. "Danki again for watching the kinner while we worked," he said to her. "We couldn't have done it without you."

Gwen reddened. "I love kinner. I'm the schoolteacher here, and I can't wait to have Timmy in my class in two weeks' time."

Right. School would start soon. Agnes didn't pay much attention to the schedule, since she didn't have kinner, and her youngest sister had graduated eighth grade the year before…the year before the fire had taken her life.

A heavy weight settled on Agnes's heart. Tears burned her eyes. *Lord, I miss my family.*

Isaac frowned, and his gaze held a measure of panic as he locked eyes with Agnes. "School? Timmy's old enough for school?"

Gwen's brow furrowed. "Katherine Brunstetter told me he'd be starting."

"Jah, he's old enough," Agnes managed to squeeze past the lump in her throat. Odd how the littlest things could stir up her grief.

After serving everyone else, Isaac turned to Agnes, the last of the women in line. He waited while she arranged a sliced banana in her bowl, then took the plastic dish from her. "What flavor do you want? One of each?"

"Just chocolate, danki. Chocolate is my duct tape. It fixes everything."

"Really." Isaac hitched an eyebrow. "If I'd known that, I wouldn't have called a glass repairman or fixed the drywall. I would've let you smear it with chocolate." He added a sardonic grin that included flashing dimples.

"I meant emotionally." Agnes blew out a puff of air and tried to ignore the sparks in her stomach brought on by the sight of his dimples.

"Emotionally," he repeated. "Hmm. Are you saying you have emotional problems?" He winked.

Agnes squirmed. She could almost feel everyone in the room watching her, possibly judging, even though she considered each of them a friend—of sorts. Waiting, like vultures, to hear her admit that, jah, she had emotional problems. Or waiting for her to deny the whispers about her being "off in den kopf," and that the tragedies that had befallen her were affecting her, mentally.

Then again, Isaac had walked in on her while she talked to a row of silent plants about aliens….

Nein. She couldn't admit it. Wouldn't. She should have taken the time to think about a response instead of opening her mouth and spewing out uncensored words.

Somehow she managed a shrug. "Everyone has their own opinion." Ouch, that sounded bitter. She forced a laugh. "I'll never tell."

Chuckling, Isaac leaned closer until his breath tickled her ear. "Then I shall look forward to peeling back the layers of Agnes and discovering the truth for myself," he whispered.

Something in his eyes both excited and terrified her at the same time. But she didn't understand what it was, and she didn't dare ask. Besides, what if he did learn her secrets and decide she truly was off in den kopf?

Then again, what did it matter? He wouldn't have her. Nobody would. They'd just support her by buying candy from the crazy lady.

She choked back a sob, tried to force her quivering lips to be still, and avoided Isaac's gaze. But her hand trembled as she dipped her spoon into the chocolate ice cream he'd piled atop the banana in her bowl.

His fingers grasped her wrist, searing her skin and keeping her pinned there. Her gaze rose to meet his once more.

Seriousness colored his blue eyes a shade of bluish-gray. "You do know that, whatever the problem, duct tape is only a temporary fix."

She nodded. Sometimes, temporary was as gut as it got. Especially when nein permanent cure existed.

Gott Himself couldn't—or wouldn't—heal certain wounds.

She swallowed the lump in her throat, forced a bigger and brighter smile, and blinked against the burn. "Danki for the unexpected treat."

His fingers moved against the sensitive skin on her wrist, but he didn't let go. "I'll expect payment later. With childcare, of course."

The hint of mocking, mixed with a promise of something she didn't quite understand, made her pulse race. "Of course," came her breathy answer.

He released her arm and turned his attention back to designing his own banana split.

Agnes wanted to bury herself in the coldness of the treat. Maybe it'd help cool down the fire Isaac had lit inside her.

⌒

Finally, he was alone with Agnes.

Alone, except for the three kinner. But did they count?

At this moment, Isaac didn't think so. Timmy was the only one still awake, and he was occupied with a plastic farm set Isaac had found at the Amish surplus-grocery store he'd visited earlier. A miniature farm now thrived in the forest of plants on the front window ledge of the candy shop.

Agnes had put the two girls down for a nap on a wooden pallet spread with a buggy quilt on the floor of her future bedroom.

And now he and she were alone in the kitchen. Silence—blessed silence—ruled, and not a single sound intruded, except for the low murmur coming from the front room where Timmy played.

Agnes deftly poured the latest batch of delicious-smelling candy into a mold to set. She slid the mold in place alongside several others on a shelf inside the gas-powered refrigerator, then closed the door.

"I think that'll do for today." She put her hands on her waist and twisted her back from side-to-side again. Fascinating move. It did strange things to Isaac's insides.

He forced himself to look away. "You've been doing dishes again."

"Only a few." Red rushed to her cheeks. "I needed to reuse them. They need to be clean, you know. I can't mix—"

He rested his finger against the softness of her lips.

Her eyes widened, and she stared at him, not moving.

Except maybe for leaning ever so slightly in his direction.

His pulse pounded. Thudded. Galloped out of control. He sucked in a shaky breath and jerked his finger back, wishing he dared replace it with his own lips.

He wouldn't have hesitated to do so if Agnes had thrown herself at him the way Sarah Fisher had. But a man shouldn't take advantage of a woman he respected. Any woman, for that matter.

Isaac cleared his throat. "I'll finish the dishes while you clean up." He swept a hand around to indicate the splatters on the counters and floor. "It won't take long. Then we can go check on the progress of Sam's haus." And pray the women cleaning it weren't nearly as efficient in their work as the ones who'd kum to help at the candy shop.

He wasn't ready to go solo, and Agnes was quite proficient at filling multiple roles. Not surprising, considering she'd had lots of practice. While he, on the other hand....

He swallowed the lump that had suddenly formed in his throat.

He. Could. Not. Do. This.

It'd been wishful thinking to believe he could. And even though young Timmy was a delight, Isaac couldn't be responsible for his brother's *kinner*. Not after....

Nein. Isaac sucked in a noisy breath. He should quit. Right here. Right now. Just turn and walk away.

Nobody would blame him if they knew the truth.

Except, he always honored his commitments.

Whatever had possessed him to make those bold, boastful claims to the bishop and Agnes?

He plunged his hands into the steaming-hot water, relishing the burn, the pain, the—

Agnes's softness brushed against his arm as she added another dish to the pile on the counter, effectively sidetracking him from his darkening thoughts.

"I really appreciate your help, Isaac." She moved away, probably not even realizing what she'd done.

He clutched the edge of the sink, his knuckles turning white, to keep himself from reaching for her, from tugging her into his arms and tasting her sweetness.

His next auction couldn't *kum* too soon.

Maybe it was time to put another call in to Jenny and find out when he could expect her and Sam to *kum* home and relieve him of his duties.

A man could take only so much.

In the area just a little over twenty-four hours and already he'd reached the end of his endurance.

"The floor's scrubbed. Counters are clean. It feels so *gut* to be busy making candy again." Agnes paused beside him. "Are you almost done?"

He pried his fingers loose from the edge of the sink. "*Jah*. Just a couple more."

"I'll get Timothy to pick up his toys, then. Perhaps he could leave them here for tomorrow. He seems to enjoy them." Agnes hurried toward the swinging door, her hips gently swaying. She was still chattering away as the door swung shut behind her.

Isaac finished the few remaining dishes, then drained the water and dried his hands. He peeked in on the girls. Mary was beginning to stir, so he woke her the rest of the way and sent her to the bathroom. Next, he gathered Martha in his arms. Cocooned in the buggy blanket, she continued to snooze while he entered the main room of the shop.

Timmy hadn't picked up his toys. Instead, Agnes was down on her hands and knees, helping him round up a herd of multicolored plastic cows. Complete with moos, and yips from the working dogs. And further testing the ends of his endurance. She was overdue for a gut kissing.

Something deep inside him shifted. What would it be like to someday have a family of his own with Agnes by his side? He wanted to embrace the idea, but….

A memory turned like a knife inside his heart, the pain compromising his oxygen supply and causing his eyes to burn.

He pressed his lips together and blinked, looking away from the playing twosome.

Mary ran into the room, bumping against his legs as she passed. "I play, too."

Isaac made a roaring sound. "Here comes a tornado."

~

Startled, Agnes glanced out the window and had to squint at the bright sunshine. "Tornado?" She turned to Isaac.

He scooped up Mary in his free arm, and the little girl squealed.

Agnes smiled, thankful that he'd stopped the energetic toddler from stomping through the collection of animals. But the sight of him with a child in each arm did strange things to her heart. She swallowed hard and looked away.

"I'm going to get these two into the buggy and then drive around front," Isaac said, the teasing tone gone from his voice. "Timmy, pick up your toys, but leave them here for tomorrow. Agnes—"

"I'll make sure everything is closed and locked." She stood. He didn't need to waste his breath telling her what to do. "Sorry, I got sidetracked." She bustled past him into the kitchen, ignoring the tasks that lay behind her closed office door. She'd deal with those tomorrow, since she wouldn't have to do any candymaking then.

She checked to make sure the door was locked, then turned off the gas-powered lights before returning to the front of the store, where she repeated the routine.

Timothy had left the plastic bag full of farm animals in the middle of the floor. Agnes picked it up and put it on a table, then locked the front door on her way out. She hurried down the stone steps to the waiting buggy and climbed in.

Martha, still asleep, lay wrapped in the blanket on the floor in the backseat. Somehow, Isaac had talked both Mary and Timothy into sitting back there, too. Or maybe they just wanted to escape the humid air. Agnes waved away a swarm of black flies that had followed her into the vehicle.

Isaac glanced at her. "I figured we'd check on progress at Sam's haus, unless you needed to go home first."

"That's fine." Agnes squirmed into a more comfortable spot. "But I'm sure it's spic-and-span by now. Someone's probably brought a meal by, too."

Isaac's breath caught. A flash of panic lit his eyes before he looked away. He nodded. "You might need to give me directions."

"Of course." She shifted again. "You'll follow this road a little ways, then take the first turn on the left. If everything is as clean as I'm anticipating, perhaps you'd like to take the kinner to the p-o-n-d to s-w-i-m." She spelled the two key words, not wanting to get up the hopes of anyone who might be eavesdropping.

Isaac stiffened. "Nein."

The curtness in his voice surprised her. Maybe he thought she was suggesting he go alone. "I'd kum along, of course."

"I said *nein*," he snapped.

She nodded, pressing her lips together.

He made a left turn and maneuvered the buggy onto the road where Sam lived.

"Third haus on the right." She motioned. "Still about half a mile or more to go, though."

"I need to call Jenny." He glanced in her direction, his eyes a stormy gray.

Ach, so his "nein" wasn't firm until he talked to his sister-in-law. "I'll get them ready, then. It'd be nice to cool off—"

"Nein!" He glared. "Don't you listen?"

Agnes hugged herself, shocked by his rudeness.

"Sorry," he muttered. "I don't mean to be unkind, but nein."

She managed a nod, then turned to look out her side of the buggy. She'd go swimming by herself after supper. It'd be easier alone anyway. She wiped away the beads of sweat on her forehead, then plucked at her dress to free it from the grip of her sweating back.

Isaac parked the buggy in the driveway in front of his brother's haus. The windows sparkled in the sunlight.

Agnes smiled. "The haus looks spotless. Guess you can stay here to-nacht."

Isaac grunted.

"I'll take the kinner inside and see if anyone left supper."

"You think Bishop Miah will let us eat there and maybe spend one last nacht? Since our clothes are there?"

Agnes studied him. Or tried to.

He didn't look at her. But his fingers were white-knuckling the reins.

She climbed out of the buggy and turned to help Mary down.

"Mamamamama." Martha reached for her.

Agnes set Mary on the ground, then gathered Martha in her arms. "Scared, Isaac?"

She'd tried to tease, the way he was always doing, but the attempt fell flat, landing in a heavy weight between them.

For an endless moment, he sat there. Silent.

Timothy climbed out. "We're home!" He ran toward the haus. "Mamm! Daed!"

Isaac drew a deep breath and nodded. "At first, I was afraid. Now I'm petrified."

10

Isaac walked out to the road in search of better reception for his phone. He had to climb up a low-rising sand hill before he finally had enough bars to hope for a decent conversation. He keyed in the number that Jenny had written in her letter, which connected him to the hospital where Sam and Jenny were staying in Minnesota.

A switchboard operator answered.

Isaac cleared his throat. "Samuel Mast's room, please."

"Just a moment." There was a series of clicks, and then, a few moments later, the sound of a phone ringing. Once. Twice. Three times. Just like the last two occasions he'd called the hospital.

Isaac curled his fingers into his palm. "Please answer." Though he didn't know what he would say if someone did. How could he admit to Jenny—or Sam—that he wanted out of this deal? That he was irresponsible and cowardly?

He *was* a coward. He'd hastened to make his phone call, leaving Agnes to deal with the crying kinner when they realized their parents weren't home waiting for them. He hadn't even left her the rock candy he'd bought yesterday to distract them.

"Hello?" Jenny's voice sounded soft and sweet, like he'd always thought of her as being.

His jaw flexed. Who was he to condemn Agnes for loving a married man?

In all fairness, though, he didn't love Jenny any longer. Hadn't for years.

He cleared his throat again. "It's Ike."

Jenny let out a noisy breath filled with tension. "Everything okay?"

"Jah, fine. We're at your haus. Agnes Zook is with the kinner. I walked out to the road so I'd be able to call and check on you both." And to quit. "How's Sam?"

"Asleep. He's on strong pain meds again. They need to do full-thickness grafts for reconstruction surgery because he was burned so deeply. They took skin from his inner thighs and his backside and used it to replace some of the burnt skin, but they're saying he'll have extensive, noticeable scarring, and will never look the same. There are supposed to be several more surgeries after this." Her explanation sounded like a rote recital.

A doctor Isaac wasn't. "Just thankful he's alive. How long do you think you'll be there?"

A pause. "I wouldn't have asked you to kum, Ike, but we have nobody else. We need you."

How had she detected his underlying message? Isaac shifted. "There *has* to be someone else."

"There's not. We'll be here possibly six weeks yet, though maybe as few as three. It depends on how the surgeries go, and whether he gets infections and other complications."

"Three weeks." Isaac kicked a rock.

"Plan on six, worst-case scenario. Besides, we'll need you a little while more after we kum home because he won't be up for doing chores just yet."

Isaac kicked another rock in the same direction as the first. "Think, Jenny. Who else can care for the kinner, since the bishop and his frau are backing out?"

Jenny laughed, but she didn't sound amused.

"Another preacher, possibly?" Jah, Isaac knew he was pushing.

"There's nobody else. Samuel Zook was a preacher, and he died in the fire. Gabe's daed, Gabriel Lapp, planned to move up from Florida to fill the position. He's a preacher there. But last I heard, he hadn't arrived. I'm not sure if he's still coming. There are rumors he might not be able to. The other preachers from our district evacuated during the fire and, as far as I know, haven't returned. The bishop's been shouldering all the work himself."

"But...." Isaac raked his fingers through his hair. "Jenny, you *know* I can't do this."

"I know you can. It was a freak accident, Ike. It won't happen again. You're responsible. You *can* do this. I need you. Sam needs you. The kinner need you." A pause. "Besides, you have Agnes." A hint of something that strongly hinted of matchmaking filled her voice.

"Agnes has a business to run. School will be starting soon, but that's only helpful with Timmy. Another girl I met—odd name; I think she said Paris—is working in a bakery.... I suppose I could ask Sarah Fisher...." Though he wasn't sure he could trust her, based on her actions at the candy shop.

"You are *not* leaving my kinner with Sarah Fisher. In fact, if you're wise, you'll stay far away from her."

Jah, he'd gotten the same impression. "But...."

Moaning sounded in the background.

"Ike, this discussion is over. Sam is waking, and he needs to be kept quiet, not stressing over things at home."

Isaac hadn't known Jenny could be so firm.

"He's happy you have the kinner, Ike. So am I. Please, do it for me. Do it for Sam." A pause. "Do it for yourself."

"Jenny—"

He heard a click. She'd hung up on him.

Isaac muttered a curse, pocketed his phone, and headed for the haus. Hopefully, Agnes had gotten the kinner quieted. Perhaps he should also check the barn to see about the animals and those chores, too.

He stopped to retrieve the crumpled candy-shop bag from the back of the buggy. If he and the kinner could stay one more nacht with the bishop and his frau, then once the kinner were in bed, Isaac would invite Agnes on a walk and discuss alternative caregivers with her. He might have to confess to her why he wasn't capable, in which case she would surely concur.

Jenny must not be thinking clearly. Even if there wasn't anyone else, he was the last person to entrust with her kinner.

"Do it for yourself," he muttered.

Agnes looked over her shoulder at him. She'd opened a cupboard door, but he couldn't see what the cupboard contained. "Hmm? Do what for yourself?"

"I have the rock candy for the kinner. Where are they?" Isaac glanced around.

"They went to their rooms to fetch a toy or two for to-nacht. Nobody left any prepared food and, oddly enough, the only canned items someone left are beets and venison. I could do something with those for your supper, though, if you wanted to stay here."

"Ah, nein. Danki. We'll stay with the bishop to-nacht and I'll stop by the grocery store tomorrow, I suppose."

"I'll make sure the word gets out that you need food brought in. It's canning season, so there should be plenty of fresh vegetables and recently canned goods. And there is supposed to be a fund to help the needy, though I'm not sure who's in charge of it now." She frowned.

"I need to talk to you about something after we get the kinner to bed."

She raised her eyebrows. "'We'? I got them ready for bed last nacht. You need to learn to do it alone. You're the one who'll be doing that starting tomorrow nacht." She put her hands on her shapely hips and glared at him.

Was she tired of the kinner already? Or just too hot to try to be nice any longer? He eyed the damp tendrils of hair clinging to her neck.

"Ach, sure, bail on me just when I need you most." He feigned a pout.

She shut the cabinet door. "You don't need me."

Mary ran into the room carrying a baby doll by its arm. She reached for Isaac.

He bent and picked up the little girl, then settled himself in a kitchen chair and opened the bag of rock candy. "Pick one."

She leaned forward and peeked inside. With a squeal, she squirmed off his lap and ran from the room with the bag, leaving him holding the doll.

"You're a natural with them, Isaac." There was a hint of sarcasm in her voice.

Isaac glanced up at Agnes. "What would it take to get you to help me out here? I'll do anything you ask."

Her forehead wrinkled. "I'll help you, but I'm not going to move in with you as a full-time nanny. That'd be inappropriate."

"Then marry me." He meant it as a joke, but more than half of him wished he were saying it in earnest.

She stared at him, a strange look on her face. "Sure, Isaac."

Her lips curled into something that might've been a sneer, but he wasn't sure.

"*Sure.* You'd marry the crazy lady just to have temporary childcare. That says bushels about how desperate you are."

"I *am* desperate, but—"

"I'm *not* desperate. I'd rather be single than married to a mistake."

Ouch. He winced.

She strode out of the kitchen and didn't look back.

Never mind that he'd intended to tell her she wasn't crazy. Only "crazy beautiful," "crazy sexy," and "crazy appealing" to him.

"*Married to a mistake*"?

⌣

That evening, back at the bishop's haus, Agnes stood in the bedroom doorway, supervising as Isaac got the kinner ready for bed by himself. She kept her mouth clamped tight, even when he did things differently than she would have. They were *his* responsibility now. Not hers. She wouldn't go with them to Sam's haus when they left the Brunstetters'.

She'd only care for them when Isaac had to leave town for an auction.

The first one was in nine days, the bishop said. Nobody knew how long he'd be gone.

The pinched look Bishop Miah had worn when he'd mentioned the trip made Agnes wonder if Isaac would ever return.

He'd said he wanted to talk to her to-nacht, but she wasn't sure she wanted to talk to him. She had nothing to say. Memories of their last conversation still raced in confusing circles inside her head. *Marry me... desperate...crazy lady...mistake.*

Three of those were not phrases she ever dreamed of when she imagined her nameless, faceless hero asking her to be his bride.

Nein, she had kum up with all sorts of elaborate methods of the unknown hero proposing—fueled by romance books, no doubt—and flowery words that probably weren't remotely realistic.

Ich liebe dich.

If those words ever were directed at her, she'd probably faint dead away.

Maybe "I'm desperate" was as gut as it got for someone like her.

Agnes spun away from the room as Isaac began reading the kinner a bedtime story—something she never took the time for. She grimaced. Isaac truly was a natural at certain aspects of this parenting thing.

In her own bedroom, Agnes changed into a pink tankini swimsuit with boyshorts that the bishop would surely forbid if he knew about it. She put her dress back on over top, pinned it shut, and tiptoed downstairs. In the kitchen, she slid her feet into her pink flip-flops, then opened the door and headed for the pond. She needed to be alone.

Bishop Miah, as well as Katherine and Bridget, would tell her to pray. But she was fairly certain Gott had abandoned her along with her family. Not one single prayer she'd uttered since that horrible day seemed to have made it any higher than the birds that flew. Now she had nothing left to say to a Gott who didn't care. She wouldn't dare admit that publicly. Even though most people thought she'd gone insane the nacht of the wildfire with her uncontrolled weeping, the announcement from a preacher's dochter that Gott didn't listen would give way to raised eyebrows and wagging tongues.

If He cared, though, Bridget wouldn't have married the man of Agnes's dreams. Her family would still be here and….

And Agnes wouldn't have a candy shop. She wouldn't be proving she could survive. She wouldn't be harboring a crush on a handsome auctioneer with a silver tongue….

She waved away her disjointed thoughts.

It was pure foolishness to set her heart on Isaac. He wasn't staying. He was just a flirt who toyed with her emotions, luring away any remnant of affection that might've been left for Gabe and making her dream of things that could never be.

"Agnes!"

She didn't answer Isaac's distant shout. She wanted to be alone. To cool off. To think. And maybe to rant at Gott.

She needed to burn off her runaway emotions through exercise. Nobody would know. Nobody ever knew.

Especially not confusing men who messed with her mind.

⌣⟩

Isaac scratched his head and turned to go back inside the haus. He'd thought he heard the back door shut. Both Bishop Miah and Katherine were reading in the living room, while Agnes was nowhere to be found. She must have gone somewhere.

He scanned the shoes lined up by the door. Her pink flip-flops were gone.

The floor creaked behind him, and Isaac turned.

"She needs to be alone." The bishop walked over to the stove and poured himself a cup of koffee. Apparently, Katherine's brew didn't bother him.

"She does this often?" Isaac glanced out the window but didn't see anything moving.

Bishop Miah shrugged. "Not often. She hasn't done it for a while. You probably stirred things up."

Isaac cocked an eyebrow at him.

"She yells at Gott. I daresay she doesn't want anyone to know, but I've followed her a few times, just to make sure she was safe. She's stronger than the community gives her credit for being, that's for sure. But she needs to let her suppressed emotions out, and this is the only safe way for her to do it. Nobody knows. Except der Herr and me. And, now, you."

"Why'd you tell me?"

The bishop half-smiled. "You needed to know."

Something lurched in Isaac's chest. He wouldn't ask why the bishop would say such a thing. He was pretty sure he didn't want to hear the answer.

"I needed to talk to her." Isaac glanced out the window again.

The smile lines faded from the older man's face. "Isaac…." He sighed heavily, then shook his head as if deciding against what he'd been thinking of saying. "I can tell you where she is, but you'll need to proceed with caution. You might see and hear things that are meant to be private."

"I'll take that risk." Agnes tended to blurt out what was on her mind, regardless of who might be around, so he wasn't too worried about hearing anything he wasn't supposed to. Though, with her calling herself a crazy lady, maybe he should be concerned if he overheard her babbling nonsense.

The bishop frowned. His expression slowly deepened as he studied Isaac, as if the man were trying to decide if Isaac was worthy of discovering a well-kept secret about Agnes. Finally, Bishop Miah said, "Behind the barn, to the right. Opposite direction from your brother's haus. Her old home is there, not that there are any buildings left. Just the pond. Someone else owns the property now, but they haven't built anything yet. She goes there to pray—usually shouting, as if she believes Gott is hard of hearing. And she...." He cleared his throat, a slight tinge of pink coloring his cheeks. "Well, you'll see."

Isaac's brow furrowed.

"I'm trusting you with this knowledge, Isaac. Don't abuse it." And with that warning, the bishop shuffled out of the room.

Isaac stood there a moment longer, then put on his tennis shoes and went outside. The stars and moon shone so brightly that he didn't need a lantern. He followed the bishop's directions, though it was a farther distance than he'd expected, and finally came to a pond.

He could hear splashing sounds. He thought he might like to get in and join her.

As Isaac stepped closer to the pond, he tripped over something. He bent and picked it up.

Agnes's dress? His breath caught. A handkerchief she'd likely used as a head-covering was wrapped inside it. Was she okay?

Someone gasped, and he glanced at the pond. Agnes dipped down in the water to her neck. And stayed submerged. "Go away."

Her voice sounded strangled.

Nein wonder the bishop had seen fit to warn him. The man of Gott must've been thoroughly shocked. Maybe even too embarrassed to bring it up to her.

Though, if that were the case, it was surprising he'd told Isaac where to find her, considering what he'd known Isaac would stumble upon.

"Are...." His face burned. He half-coughed, half-chuckled. "Um, are you naked?"

11

What? Nein!"

Isaac wasn't sure how long he stood there staring at Agnes. It might've been just a few seconds, but it also could've been hours. Nothing existed but the woman in the water, her dress smoldering in his hand, while his mind went to places it had nein right going.

Bishop Miah had warned him not to abuse this knowledge, but Isaac dearly wanted to investigate further.

Isaac licked his lips. He had to be the gentleman, whether he wanted to or not.

He returned the dress to the rock where he'd found it, then turned his back on Agnes. "I wanted to talk to you," he said over his shoulder.

"And I didn't want to talk to you," came her tart reply. "You're conceited and cocky, thinking I'll fall into your arms because you're desperate or you believe I am. I'm not going to marry you just to give you a free pass on your obligations. I love those kinner and I don't know what your problem is. I would expect you to jump at the opportunity to get to know them."

Isaac coughed. Apparently, being half-naked in a pond did nothing to diminish Agnes's ability to speak her mind. "I've known a lot of Amish women, Agnes, but none of them has been as know-it-all and bossy as you."

"Funny, I was just thinking the same complimentary things about you."

"Thinking and saying." Of course, he'd done the same.

She spluttered.

An owl hooted in a nearby tree. Another owl answered.

"Listen, Agnes. I have my reasons for not wanting to do this. Valid reasons, I might add. I need someone else to watch the kinner." He folded his arms across his chest, feeling ridiculous at having this conversation while facing an audience of trees.

"Your reasons can't be considered valid unless you share them. Even then, they'd be subject to dissection and discussion."

Isaac blinked. Dissection and discussion? "What?"

Behind him, the splashing sounds grew louder, as if Agnes were moving toward him and into shallower water, possibly revealing whatever it was she did or did not wear. He fought the urge to turn around.

The bishop had trusted him with this knowledge. He couldn't abuse that trust, misplaced though it was.

Sam and Jenny trusted him, too. And yet, he would abuse their trust by abandoning his duties?

He pulled in a deep breath. Shuddered. And swallowed hard. He wasn't worthy of anyone's trust. "Fourth of July. Titus went out in the backyard after supper to see the fireworks...and fell down the well and drowned."

And there it was, laid bare in all its messiness. Even if she didn't understand the full story or know who Titus was.

Tears burned his eyes. Tears he hadn't allowed to escape since that unspeakable day six years ago.

Silence. Then a wet hand touched his shoulder for a brief moment. "Ach, Isaac." Then both her arms wrapped around his waist from behind. Her softness pressed against his back. Water droplets soaked through his shirt, cold against his skin. The sensation somehow worked to release a heavy flood of tears from his long-held dam.

"H-he was eighteen months old, like Martha now. I didn't know Sam had left the cover off the well. I'd promised to take Titus out to see the fireworks, so I told him to go out ahead of me, that I'd be right there, but...." Here came the worst part. "I was too busy flirting with Jenny." Who was married to his brother. "I...I drowned the only child they had, and now they trust me with the three they've had since?" He closed his eyes and shook his head. "I can't do it."

"Shh. You have to do it. I'm here for you." Her hand moved slightly, as if she considered rubbing his chest, but then it froze in place.

Despite his crippling grief, something exciting swirled inside him. He trembled.

Her arms tightened. "I'll help. We'll all help. They'll be fine. You'll be fine. Trust me," she murmured.

His throat hurt from the flood of tears he hadn't been able to contain. He sniffled as he twisted in her arms, needing to hold on to her as much as he needed her holding him.

"I can't be responsible for them, Agnes." He wrapped his arms around her and clung tightly, his hands flat against her back...except for the heavy wet rope under his palm. He fingered it. Her hair. Her glorious hair. He fisted the braid. The backs of his fingers brushed against bare skin.

His breath hitched.

"It wasn't completely your fault," she whispered. "Sam should've covered the well. Jenny and Sam were just as responsible for the tragedy as you. Maybe more so. But nobody blames you."

He blamed himself. He swallowed again, letting his free hand slide down the wet swimsuit material covering her back.

Desire swelled. He bent his head and brushed his lips across hers.

She sucked in a gasp. Stiffened. Then relaxed in his grasp.

Sort of. There was a hint of something that might've been expectancy in the way she tilted her head.

He shouldn't....

But he could nein more stop his lips from finding hers again than he could halt the passing of time.

⌒

Agnes trembled against him, unable to keep herself from surging into the kiss—her first kiss. She unclasped her hands from Isaac's waist, circled her arms around his neck, and held on for dear life, wrapped in the ebb and flow of his masterful lips.

His face was wet with his tears, and he tasted of salt. Of desperation. Of need. And, oh, how she wished to soothe his broken heart. She knew what it was to carry guilt over the loss of a family member.

The cooling evening air hitting her damp, exposed skin did nothing to extinguish the fire that roared to life inside her at his touch, his kisses, and his barely restrained passion.

Her stomach clenched, and she pushed herself more firmly against him. His fingers brushed against the bare skin exposed by her swimsuit, and he groaned, his arms shifting, tightening, bending her backward....

He stopped with a jerk and, with shaking hands, raised her up again. He released her braid, moved his hands to her waist, and set her away from himself, but she kept her arms loosely wrapped about his neck. His fingers trembled against her sides.

She didn't want to stop. "Nein." She leaned against him again, her lips pursuing his this time. "Kiss me."

"Agnes...." Her name emerged as a warning growl. But he did as she asked, his lips teasing hers for long minutes of pure bliss.

Delinquent morals, lips bruised, insides melting. Things were out of control. Deliciously so.

Her back arched, and she moaned, pressing herself more tightly against him. His hands slid from her waist to her hips, lingering there a moment, then slowly rising to grip her by the upper arms.

This time, he put more than a foot between them.

All physical contact removed.

And he didn't turn his back. His gaze was fixed on her. As if she were his opponent, and he watched for her next move.

She fought for her breath. For control of her shaking limbs. For....

For some semblance of pride.

Of course, he didn't want to kiss the crazy lady. She'd thrown herself at him, demanding his unwilling attention.

She sucked in a breath, dipped her head, and grabbed her discarded dress, clutching it to her heaving chest.

How would she ever face him again?

How would she ever live without this...this wondrous discovery?

"Agnes." He sighed her name. "I'm sorry. I shouldn't—"

"Don't." The word sounded harsher than intended. "Just don't."

He couldn't destroy this verboden memory with an apology. He couldn't.

But he had.

The damage had already been done.

Isaac nodded, his hands clenched into fists at his sides to keep himself from reaching for her again and finishing what he'd so foolishly started. And after the bishop had trusted him.

Trust.

The weight of all the unwarranted trust almost crushed him. He swallowed again, his throat still raw from his unrestrained grief.

His confession and tears hadn't been freeing at all. Instead, the guilt and shame were compounded by his lustful behavior, even though it'd been wonderful at the time, and he'd wanted to…to anticipate his wedding vows.

Assuming he'd ever marry. And assuming Agnes would be his bride.

"I'd appreciate it if you didn't mention our, uh, conversation to the bishop," he said gruffly.

"Conversation." She sounded breathless.

He shoved his fists into his pockets. "About…about the kinner. And about…us. Me. My behavior."

She pursed her lips and nodded. She adjusted her grip on her dress material, with the effect that more skin was revealed.

"Shoot, Agnes. For my sanity's sake, cover yourself."

She blushed. "A gentleman would turn his back."

"I think we've already established I'm nein gentleman." He half-smiled, his gaze dipping to her lips.

She stood there another moment, her mouth working. Then, as she gave a huff, the dress whipped around her shoulders, its hem falling below her knees. She quickly pinned it shut.

Covering those amazing curves that still burned his senses.

Too bad she'd refused to marry him. He could've gotten used to that idea.

He inhaled deeply. Exhaled.

If only he were still a praying man. But how could he approach a loving Gott after his sins? He was unworthy beyond repair.

He shuddered.

Nein, he wasn't gut enough for Gott, and now he might have gone and ruined his chances with the amazing woman standing before him.

He couldn't manage without her. Not if he intended to walk away a hero in somebody's eyes.

Not that such a feat could be done.

He'd already betrayed the bishop's trust.

But Sam's?

Blast it all. With his brother lying in the hospital, suffering painful skin grafts, the least Isaac could do was try.

But for six weeks, possibly longer?

"I can't do it alone, Agnes. If I promise I'll never touch you again, you'll still help me, ain't so?"

She looked down, staring at her feet. Her shoulders slumped. Shook.

Oh, shoot. She'd *told* him to kiss her.

More accurately, she'd demanded he do so. He tried to fight the humor, but his lips started to rise.

He sucked in a shaky breath. "Or should I promise to kiss you every day?"

12

Every day works. If you can catch me." Agnes slapped her hands over her mouth as her blurted-out words registered. Why couldn't she keep herself from voicing her every thought? And after Isaac had apologized for kissing her in the first place.... But since he'd offered to do it again, maybe he wasn't sorry for that amazing kiss.

Should she turn and run away? Or stand there and try to retract her words?

He laughed. *Laughed!* As if she'd said something funny.

Which, she had. She sighed heavily. Not only had she just proved she was off in den kopf, but she hadn't left any room for doubt.

She glanced around at the moonlit surroundings. If she were to run, which way would be best? Back into the pond? Through the forest? Toward the rubble of her former home? Or should she shove past Isaac—

"If you run, I will catch you." Isaac wore a lazy half-smile, like a cat with one paw holding a mouse, toying with it for some sick enjoyment before going in for the kill. Despite his casual stance, he definitely seemed poised for the final pounce.

She didn't intend to be killed—er, caught—to-nacht.

"Promise me you'll forget this happened."

His smile widened. "I never make stupid promises. I plan to fall asleep thinking about this. Dream about it. And you'll remember it, too."

Jah, she would. The kiss—and the apology. She firmed her shoulders. There was only one reason he would apologize for kissing her and that was because she lacked in some way. But it had been her first time.

First and probably last, so she wouldn't get better with experience.

Of course, it might be a factor of his not being physically attracted to her. She would understand that. Nein man ever had been. Men were interested strictly in her candy.

Yet, he'd said he would catch her, implying he wanted to kiss her again, and maybe just as passionately. Her face burned. Her lips tingled. She forced her feet to stand still, even though she wanted him to catch her, just for the kiss he'd alluded to. Then again, he was the one who'd offered to kiss her every day, so maybe there was more than just an implied promise. But in spite of her habitual "verbal vomit," she could never bring herself to ask him what he was really thinking.

"Cat got your tongue, Agnes Zook?"

She hunted for a sarcastic response, but his use of the word "cat" conjured once again the image of a feline toying with a mouse, scrambling her brain. At a loss for words, she merely grunted. Like Isaac often did. Maybe he'd understand the typical male sound as well as she did—not at all.

He chuckled. "I never thought you'd give up so quickly."

Give up? She wasn't sure what he meant. She hadn't given up. On anything. Except for Isaac, and, right now, her hopes and dreams were in a messy jumble because of him. "I haven't quit."

"I know you well enough to know you always say what's on your mind."

She looked down to hide her burning cheeks. "It's a bad habit, I know. But I can't seem to manage my tongue."

Another chuckle. "I can manage it quite well. Want me to prove it?" He took a step toward her.

Her heart rate increased. But saying jah would only make her look desperate. She sucked in a noisy breath. "Did you come out here for a reason other than to harass me?"

He cleared his throat. "Jah, I did. And we discussed it, briefly." His voice had turned husky. Was it because of the memory of their kiss? Or from his teary confession? "It was the reason I'm not able to take long-term care of Sam's kinner. You heard my *valid* reasons. And you agreed we would find someone else as soon as possible."

Agnes's brow wrinkled. "I'm fairly certain I didn't agree to that. I think I said you could do it with my help."

He gave her another half-smile. "You're gut, Agnes Zook."

Apparently, not as gut as he was, because she was the one off-kilter and flustered, while he seemed in control of the game.

Too bad his abundance of self-confidence didn't extend to his ability to watch three young kinner. It wasn't that hard. She and Katherine had done it for almost six months.

She couldn't remember how long Isaac would be around, or if he'd even shared that information. She was fairly positive he hadn't because those details would've been engraved in her mind.

"Um, how long did you say you'd be here?" She glanced at him.

A muscle worked in Isaac's jaw. "I don't know. Jenny said Sam might be in Minnesota for as many as six weeks. But they'll still need me for some farm work for a while after that."

"So maybe seven, eight weeks?" She crossed her arms over her chest. Not as much to warm herself as for protection from what he'd said—and from what he might say.

He shrugged. "Could be. More or less."

She had less than two months to win his heart.

Um, nein. Two months to steel her heart against him so he wouldn't steal her heart.

"Of course, I'm booked for auctions every weekend and I'll have travel time so it will be a few days more, depending on how far I need to go."

Ach. *Much* less than two months.

Gut thing she was resigned to her fate.

Sort of.

⌒

Isaac glanced around as he walked in the direction of the rubble of Agnes's former home. "The bishop said you used to live here. Tell me about your haus. Your family."

"The bishop said…?" She sucked in a noisy breath. "Wait. He knows I kum here?"

"How do you think I knew where to find you, Agnes Zook?"

Agnes frowned. "Why are you calling me by my first and last name?"

How could he tell her he needed to emotionally distance himself from her, at least for now? He forced a chuckle. "Would you rather be called 'my love'? Or perhaps 'süße'?"

"Not if you don't mean it."

He grinned. "I like your ability to speak your mind. Nein second-guessing what you're thinking."

"I'm thinking you didn't answer my questions," she said tartly.

"And you didn't answer mine." With his toe, he shoved at a tree branch. It rolled aside, revealing something white. He bent down, picked it up, and studied it a moment. "A teacup?"

"Nein way." Agnes hurried over and gently took the teacup from his grasp. Her fingers brushed against his, igniting sparks. "How did this survive the fire? And how kum Bridget and I didn't find it before?"

Isaac shrugged.

"It was my mamm's. Or, rather, her family's. I guess it was brought over from the old country, but I can't verify that. Mamm cherished it. I used to dream over this teacup, imagining the day when I would display it in my own home...." Her voice caught. "I guess I will, still, just not the way I'd dreamed."

"I'm glad you found it. Maybe it'll bring you comfort."

"Or guilt." Her voice shook. "If I hadn't been chasing after Gabe, I could've saved my family."

And if he hadn't been flirting with Jenny, Titus wouldn't have died. He swallowed hard, forcing those thoughts away, and focused on what she'd said. "How could you have saved them? More than likely you would've died along with them." He let his finger trail down her cheek. It was damp, whether from tears or the pond water, he didn't know. "And I'm glad you're still here."

"Right. So I can watch your nieces and nephew." There was a hint of bitterness in her voice.

"Nein. So I can get to know you better. As my future frau." He inhaled deeply. That had kum out of nowhere, but he liked it, even though he had nein business thinking such a thing, much less saying it. Her unhinged tongue must be affecting his.

She snorted. "Like I said. So I can watch your nieces and nephew."

"You can watch them without the benefit of marriage. I can think of other reasons."

She gasped and lowered her head, hiding her gaze.

He derived way too much enjoyment from flustering her.

"Let's start over. How did the bishop know where I was?" Her voice hitched.

"I think there are very few things Bishop Miah doesn't know. He seems to have an insider's view of people here." Isaac included. But how? Sam and Jenny wouldn't have talked about him very much. And, even if they had, it'd been years since they'd really interacted with him. "He said he'd followed you a few times."

"What?" She gasped again. "He followed me? Here?"

"To make sure you were safe. He warned me about what I might see or hear. Told me he trusted me to not take advantage of the knowledge." He cleared his throat. "And that is why I pushed you away, Agnes Zook. And it's also why I'm using your last name. You're entirely too tempting."

"And you are such a liar. Probably why you have such success as an auctioneer. Your silver tongue talks people into purchasing what they don't want or need."

He hadn't been lying.

But then, it was entirely too early in their relationship for anything. Including kissing.

Time to change the subject.

"The bishop said you kum here to pray."

She blinked. Snorted again. "Jah. Right."

"That you shout, as if you believe Gott can't hear you otherwise."

"He can't," she whispered.

"I know I'm a fine one to talk, with my sins piled up higher than the tallest sand dune, but I think maybe Gott doesn't mind your getting mad at Him and yelling. He knows you're hurting and He wants us to feel free enough with Him to let our emotions loose. Perhaps that's the only way healing takes place. Gott takes that anger and works with it to turn it into peace with the situation and you ultimately kum to the realization that He works all things together for gut."

"For those who love the Lord and are called according to His purpose. Don't forget that part." Agnes turned away as if dismissing his words. "And right now, I *hate* Him."

Isaac chuckled. "Oh, you love der Herr, Agnes. I'm sure of it. Underneath all the hurt and grief, there's a love that just won't die. Hate isn't the opposite of love, you know. Indifference is. And you are far from indifferent."

Her shoulders shook. She stiffened, jerking her chin higher. As if that posture would give her control over her emotions.

He reached for her, grasped her shoulder, and tugged her backward into his arms. He wrapped his arms around her and quickly lowered his hands to her waist when they brushed against her alluring curves.

"Don't cry," he murmured.

She sniffed. "I won't. I haven't cried since the fire."

Right. She was fighting an avalanche of tears. He should know. Not only that, but hadn't she cried when he brought the fixings for banana splits and she said "I think I love you"? He was pretty sure she had.

He started to lower his head to nuzzle her neck, wanting to distract her from her sadness, but his peripheral vision alerted him to movement nearby. He turned his head and narrowed his eyes, finally making out the shape of a hat. A man. The bishop? Probably. "Don't look now, but I think we're being watched," Isaac whispered.

Nein wonder the man knew everything. He was a master spy.

⌒

Agnes scanned the woods but didn't see anything, or anyone, who might be watching them. Even so, she stepped out of Isaac's grasp. Physical contact with him was improper, whether or not they were being watched. Plus, it made her heart rate surge dangerously. "Where? Who?"

Isaac's breath whooshed past her ear. "I'm pretty sure it's the bishop. Probably making sure I'm keeping my promise not to take advantage of the situation."

"Ach." How much had the bishop seen? Had he witnessed their passionate kisses? Was he close enough to have heard her confession? Their conversation?

"We should start back." Isaac tilted his head in the direction of the bishop's haus. "But I would like to hear about your home and family. You might as well tell me on the way. You already know how tenacious I can be."

Jah, she knew, but what should she say? Where should she start?

"You said you were too busy chasing Gabe, so you weren't home the nacht of the fire. Yet, before your daed died, he approved of your opening a candy shop and hiring a contractor. That means you knew even then that Gabe was taken. If you love Bridget like a sister, why were you chasing her man?"

Agnes hung her head and stared at the dark ground as they walked. She cradled the precious teacup in one hand. Too bad the matching saucer hadn't survived. Or maybe it had. She needed to return in the daytime and search. She sighed. "Daed said nein man would ever marry me if Gabe didn't. And that Gabe wasn't really taken until the vows were spoken." She shrugged. "Like most Amish girls, I wanted an ehemann and kinner. And Daed said Gabe was my only hope."

"Your daed said...*what?* Why would he say such a thing?"

"I'm different from other Amish girls. Outspoken. Emotional. Maybe too homely. I don't know. My sister Caroline was two years younger than me and she had buwe asking her on buggy rides all the time. Nobody ever asked me. Even my youngest sister, who wasn't even old enough to go to singings, had buwe giving her second looks and helping her carry things. Me? Never. Nein second glances, nein offers of help, nein invitations to go out. Nobody ever wanted me. They just wanted my candy. Whoever said that the way to a man's heart is through his stomach obviously never met any of the men from around here."

"The men around here are blind. You're not homely. You're beautiful. Someday, a man will look at you and think, *She's exactly what I want in a woman.*" There was a hint of warm conviction in his voice, even though she searched for a touch of teasing, as if he were merely trying to cheer her up.

"Were those your thoughts when we met, Isaac Mast?"

He grunted. One of those noncommittal answers. So irritating.

"Of course, you didn't. Be honest and admit it. You used the word 'someday.' I'm smart enough to realize you meant it hasn't happened yet. My daed was a preacher, Isaac. He heard from Gott. He knew these things. Gott inspired every word that came out of his mouth." Or so he'd said. She'd never imagined the possibility that he could be wrong.

"Uh, I'm pretty sure that not every word a preacher says is inspired by Gott. The Bible says all Scripture is inspired by Gott. Not men."

She waved her free hand dismissively. "Nein, he said he was insp—"

"Nein, listen to me. The Bible says, '*All Scripture is given by inspiration of God, and is profitable for doctrine, for reproof, for correction, for instruction in righteousness,*' and the reason is '*that the man of God may be complete, thoroughly equipped for every good work.*'" He caught her elbow and pulled her to a stop. "None of those reasons has anything to do with the idea of Gabe's being your only hope. That was unkind of your daed to say, not to mention untrue. I can't imagine why he'd say such a terrible thing to you. If I dared to dream of taking a frau, you are exactly what I would want."

Agnes rolled her eyes. "Of course. Because as you've said, you're *desperate*." Her eyes burned. She blinked to keep the tears at bay.

"Nein." He turned her to face him. His fingertip traced gently over her cheek, her jawline, her chin, then her lips. She trembled. He leaned closer. "Because you're beautiful, fun, caring, talkative, and passionate. And I like that combination."

If only she could believe him. Beads of moisture fell on her cheeks.

"I think I caught you, Agnes Zook." His lips claimed hers, ignoring the drops of water that now fell from the sky. Kissing in the rain…. Her heart raced.

Wait. Caught? In what? A web spun from his lies?

She jerked out of his loose grasp and raised her free hand.

And slapped him in the face.

13

O uch. Isaac resisted the urge to rub his stinging cheek. Instead, he stood there, silent, and watched Agnes stride briskly away, her back ramrod stiff, the teacup still cradled in her hand. How could the woman be so tender with a teacup and so harsh and unforgiving with him?

But then, she had been tender and forgiving with him. Until he took his teasing, flirting, and advances too far. There had to be some consequences for his actions. But he had been telling the truth. She was exactly the kind of woman he wanted for a frau.

Isaac puffed out a breath and, with Agnes out of sight, allowed himself to rub his cheek. He picked up his straw hat that'd fallen off sometime during the exchange—either while he kissed her or when she slapped him, he wasn't sure which.

Inhaling a breath for much-needed strength, he trudged through the light rain to the bishop's haus. Surely, Gott had known what He was doing, sending an unsuspecting man here. Isaac had expected some emotional trauma because of the kinner and had hoped to find an alternative caregiver. Instead, he'd found Agnes. And she messed with his mind. His thoughts. His pulse. His dreams. His...everything.

When Isaac finally entered the haus, he found Katherine sitting alone in the living room, darning socks. The older woman pulled the needle threaded with black yarn through the sock and glanced up. "The kinner are asleep."

Gut. Because he wasn't in the mood to be nice to them. Or to anyone. He managed a curt nod, not bothering to remove his shoes. "I'll take myself off to bed then." Not that he'd get any sleep.

Nein, he would lie there reliving every moment of the past hour, from finding Agnes partially dressed in the pond to their painful parting.

"I'm thinking it's time for you to swim, Ike. Agnes tells me Sam's haus is clean. You and the three kinner can stay there tomorrow nacht." Katherine peered up at him.

His stomach churned. Nausea rose in his throat. He balled his fists at his sides.

"Agnes says you're a natural with them."

Agnes had it in for him.

And he'd probably just ruined any chances he'd had of getting more help from her.

He tried to nod but wasn't quite sure he'd managed. "Okay, then. Danki for taking care of them until I could kum."

When he reached the bottom of the stairs, he heard the door open. Isaac paused, one foot on the bottom step, and glanced over his shoulder.

The bishop took off his hat and laid it on the back of a chair. He looked up at Isaac, his eyes serious. He looked sad. Or maybe disappointed.

The man had seen or heard entirely too much. Maybe both.

Isaac ducked his head and rounded his shoulders—as if that would enable him to escape unnoticed—and climbed another step.

"Life, for most of us, is a continuous process of getting used to things we hadn't expected," Bishop Miah said.

What? Isaac raised his head and glanced back. Had the man read his mind, perceiving his thoughts about not having expected Agnes?

The bishop shoved his glasses higher on the bridge of his nose. "People do not lack strength. They lack will."

Looking back had been a mistake. Isaac wasn't in the mood for unsolicited advice regarding the kinner either, nein matter what form it came in. He firmed his jaw and climbed another step. Two. Three.

"Let prayer be the key to the day and the bolt to the nacht."

Isaac reached the landing and turned toward his...*whoops*. He'd forgotten he slept downstairs on the sofa bed. Now he'd have to face Bishop Miah and Katherine with his tail between his legs. Might even have to listen to more of the unwelkum proverbs spouted off by the older man.

Or he could step into the kinner's room and take the bishop's advice to pray.

Pray that the kinner would survive him.

Or that he would survive them.

～

"One, two, three, four, five, six, seven, eight." *Pivot.* "One, two, three, four, five, six, seven, eight." *Repeat.* Instead of ranting about Isaac—his behavior and his words—Agnes focused on counting aloud her steps as she paced her floor. She was on her fifth trip across the room when she noticed the irritating man in question standing just inside her closed bedroom door.

Or maybe it was a mirage, because, surely, she would've noticed the door opening and him entering.

Unless he could walk through walls.

She shivered at the frightening prospect.

Or perhaps her out-loud counting had masked his entry, in the same way that her discourse to her plants had drowned out the candy shop's bell the previous day.

She could imagine perfectly the smirk on his well-formed lips. The teasing light in his blue eyes. The slight curl in his dark blond hair.

She turned her back on him. To walk over and poke the "phantom Isaac" in the chest, she'd be not-so-silently telling him what she thought of him and his behavior. How he made her feel. What he made her want. And, well…. She probably appeared desperate enough without having to shout the words "Pick me!"

She paced to the window. Stared out into the darkness. "What part of 'nein' don't you understand?"

Except, she hadn't exactly said "Nein." Instead, it'd been a nonverbal "Please, please, please."

It was easy to talk to an Isaac she couldn't see reflected in the glass. Not that he was real to begin with. Nein Amish man would go upstairs in the home of the bishop, open the bedroom door of a maidal, and kum inside, shutting the door behind him. Nein. If he were real, she wouldn't be turning her back on him. She'd be in his face, telling him off.

And driving home the fact that she was an outspoken, intractable, tradition-defying Amish woman who'd make an absolutely terrible frau. Nein wonder Daed said she'd never marry.

In fact, it probably wasn't wise to turn her back on a phantom Isaac either. Just his imagined presence turned her insides to mush. She whirled around and marched across the room to the very real-looking mirage in front of the shut door and shoved a finger at his nonexistent chest. "To put it plain and simple, I don't want a one-nacht stand. I want forever."

She rammed her finger into a very firm, very hard, immovable object. *Odd.* She shook her head, stepped back, and surveyed the man who simply couldn't be real. Or maybe he could be, because who, other than Isaac Mast, would have the gall to enter an unmarried woman's bedroom, in the bishop's haus and shut the door?

And then, on top of all that, to look at her with a painful longing?

He didn't make a sound. Didn't move. But there was a red mark in the shape of a handprint marring his left cheek. *Ach, my.* She struggled to keep from hyperventilating.

She needed to yell. Scream. Cry for help. Or…maybe she should've locked the door before she began pacing her room. But who'd'a thunk?

He shifted his stance. An expression she couldn't read crossed his face. Then he reached for her but quickly dropped his hands to his sides as she skittered back. "I'm…I came to say I'm sorry. Well, not exactly. Actually, I made the wrong turn. The bishop said something about praying. And I figured maybe he was right. I should. Pray, I mean. So, I intended to go into the kinner's room and pray they'd survive me. That I'd survive them. That we'd survive each other. I goofed and this"—he waved his hand—"is obviously the wrong room. I didn't mean to intrude. But I do need to apologize. I didn't intend to be, but apparently I am, a jerk."

Nein, not a jerk. More someone who said what she wanted to hear. And she didn't dare embrace the hope that he'd ignited in her. If she did, she would surely end up alone and heartbroken.

"Should we start over?" He held out his hand. "I'm Isaac Mast."

She stared at his hand for a moment before raising her eyes to meet his. "We know too much about each other to start over." She'd learned more about Isaac Mast in two days than she had gathered about Gabe Lapp in six months.

Isaac inclined his head. "That we do." And with a lopsided grin, he leaned forward, kissed her cheek, and whispered, "Gut nacht, Beautiful."

Ach, her heart. She smiled. Beamed, probably.

He opened the door.

Bishop Miah almost tumbled in.

Agnes gaped.

Isaac chuckled as he sidestepped. "Your sleuthing skills are failing you, sir." And then he headed downstairs.

The bishop stood in the doorway for a long moment, staring at Agnes. And then he turned and walked away.

⌣

Isaac sat on the edge of his sofa bed and rubbed the still-stinging skin of his cheek as he recalled the stunned look on Agnes's face following his gut-nacht greeting only moments ago.

How long would it take for the bishop to make it back downstairs to talk to him? Might as well get some work done while he waited for another proverb-laced lecture. He pulled his phone out of his pocket and opened the calendar app. He studied it for a moment, then went online to a bus company's website to start researching the schedule. He would need to leave Wednesday in order to get to Montana on time. He clicked his way through the process of purchasing his ticket. Should he make it a one-way trip? He'd have proven his ineptitude by then.

It ought to make everyone happy to see him struggle through child-care for three more days. And one of those days would be a church Sunday. Tomorrow. His stomach lurched. Jah, that'd be a hoot. Thankfully, little Amish girls didn't dress in frilly frocks and diaper covers like some Englisch ones. They did, however, wear those impossible-to-get-a-gut-grip-on straight pins to hold their dresses shut.

Speaking of diapers...ach, shoot. He'd have to change them. Would someone give him a crash course in diapering? Or would he be left to handle those events without any training?

He. Could. Not. Do. This.

The all-too-familiar weight of impending doom pressed down on him. The bishop's suggestion to pray had been spot-on. Yet Isaac had spent more time panicking than praying. Gott was more than capable of helping him; he just had to ask. To trust.

Easier said than done.

He'd include a request for deliverance in his prayer.

He puffed out a breath, lowered himself to his knees beside the fold-out bed, and bowed his head.

"Gott...help." Maybe it'd be better if he fell flat on his face before der Herr, like an old-time Bible hero. Of course, to one of them, Gott had spoken from a burning bush, telling him he stood on holy ground. Isaac should take off his shoes, too, if he was going to pretend he was on holy ground in front of a burning bush concealing the blinding magnificence of der Herr. Isaac dropped into a sitting position and yanked off his shoes. Shoved them out of the way. Then started to fall flat on his face.

He caught himself on his elbows when he found himself staring at a pair of black-sock-covered feet, one of the big toes protruding through a hole.

Isaac looked up.

With furrowed brow and parted lips, Bishop Miah shook his head. "I'm really too old for this."

14

The next morgen, Agnes dressed for church, then went downstairs to reheat the cinnamon rolls Katherine had made for Saturday breakfast. She slid the tray into the oven to warm, then lifted her arms and twisted side-to-side to stretch her back, all the while eyeing Isaac's closed door. Then she returned upstairs to wake the kinner and get them ready for church.

Their bedroom door was shut, but she heard rustling sounds coming from inside. Gut, they were awake. She opened the door to find Isaac standing in the middle of the room with Martha in his arms, the girl's bare legs dangling. The way her nacht-gown clung to her back, it was clear she had soaked it thoroughly.

Isaac turned at Agnes's entry, his eyes wide and panicky. "I can't find the clean diapers."

Agnes reached for the big boot box on the dresser and lifted out a white cloth diaper. She laid it on a dry spot in the crib. "Liners are in the box beside it, and diaper pins are in the tin. The clean sheets are...here." She opened a drawer and pulled out a rolled-up sheet of light blue fabric. "Did she get the blankets wet, too?"

Isaac's look was frantic. "You've got to be kidding me. I thought maybe you had those, um, fitted ones you can throw away when they're soiled."

"Disposable diapers? Really?" She raised an eyebrow at him. Were Amish customs so foreign to him? Or was he feigning ignorance in hopes that she would deem him incompetent and take over?

Isaac grunted. "Is the grocery store open today?"

"The Englisch one, maybe, but I don't think it'd be okay for you to shop on a Sunday."

"I don't care. Disposable diapers I could probably handle. These? I don't have a clue where to start."

"They aren't so hard. Here, let me show you." Agnes moved in front of the crib, took Martha from Isaac, and quickly stripped her of the soaked nacht-gown and diaper. The sooner Isaac learned to do this, the sooner she could rebuild the wall around her emotions. But her traitorous heart was glad for an excuse to be close to him.

"And another thing. She's a little girl. I'm a grown man. Isn't there something fundamentally wrong with my changing her diapers?"

He sounded like a little bu trying to talk his way out of having to do his chores.

Agnes smiled patiently. "You're her onkel—and caregiver. Go into the bathroom and dampen a washcloth with warm water so we can clean her."

With another panicked look, Isaac followed her instructions.

Timothy sat up on his bed, wide-eyed. "Onkel Isaac is scared of diapers?"

"He's not used to them. They aren't scary." Agnes glanced at him. "Get ready for church."

Isaac returned from the bathroom and handed Agnes the warm washcloth. He leaned closer and muttered, "You lie. They're terrifying."

Agnes rolled her eyes as Mary stood on her bed and lunged for Isaac. "Up."

He caught her in his arms and held her, watching with one hip leaning against the side of the crib, as Agnes cleaned Martha and then put the clean diaper on her. She pulled a pair of plastic pants over the diaper. "There. Easy as pie. You can do the next one."

He grinned, and her heart fluttered at the now-familiar sight. She tried to shore up her internal defenses.

"Except, we'll be at church, and she'll be sitting with the women. And I'm going to town for disposable diapers immediately following."

Not on her watch. Agnes pursed her lips as she pulled off the plastic panties, unpinned the fresh diaper, and unfolded it. "Have at it, Mast." She stepped aside.

"You're cruel, Zook." He put Mary back on her bed. "Get dressed, sweetheart."

"Okay, Onkel Daed." She jumped off the mattress, arms swinging, and ran to the closet.

"Onkel Isaac!" Timothy shouted.

Isaac turned to him. "What?"

That very second, Martha lobbed her stuffed hippo, striking him square in the cheek. He looked down and picked up the stuffed hippo just as Martha reached for a stuffed dog and took aim once more.

"Hey, now." Isaac attempted to catch the dog but missed. Meanwhile, Martha got to her feet and clambered out of the crib. Two seconds later, her naked body was running out the door.

With a giggle, Agnes leaned back against the crib, settling in to watch the show unfold. How would the competent auctioneer handle things so far outside his comfort zone.

Isaac dropped the hippo back in the crib and turned to Agnes, hands outstretched toward the heavens. "Now what?"

She smirked. "Now you catch her and bring her back before she finds a mud pit to play in."

"You won't help?" He pouted.

"You're on your own, Mast." It served him right for messing up her sleep with dreams of kisses by the pond...and a butterfly kiss on her cheek. His whisper that she was beautiful...

Isaac turned to Timothy and Mary, who were shoving their arms into their sleeves. "Has either of you ever heard of 'the tickle monster'?" He held up both hands, fingers spread and slightly bent, and stiffened them. "It's going to get Aenti Agnes." He turned to Agnes with a wicked grin.

With a squeal, she straightened and dashed from the room, Isaac on her heels, two partially dressed kinner screaming in hot pursuit. She ran into her bedroom, slammed the door shut, and spun around to lock it.

Except, Isaac was already there, reaching for her. "You can run, but you can't hide."

She squealed again as his fingers brushed over her ribs.

"Kinner!" Katherine bellowed from downstairs. "Behave yourselves! And someone please kum and collect the escapee."

Isaac's hands slid away from Agnes. "Later, Zook. And I will catch you." He winked and then strode off.

She looked forward to getting caught because of his promise of a kiss. She wanted to get caught like this every day for the rest of her life—rather than get caught in a web of lies.

"Go get dressed," Agnes ordered the two gaping kinner. Then she shut her door once more, twisting the lock, and slumped against it.

Relief and disappointment warred within her.

⌒

As soon as church was over, Isaac glanced around to make sure the coast was clear for sneaking off to town for some much-needed supplies. He'd be scolded for shopping on the Lord's Day if the bishop found out and since Isaac would be taking the three kinner home when he returned, he preferred to escape unnoticed.

Today at church, they'd taken names and drawn lots for a new preacher to replace one who'd decided not to return, meaning the bishop would probably spend some time talking to the newly called preacher—whoever he was—about his duties going forward. Hopefully, those duties wouldn't include lurking in the shadows, watching unsuspecting men and women.

Isaac had been excused from this final part of the service, since he wasn't a member of the district, making his escape easy. He'd leaned over and whispered to Noah Behr, seated beside him, that he had an errand and would be back later.

Noah had nodded.

Only Timmy had noticed and he now trotted beside Isaac, chattering away about something. But Isaac wasn't listening. Instead, he prepared a mental shopping list for his verboden Sunday grocery run. *Diapers, cold cereal, canned soup....*

"...Agnes?" Timmy asked.

Isaac snapped to attention and looked at the bu. "What?"

"Why did you call Agnes 'Aenti'? She's not our aent. Is she yours?"

How could he answer that without telling Timmy that Agnes made him think about marriage? He couldn't say that. Timmy might blab it around to his young friends and it wouldn't take much snooping at all for the bishop to uncover that—if he hadn't already.

Isaac shook his head and frowned. "She's not your aenti? She's not mine either."

"So, not our aenti." Timmy sighed heavily, as if the news saddened him. "I like her. She's fun sometimes. She's a grown-up, but she doesn't act like it all the time. Neither do you."

Isaac had always been the prankster, while Sam was the serious one. Isaac smiled. "All work and nein play—"

Timmy grabbed Isaac's hand. "You have to marry Agnes. Then she would be our aenti and you wouldn't have to leave. You'd have a home."

Ach. He should've expected that.

He opened his mouth. "I don't need a ho—"

Timmy tugged on his hand again. "Agnes lost her whole family, you know. She's all alone. If you marry her, then she'll be part of our family and she won't be lonely anymore. Besides, she likes us. She doesn't treat us like just another job she has to do."

"Agnes is nice, but—"

"Gut. Then it's settled." Timmy sighed again, this time contentedly, as if a great weight had been removed from his shoulders.

Isaac's heart broke for the poor bu holding tightly to his hand. If only it were truly so easy. But he and Agnes….

His heart rate increased.

Ach, jah, he was definitely interested. But it didn't work that way. Besides, most communities had a planned wedding season, generally in the fall, after harvest. And how could he court her when he didn't have anyone else to watch the kinner? Instead of wooing his woman in private, as was the custom, he would have three youthful chaperones along at all times…which would only make Agnes suspect his interest was only in getting handy childcare. He'd have to wait for Jenny and Sam to return before he could court her freely.

Nein, Agnes had fixed it well and gut. He was out of the bishop's haus, on his own, with nein time available to tease, woo, and win the first woman in years to catch his attention in that way. Maybe the first woman ever because what he'd felt for Jenny might have been mere puppy love. His heart hadn't been broken, only wounded, when she'd picked Sam.

He'd have to outsmart Agnes somehow. But now wasn't the time to kum up with a devious plan. They'd reached his brother's home. He needed to hitch the horse to the buggy and drive to town so he could return armed with bachelor-friendly boppli supplies and food, since he'd lost a cook, too.

The heavy weight returned. He'd also lost a haus-keeper, a laundress—he added laundry soap to his mental list—and probably the help of all the men who'd been coming to take care of the farm animals.

He. Could. Not. Do. This.

Let prayer be the key to the day and the bolt to the nacht.

That really had been gut advice.

Lord, help. I can't do this without…Agnes. I mean, without You.

An hour later, with a box of disposable diapers and several bags' worth of assorted bachelor-friendly canned items purchased, Isaac and Timmy returned to Sam and Jenny's home. Isaac parked the buggy in front of the barn but left the horse harnessed, since they had to return to the Brunstetters' haus to collect the girls and their things, plus Isaac's luggage.

And eat lunch. If it wasn't too late for that. But it probably was.

Isaac huffed out a breath, grabbed the plastic bags full of his purchases, and strode toward the empty haus, Timmy by his side. That part felt gut, as if he'd at least sort of figured out how to keep an eye on one of his charges. Timmy stayed close to him rather than running away, like Martha. Isaac smiled as he remembered Agnes chasing after the naked girl the day he'd arrived. He couldn't wait to catch Agnes later. He had promised to, after all.

The door opened and Mary ran out. "Onkel Daed, you came!"

"Onkel Isaac," Timmy corrected.

"Mary? What are you doing here?" Isaac opened the door and tripped over his own suitcase. He frowned as he stepped around it.

Mary didn't answer his question, but she didn't need to. He'd been officially evicted from the Brunstetters' haus.

His chest hurt.

He strode into the kitchen and set the grocery bags on the table. A kettle sat on the stove, simmering, but nobody was in the room. He lifted the lid. Chicken and dumplings? On a Sunday? His mouth watered. He replaced the lid, then turned as Agnes came into the room.

She hesitated when she saw him, her eyes widening.

Isaac pressed his lips together. A muscle jumped in his jaw.

"I saw you sneak off. I guess Bishop Miah did, too, because he sent me over to help you and the kinner until to-nacht." She bit her lip.

Which meant the bishop was probably lurking in the shadows, chaperoning. Isaac resisted the urge to peek out a window. He went to the table and unloaded the canned goods he'd bought. Soup, pasta, tuna, peanut butter, jelly. Shoot, he'd forgotten bread. He glanced toward the stove. "He let you cook today?"

"I made it yesterday. All I needed to do was drop the dumplings in and warm it."

Isaac nodded. "It smells great. Can't wait to enjoy your gut cooking when you're my frau."

Agnes's lips curled, then formed a straight line.

"Timmy's of the opinion that I should marry you." He knew he shouldn't push it, but he couldn't resist the lure of her pink lips and the memory of her curves pressed against him.

"You already asked." She wouldn't look at him.

"And you rejected me." It still hurt, strangely enough.

"You only asked because you were desperate. Not because you love me." She held up a can of pasta and beef—probably imitation—in tomato sauce. "Really?"

He shrugged. "I can't cook." Much.

"You can't diaper either. Thankfully, I caught Martha concentrating in church this morgen and took her to the bathroom or we would've had a mess."

Isaac frowned. "What?"

"Potty training, Mast." She set the can down and picked up another one. "Chicken noodle soup. That actually sounds gut."

"Potty training?" He couldn't keep the panic out of his voice.

"It's easier than changing messy diapers. And considering how poorly you diaper, you would have a serious mess."

Gut thing he'd bought disposable diapers. He scanned the table. That box wasn't on it. He'd probably left it in the buggy with the laundry soap. He'd get it later so Agnes wouldn't know. She would probably insist on another lesson using those rectangular-shaped cloths.

Though he wouldn't object to another lesson, especially if it ended the way the last one had. Or, even better, with her squirming into his arms, raising her head for his kiss....

He blew out a breath of frustration. If he wanted her help, he'd need to make sure he kept his hands off her.

She returned the can of soup to the table and moved to the opposite side of the piece of furniture, as if she were afraid to kum near him. Skittish.

He sighed.

"Look, Zook—er, Agnes. I'm a tease. I'll freely admit it. It's how I am. I tease people at auctions. I greet complete strangers that way. It's my 'coping mechanism,' as Englischers would call it. I don't mean to make you uncomfortable."

She gave him a dark look. Not a glare, exactly. Just dark.

"I probably take it too far sometimes." And he usually kept his hands off the women he flirted with and dated in other districts, unless they made it clear they were interested in a kiss or two. He'd never slept with any of them. He didn't want to ruin his reputation that way. He hadn't even been tempted. By anyone.

Until Agnes. He would never get enough of the sparks between them. Probably the wrong thing to say right now, especially after her comment about not wanting to be a one-nacht stand. He hadn't denied being interested in that. She probably thought it was all he wanted. It wasn't. He wanted more. All. He wanted it all. Complete with the marriage license.

An impossible dream. Maybe if he survived this season without accidentally killing any kinner and maybe if he repaired his relationship with Sam and Jenny…

He groaned.

If—if—he succeeded with his impossible mission, he'd need to show Agnes respect and then kum up with a rejection-proof method of proposing. Like the snow-crunching stroll by a Christmas tree she'd mentioned.

His thoughts went in dangerous directions. He swallowed hard. "I'm sorry if you feel I disrespected you. It wasn't intentional."

She gave him another look. This one not as dark, but still indecipherable. "Dumplings are ready. Call the kinner for supper."

He nodded. And instead of bellowing—as he normally would've done—he walked down the hall to the bedrooms. He peeked into the doorways as he passed.

All three kinner were on the floor in the girls' room, the open package of diapers beside them, and diapers scattered were across the room.

Diapers on their heads as hats. Baby dolls diapered. Diapers taped to each other in a long line. Diapers ripped and shredded. The empty plastic bag bundled in a misshapen ball.

The diapers were ruined.

He sagged.

Mamm had always said she could tell when Isaac and Sam were being naughty because they'd get quiet. Why hadn't Isaac remembered that until it was too late? The lack of noise hadn't even registered.

Just a few hours into a solo act and he'd already failed. He whispered a prayer for Gott to remind him the next time things got too quiet.

Nothing to do about it now. Maybe he could safety-pin shut any salvageable diapers.

"Dinner's ready." Hopefully, he sounded calm. He took a deep breath, plucked a diaper off Timmy's head, and tossed it on the floor. "Hats off inside."

"They cute kapps." Mary tugged on Isaac's pants. "They bugs on them. Agnes want one." She bent and picked up the diaper Isaac had removed from Timmy. It was decorated with blue ants and dragonflies.

There was nein hiding the diapers from Agnes now.

Isaac lifted Martha in his arms and led the way back to the kitchen.

On the table were spoons and three bowls with kinner-sized helpings of the meal. The fourth bowl was empty. Agnes looked up room and gaped. "What's that on their heads?"

"New kapps!" Mary announced. "Yours." She held one out.

Agnes took it. She studied it a moment, then shook her head and glanced at Isaac. "Really?"

He shrugged. "You said I did a terrible job diapering."

She flapped the diaper. "So you're just going to quit? I never took you for a quitter. You said you upheld your responsibilities."

At least her verbal sparring was better than her dark look.

He pressed his lips together. He'd quit a lot of things, the biggest being his family. But despite the strong temptation to leave again, he wouldn't do it. Never again.

If he left, he'd leave Agnes. And he wouldn't quit on her either.

He glanced at her. "Is it wrong to meet a responsibility in an alternate way? Please don't tell me the Ordnung says 'cloth diapers only.' I already told you, I follow my own rules."

Agnes set the diaper down on the counter and shoved away a dangling kapp string. "Some young mamms use disposable ones sometimes, for church Sunday or while they're grocery shopping. But Katherine used only cloth and she taught me."

Isaac raised his eyebrows and tried not to smirk. His attempt must have failed, since Agnes swatted at his arm.

He grabbed her hand, lifted it to his lips, and pressed a kiss to the palm. "Danki for everything, Beautiful."

She clenched her fist. Blushed. And with her gaze still resting on him, dropped into a seat.

Isaac leaned close to Timmy. "I'm gonna marry that girl someday."

⁓

He'd marry her someday? If only. He was a tease. Nothing but a tease. Well, a tease and a flirt.

Agnes's palm tingled and her heart raced as the kinner cheered.

But it wasn't true. It was a lie. False hope. And he'd told her he was a tease—admitted it with his own kissable lips not ten minutes ago. A coping mechanism, he'd said. For coping with what? For hiding his grief and guilt over the death of his first nephew?

She huffed and then eyed him, waiting for his adamant denial. His laughter. Or whatever it was that would prove it was only a joke.

Isaac grinned. Winked. "Let's pray."

The grin and the wink seemed to confirm her suspicions. Her hope withered and died. With a sigh, Agnes closed her stinging eyes. She wasn't sure she could manage anything beyond the Lord's Prayer. She'd make a trip back to the pond to vent before returning to the bishop's haus that evening. Not that the Lord Gott heard her shouts any clearer than He did her silent prayers. It was as if He had her on mute. Or had more important people to listen to and answer than Agnes Zook. Either that, or Daed now had the ear of der Herr and daily reminded Him that Agnes would never marry since Gabe had rejected her, so the two now teamed together to taunt her.

But...Isaac had asked. Admittedly, at the time, they'd known each other for less than twelve hours. And he'd said he was desperate. But he *had* asked.

What would've happened if she'd said "Jah, please"? Would he have asked the bishop for a marriage of convenience—for him? Or would he have laughed in her face and called her desperate?

Did Gott even care how much it hurt to have Isaac here, teasing and flirting? How much more strongly it made her long for the nonexistent man who would sweep her off her feet and whisk her off into the sunset?

Foolish hopes and dreams.

"Amen," Isaac said.

He didn't need to agree.

Agnes hiked her chin up, lurched out of the chair, reached for Isaac's bowl, and ladled some chicken and dumplings into it. "Tell me when."

"I'm thinking as soon as possible."

15

Agnes was sorely tempted to dump the bowlful of chicken and dumplings over Isaac's head. But that would accomplish nothing, except to scald him and make a mess for one of them to clean up later; plus, she'd feel worse for giving into her temper.

Instead, she tried to calmly ladle in another scoop, then set the bowl in front of him. But her hands trembled. Nerves.

"Sure, Mast." Jah, she was being a bit sarcastic.

His grin widened. He'd either missed the sarcasm or was choosing to ignore it. "Seriously?" He stood.

"As serious as you are." *Not at all.* Except for his desperation for help. A marriage of convenience. For him.

He whooped, then lifted her up and spun her around, to the kinners' squeals and shouts. And then he noisily kissed her. Nothing spine-tingling about it at all. But then, it'd been brief. Too brief. A forecast of things ahead if she succumbed to his foolishness?

Now the news would be spread around the community by the wide-eyed kinner. Didn't Isaac have any idea what he'd done? Agnes slumped into her chair, her appetite gone. Still, she ladled out a little bit for herself. She had to eat something.

"I'll talk to the bishop tomorrow when we pick you up to go to the candy shop."

She looked at him. Frowned.

"I'm serious, Agnes."

Sure, he was. Because he was desperate. But the bishop wouldn't see it that way. He would say "Nein." He would realize—he had to realize—that as soon as Sam and Jenny returned and Isaac didn't need Agnes's help anymore, he'd go away. And since divorce was verboden, they would be tied to each other for the rest of their lives. Not to mention, the bishop would also get direct revelations from Gott, like Daed claimed he did, and he'd know Agnes must never marry because—

"Don't listen to the lies, Agnes." Isaac's thumb grazed the back of her hand. "I know what you're thinking. Prove your daed wrong."

Prove him wrong? Was it even possible?

Daed had said she would never marry and now marriage was within her grasp.

Would it be better to be married and then abandoned, or to be an old maud in a society that believed a woman's highest duty was to marry and raise kinner?

If only she could talk this over with Daed. Find out what Gott had to say about this.

Neither option sounded appealing to her, but the bishop would know which one was better. She pressed her lips together. A trip to the pond to vent noisily was a necessity.

Isaac looked at the kinner and put his forefinger over his lips. "Shush, now. This is our secret. You can't tell anyone, okay? Not one person. Promise."

Timothy and Mary both nodded solemnly, while Martha whammed her spoon on the table once more. Gut enough, since nobody understood much of her babbling anyway.

Isaac smiled. "Danki. Now eat your dinner. And after we eat, we'll do something fun."

"Yay!" Mary cheered. Timothy dug in.

Agnes glanced at the clock. It'd be naptime for the kinner right after they'd eaten. She forced her food down, though her stomach threatened to revolt.

A marriage of convenience, for him—with a future abandonment for her—had never been in her dreams.

But maybe they were her reality.

The thought was depressing.

Agnes sighed.

Dinner eaten, Agnes collected the dishes and carried them to the sink. She turned to Isaac and nodded toward Martha. "She needs a bath, then put down for a nap. The other two need naps, too."

Isaac brightened. "I'll do the dishes while you get them ready for their naps, then. I'm sure I can handle dishes." He winked. "I've had to do them as a bachelor, you know."

Agnes tried to smile. "You're doing more than the dishes. You've got it all. I'm just here to supervise."

Isaac's brow furrowed. "You said you'd help."

"I *am* helping."

He pretended to pout. "Your version of 'helping' and mine must be vastly different."

At least she'd have some self-respect and would not have bowed to his "convenience" until any vows were made.

"Kinner first, Mast." Agnes pointed toward the stairs. "You can do the dishes while they sleep. I'll even dry and put the dishes away for you."

Isaac huffed, then scooped up Martha in his strong arms and nodded to the other two kinner. "Kum on, now. I'm told it's naptime."

"Do we get a bath, too?" Timothy yanked his socks off and let them lie where they'd landed.

"Bubble bath!" Mary yelled.

Isaac shrugged. Glanced at Agnes.

She shook her head. "We're giving Martha a sponge bath. This isn't playtime. Pick up your socks and get into bed. You, too, Mary. We'll be there shortly."

Agnes followed Isaac upstairs and to the bathroom, then leaned against the doorframe. "First of all, remove her diaper and set her on the potty. Then, run lukewarm water in the sink, add a drop or two of soap, and wash her hands and face."

"Sounds easy enough." Isaac did as instructed, washing the messy food off her face and hands with the soapy washcloth, then handed Martha a couple squares of toilet paper. She seemed to know what to do with it. Afterward, he carried her back to the bedroom, laid her in the crib, and picked up a disposable diaper from the floor. Thankfully, it was one the kinner hadn't ruined. "Might as well start where I intend to go."

Agnes scowled.

He shrugged. "I'm a single man. I'm going to spare myself the laundry—which I really don't know how to do. When I'm traveling, I add a few coins to a machine, buy a box of soap from a container hung on the wall, dump it and the clothes into the machine, and then sit down and read until it's time to move the clothes and feed money to another machine. I'm fairly positive Jenny has something like what my mamm had—an antique scrubbing board and an equally antique machine and washtub."

"You're right." Agnes nodded. "Go ahead, then. Although, Katherine will have something to say about your not being a gut steward of Gott's blessings and wasting Sam's hard-earned money."

"I'm not asking Sam to pay for it. This is just to make it easier for me. I'm already in over my head here. And these diapers are pretty self-explanatory." He fitted the diaper on Martha and taped it shut. "Easy, breezy. Not nearly as complicated as that one movie I saw where the baby crawls off leaving the diaper behind."

Agnes blinked. His world was so Englisch, it was a marvel he wore Amish clothes. But then, he'd warned her when they first met that maybe he wasn't Amish at all.

Except, he'd joined the church. Someplace. Even if he didn't claim to follow any particular Ordnung.

Even if he was wholly Amish and they courted, Bishop Miah would still have questions, wanting to make sure he was a fine, upstanding man who followed the faith. And he'd want them to choose a permanent district.

Nein. Marriage to Isaac would *not* be approved. Assuming, of course, that Isaac was serious enough to actually talk to the bishop. And his comment about being a single man seemed to indicate he wasn't. Agnes sighed.

But Isaac seemed blissfully unaware of her misgivings as he turned toward the door. "Have a gut nap. I might take one, too."

It was Sunday, meaning they weren't allowed to do work other than what was absolutely necessary. But what was she supposed to do while he napped?

Work sentry duty, to make sure none of the kinner wandered off?

Or maybe she could go to the pond and vent sooner than expected.

When they reached the bottom of the stairs, Isaac reached for her hand, entwined his fingers with hers, and led her toward the living room.

He sat down on the old, ragged sofa, tugged her down next to him, wrapped his arm around her, and bent his head toward hers to steal a kiss.

"You need to do dishes." She pushed against his chest. "And we need to talk."

And she didn't mean have a "conversation" like the one they'd had beside the pond.

"Dishes will wait." So would talking. Isaac was pretty sure that whatever Agnes wanted to say, he didn't want to hear. He'd seen her expression earlier. She didn't think he was serious about a proposal. Thankfully, the sofa sagged badly enough that she didn't get far. She was still pressed against his side.

Exactly where he wanted her to be.

Well, close enough anyway. For now.

He stroked her upper arm, sheathed in a sleeve of maroon fabric, and sighed in contentment, a small smile on his face. "If I was able to court you, I'd ask you to sneak out early from to-nacht's singing—"

"I won't be there. Nobody will ask to take me home. All I get are looks of pity and compliments on my fudge." Agnes pushed away from his chest again, gaining a little leverage.

He tightened his hold on her, pulling her tightly against his side. Her heat burned through his clothes. "I'd ask you if we were both there. But I won't be attending either, for obvious reasons. So, this is a pretend date, okay?"

"We're on a pretend date?" She twisted her head and looked at him, putting her soft lips in the perfect position for him to steal a kiss.

He swallowed and looked away. "Jah. So, I ask you to sneak out of the singing early and I pick you up on the road so nobody knows who you're with. I'll be the 'mystery man.' And we'll go into town and order pizza for dinner."

She laughed. "There's nein pizza place in town."

He raised his hand and pressed his forefinger against her lips.

She sucked in a breath, her eyes widening.

"A pretend date, remember? We can have a pretend pizza place. What kind of pizza would you like?" He slid his finger off her lips and caressed her cheek, her jaw.

"Supreme, with mushrooms and onions and everything. And extra cheese." She hesitated. "And pop to drink. I can't remember the last time I had either of those."

Isaac grinned. "Then that's what I order. And after we eat, I take you to a miniature golf course for a round of putt-putt." His fingers slid slowly down her neck.

Her breath quickened. "What's that?"

He toyed with her kapp strings. "Your education is sorely lacking. I'll teach you to play. You'll love it."

"It's a game?"

"Hmm." He raised her chin with his fingers. "And then, after dark, I'd take the scenic route home. And maybe, if you asked...I'd pull off someplace private and steal a kiss. Or two."

Her gaze lowered to his lips and she sucked in another breath. "If I'd asked, you wouldn't be stealing. You'd be taking what I willingly gave." Her cheeks turned a lovely shade of pink and she shivered.

"Hmm. You are so common-sense, Zook. Give in to the madness." He brushed his lips over hers and started to pull away. That was all he would allow.

She surged into his kiss, wrapping her arms around his neck.

His stomach clenched. He supposed he had told her to give in to the madness. He just hadn't expected she would listen.

Maybe a little longer wouldn't hurt.

He deepened the kiss, taking what she so willingly offered.

This was pure bliss. Who knew kissing could be so wunderbaar? Agnes could never get enough of this. She could get addicted to it, easily. Would she go through withdrawal when Isaac left for his auctions? Undoubtedly. Especially if he kissed her like this every day.

She wasn't sure how long she lay in his arms, kissing him, and she didn't care. It could last forever, as far as she was concerned. His kisses strayed from her lips across her cheeks to her eyelids and ears, then down her neck, where he nibbled at the place where her pulse pounded. She arched against him, a moan escaping. He growled deep in his throat before returning his attention to her lips, these kisses more heated, more demanding, more—

A hand landed heavy on her shoulder and squeezed. She whimpered and tried to shove it away. It didn't belong. But the grip tightened, becoming almost painful.

She opened her eyes as Isaac raised his head.

Bishop Miah stared down at them, his brows drawn, his eyes dark, and his lips curled down. His other hand was clamped on Isaac's shoulder.

"Oops. We've been bad." Agnes struggled to scramble out of Isaac's arms as the bishop released them both and stepped back.

She would get a Daed-worthy lecture from the bishop, for sure.

Isaac let her go. "We weren't bad." He glanced up at Bishop Miah. "I asked her to marry me. She accepted."

Agnes lurched to her feet. She wobbled and grasped the back of a chair for support. Had she accepted? It'd been a sarcastic answer to his facetious announcement, but he'd taken it as fact, apparently, despite his warning to the kinner not to say anything to anyone.

"Getting married is serious business. It's for keeps." Bishop Miah's stern expression didn't ease. "You two haven't known each other for even a week yet."

"Love's a decision. I made a decision." Isaac set his jaw.

What about the sparks? The excitement? The passion? Agnes tightened her grip on the chair. He made it sound so clinical. And yet the memory of his kisses on her lips still sent sparks shooting to her heart. Was there any hope that maybe he could kum to love her?

The bishop sighed, then pulled up a chair and sat. "I realize you're desperate for a husband, Agnes, but falling willy-nilly into the arms of the first man to kum along, and begging him to marry you, is not the answer."

Agnes gaped. Spluttered. "I—I didn't say jah. I mean, not exactly. I definitely didn't beg. I said I'd rather not marry a mistake. I am *not* desperate." Except, she sort of was.

Isaac winced. "You said, 'Sure, Isaac.'"

"I was being sarcastic!"

"I'm holding you to it." Isaac looked at Bishop Miah. "You and Katherine both said I need a frau. I *am* desperate, I'll willingly admit that. Agnes is available—"

"Ach, that's so romantic!" *Not.* Agnes's eyes burned. She stood. "I'm going to do the dishes."

She was free from being a mere convenience to Isaac…and yet it stung to still be an aging maidal whom the bishop had accused of being desperate enough to beg any man to marry her. If only Isaac had been serious. And if only the bishop had approved. Then maybe Agnes could prove Daed wrong. This incident had only served to reinforce what he'd always told her: that nein man would ever marry her.

"The situation is simply outrageous," Bishop Miah said. "Even if you both were serious—which neither of you is—I'd have to say nein."

Jah, that was what she'd figured. Agnes blinked against the burn once more as she stomped toward the other room.

"I'm very serious." Isaac seemed prepared to argue the point. "We could elope, you know. You wouldn't be able to stop us."

She slowed her steps. That was a possibility….

Except, they would be shunned, and both her candy shop and his calling as an Amish auctioneer would suffer. And possibly die.

"Isaac." The bishop's voice was calm. Too calm. "Desperation is not a gut reason to marry."

Agnes stumbled to a stop in the kitchen doorway. Was that comment directed at her or Isaac? Maybe both of them.

"There are many single daeds in the world and they manage. You need to learn that you are capable. And Agnes needs to learn that—"

"Capable." Isaac scoffed. "My world is falling apart and you say…."

Bishop Miah chuckled. "Ach, it's not falling apart. It's falling into place. And when the dust settles—for both of you—then we'll discuss marriage."

16

Cold cereal wasn't as foolproof as he'd hoped.

Isaac stared at the empty box in Mary's hand and then at the overflowing bowl of O's before her. Some of the circular morsels that had missed the container now cascaded like a waterfall to the floor.

"Oopsies. I clean it."

Isaac lurched forward. "Nein, nein—" Too late. He could hear the crunch of cereal under her feet and he shuddered at the thought of sticky powder being tracked across the floor.

Mary dropped the box and knelt to gather the survivors in her skirt. But, even then, it was a mess.

Shouldn't a three-year-old be capable of pouring cereal into a bowl? He stared at Mary.

Martha giggled.

Isaac swiveled to the right in time to watch the toddler's hand slam down on the edge of her already-prepared bowl, sending the contents of milk and soggy O's, in their entirety, all over her dress. At least the stuff had missed her hair, although how he was supposed to tame that beehive of tangles was anyone's guess.

Isaac glanced at Timmy. The bu seemed to be okay for now.

Then he looked at the empty bowl where he'd planned to sit and took a deep breath.

This meant Martha would need a bath and a change of clothes.

Except, this was her last clean dress.

Timmy scrutinized Isaac as if he wanted to gauge his reaction before producing his own.

A chair scraped the floor as Mary reached for something under the table.

Martha slapped her hands in the mess in front of her.

Gott, please get me out of this.

And here, Isaac had congratulated himself on surviving the evening and the over-nacht hours without mishap, after the bishop had escorted Agnes out of the haus and left him on his own.

To pray. To think.

Jah, like he needed to do anymore of either of those. Thinking he owed this to his brother had gotten him into this situation. Thinking he could earn his brother's trust again, that he could mend their tattered relationship, that, maybe, he could dare to dream of a relationship with Agnes someday.

It'd all been ripped out of his hands and now lay in messy heaps, like the cereal on the floor, part of it in a pool of milk from the toddler's bowl, part of it crushed beyond recognition with a giggling, "helpful" little girl in the middle of it.

His life, reduced to being compared with crushed, soggy cereal.

Isaac blew out a breath of frustration and moved the issue of *The Budget* that he'd hoped to read during breakfast to a dry spot on the table. Then, forcing a smile, he went to grab the broom and the dustpan like a soldier preparing his weapons for facing a battle.

As he turned back to the kitchen table, Timmy, apparently deciding Isaac's unspoken decision had meant "Carry on," went for the other box of cold cereal and the pitcher of milk on a nearby counter. While trying to transfer them to the table, he dumped them both, causing a new disaster.

The broom fell to the wooden floor with thunk that was almost drowned out by the shouts of the kinner.

Isaac's shoulders slumped. *Do You hate me, Gott?* He waded into the mess, moved the kinner to the clean side of the table, and started to clean up.

"Sorry, Onkel Isaac." Timmy hung his head. "I was just trying to help."

Isaac forced another smile. "Accidents happen. Can you find your mamm's pail? I'll need to scrub the floor."

The mess would be a far easier, faster cleanup if he invited Sam's hog into the haus, but Isaac didn't think either Jenny or Agnes would be impressed with that decision, and—Isaac eyed the kinner—the women would be certain to find out.

A one-way ticket out of here sounded better and better.

Except for Agnes. If he left—and didn't return—it would mean the death knell for their relationship, such as it was. At least the bishop had left them with a little hope, for the day when Isaac figured out he was capable of something more than just auctioning off other people's stuff. Maybe caring for a family. Sticking around for longer than a few days.

And for the day when Agnes realized she was worthy of love.

Convincing Agnes she had value would be easy compared to taking care of these three kinner. As Isaac swept the ruined cereal into a pile and then dumped it into the slop bucket for the pigs, his mind raced to conjure things he could do for her, get for her.

A new sink for her shop was on his mental list.

An hour later, with the compounded mess—both the kitchen and the kinner—finally cleaned up, Isaac loaded the trio into the buggy, where he could keep an eye on them while he hitched up Sam's horse.

Timothy bounced on the front seat. "Gut morgen, Chunky Monkey."

Isaac glanced at him. "What?"

Timmy's little chest puffed out. "I picked his name."

Isaac eyed the harness that strained to fit around the horse's girth. "Chunky" was an understatement. He hoisted himself to sit beside his nephew, gathered the reins, glanced over his shoulder at the two girls with their tangled messes of flyaway hair, and, with a sigh, started the buggy toward the Brunstetters.

When they got there, the haus was quiet and nobody came out to meet them.

"Stay here." Isaac gave Timmy the reins. "Don't go anywhere." He climbed the porch steps and opened the door. "Agnes?"

Katherine came into the room, wielding a feather duster. "She went to work. Hours ago." She sounded almost gleeful.

"Ach. Jah, we are considerably later than planned. And I didn't do the girls' hair. Not quite sure how—"

"Nein, danki, Ike. I can't babysit."

Isaac hadn't asked her to, exactly, but he had rather hoped she'd offer to do the girls' hair and then volunteer to keep them a while, since he was clearly inept.

At least Bishop Miah wasn't around to tell Isaac to go home and stop bothering Agnes.

Isaac nodded and headed for the door. He suppressed a gasp as Chunky Monkey took off toward the road at a fast trot. Timmy must've flicked the reins.

Isaac rushed out the door, jumped off the porch, and raced toward the buggy, grabbing the reins seconds before the vehicle reached the mailbox. He couldn't live through this nacht-mare again. How could he have been so stupid as to give the reins to a young bu?

He patted the spunky beast on the back and surveyed the kinner. *Breathe. Just breathe.* He climbed into the buggy. *Gott, if it's not too much trouble, could You please help us get to town without any more problems? And give me courage.*

"I don't think you're quite ready for driving lessons." Isaac settled next to Timmy and glanced back at the girls to make sure they were okay before he dared to take another breath.

"Daed let me drive before the fire," Timmy said.

"Not on the road, I'm sure." Isaac glanced both directions, then turned the buggy onto the road.

"On the road."

Isaac gave him a stern glance.

"Only if nobody was coming." Timmy sagged. "And he always kept holding the reins."

That made sense. Isaac's daed had done the same thing with Isaac and Sam.

Town was busy, with vehicles parked up and down the main street. As they drove past the Amish bakery, someone emerged carrying a white plastic bag of purchases. Isaac's stomach growled at the reminder of the breakfast Isaac had missed while cleaning up the spilled cereal. He drove the buggy around the corner and parked it between Agnes's and another one, which probably belonged to the baker.

After securing Chunky Monkey to the hitching post, Isaac lifted Mary out of the buggy. "Wait for me."

Mary obediently paused.

He stepped aside for Timmy to jump over the wheel, then reached for Martha. Once he'd lifted her out, he looked around. Where were Mary and Timmy? He sucked in a deep breath when he spotted them running toward the road. "Wait!" He dashed after them. He couldn't let down his guard for even one second. There was too much potential for things to go wrong. What kind of trouble would they get into next?

Timmy grabbed Mary's hand and jerked her to a stop. "Onkel Isaac said to wait."

Obedience, at last! One success today.

Isaac opened the door of the candy shop and they all filed inside. The tantalizing scent of chocolate met his nostrils. Instead of cooking, though, Agnes sat in a chair with her back toward the door. Nearby, several Englisch people in professional dress were getting ready for…something. Agnes turned with the jingle of the bells and the chatter of the kinner and her eyes sought his.

The television interview. Had she mentioned it and he'd forgotten? He glanced out the front door. There was a big van parked outside. He'd been so focused on making sure the kinner stayed seated while maneuvering through the traffic that he'd missed the biggest sign of all.

He'd need to watch the kinner himself and try to be supportive of her. Or maybe he should take the kinner back home to remove the distraction. Except, then he wouldn't be there to hold her hand or send winks her direction.

The interview hadn't started yet. An Englisch woman wearing a tight black dress was helping an Englisch man in casual clothes set up several spotlights. Isaac corralled the two older kinner, who'd snagged the bag of colorful farm animals, and steered them toward the kitchen. He glanced at Agnes once more. Her expression was tight, her eyes wide. Her hands shook. Nerves, she'd said. He should pray for her.

What was it the bishop had said? "Let prayer be the key to the day and the bolt to the nacht." Gut advice.

"Is that your husband?" The Englisch woman raced toward him on impossibly high heels and grasped his arm just above the elbow.

He pulled away. "Jah."

"Nein," Agnes said at the same time.

"Promised," he amended. Although, technically speaking, it wasn't true.

"And those are your children?" the woman pressed.

Agnes gasped, her eyes widening even more.

"No. Nieces and nephew." Not that it was any of their business, but if rumor got out that he had kinner outside of marriage, his reputation would suffer. Agnes's, too, for that matter. It did happen on occasion in the Amish community, but even so….

"What's your name?" The woman pulled up another chair, set it near Agnes, and motioned for Isaac to sit.

"Isaac." He ignored the gesture and put Martha on the floor. She hurried in the direction of the kitchen.

"Do you go by Ike?" She didn't wait for an answer. "Okay, Ike." Maybe she'd read agreement in his eyes. "If you'll have a seat, I'll ask you a few simple questions, like how you feel about your girlfriend's success in starting a candy business with such a huge level of competition, since you're located so close to Mackinac Island, world-famous for its fudge."

That was a simple question?

⌒

Agnes breathed a little easier with Isaac's unexpected yet timely arrival. His big, strong shoulders were enough to bring a measure of security to this uncomfortable predicament. He was more than capable of taking care of her. At least, it seemed that way.

"Let me get the kin—er, children—first." He disappeared into the kitchen.

Agnes's tension mounted again. If only the bishop would've said nein to doing this interview.

The woman fussed with something behind Agnes, then adjusted the angle of Isaac's chair.

The cameraman murmured something to the woman. Then he carried his camera over to the display case, focusing on the fudge Agnes had set out, then panning to the glass jars of rock candy and the handwoven reed basket filled with saltwater taffy.

Agnes's stomach knotted. Cramped. What was taking Isaac so long?

The door swung open and Isaac appeared, kinner in tow. He pointed Timothy toward the plants and handed him the bag of colorful animals, then sat both girls down at a table nearby with the play dough Agnes had made. "Stay here," he instructed them.

His lips formed that now-familiar half-smile Agnes found so addicting. "Mary had already climbed up on the counter to reach whatever was cooling," he explained as he sat. "Figured they'd better be where I can see them."

Ach, gut. He'd saved the new recipe she was trying—white chocolate fudge with dried cranberries and pistachios—from certain destruction. Maybe he'd be willing to taste-test it later and give his opinion.

Isaac aimed his grin—with considerably less wattage—at the Englisch woman. "Do you want my hat on or off?"

"Off, please. You object to your picture being taken, too?"

"Filming me from behind is fine." Isaac laid his hat on a table, then sat beside Agnes. He reached for her hand and squeezed her fingers.

She took a deep breath and clung to him. She needed his strength.

After a moment's hesitation, his hand shifted. Palm against palm. Fingers intertwined. "Breathe, Beautiful," he whispered.

She handed over her heart in its entirety. Something she'd never done, not even with Gabe. Something had held her back then. Maybe knowing he loved someone else, that he could never truly be hers. But Isaac....

Her heart would be shattered when Isaac left.

The woman sat in front of them, facing the camera situated behind Agnes and Isaac. Agnes glanced at woman's long, shapely legs, then tugged at her own boring navy-blue dress. What did Isaac think, looking at this beautiful woman? Agnes glanced down at the battery-operated microphone attached to her bodice. Maybe she had truly been abducted by those aliens she'd been telling her plants about the day Isaac arrived.

"This is BJ Donovan with Channel Nine and Ten News, broadcasting live from Sweet Treats, a candy store that's owned and operated by an Amish woman, Agnes Zook. Agnes, tell me where you got the idea for starting a candy shop."

Agnes's tongue seemed to swell to twice its normal size. Maybe three times. She opened her mouth, but nothing came out, except for a sick-sounding "eek." This woman wanted her to spill her whole sad story about having a crush on Gabe, watching him choose another, and needing to find some way of supporting herself because she was doomed to be forever single? There had to be a simpler, more condensed version to tell, but she couldn't think how it might go.

Why hadn't the television station sent her a list of questions to prepare for? Then she could have asked Bishop Miah to help her plan her scripted answers. For that matter, why hadn't they told her an exact date and time when they'd be there for the interview? Then she wouldn't have been as shocked and horrified when they'd marched into the shop a half an hour ago.

Isaac's hand tightened around hers. "Agnes has long held a reputation for being a top-notch candymaker. Amish would kum from all over to sample it and it always sold out first at auctions and farmer's markets, so it made sense for her to open a store and sell it on a daily basis. She's got quite the following and now her customers don't have to wait for special occasions to buy Agnes's fudge or brave the crowds on Mackinac Island or in Mackinaw City to get it."

Nein wonder he was such a successful auctioneer. He could talk under duress. And kum up with well-composed statements that made her sound better than she was. She squeezed his hand as a show of thanks.

"Do you plan on keeping your shop open indefinitely?" BJ asked.

Agnes managed a nod. "Jah." Her answer wasn't much louder than a whisper.

"Until we marry and she has children and becomes a full-time mom," Isaac added.

He'd summarized her dream so succinctly. Did he really mean it? Or was he being a bit of a flirt, playing with the camera?

"Rather male chauvinist of you, isn't it, Ike?" BJ sounded a bit irritated.

Agnes would gladly give up the shop when she married and had kinner. Make that *if*. Not "when." She glanced at the girls, who were now throwing play dough on her previously clean floor.

Isaac shrugged. "That's the way it is in our culture."

"When's the wedding?" There was a definite bite in the woman's tone.

Agnes lowered her head and stared at her lap. There would be nein wedding. But stating that would be to call Isaac a liar for saying they were promised to each other—and she loved the sound of the word "promised." *Promised* meant she was wanted. Plus, it would necessitate spilling that whole sad story to these Englisch strangers who would never understand what it meant to be Amish.

Isaac chuckled. "Now, now, BJ. Some things are meant to be kept quiet until they're published. How do you think my brother would feel if you—and your viewers—knew our wedding details before he did?"

And that settled the issue. Agnes shifted a little closer to the man beside her. She *loved* Isaac Mast.

There was a rustling noise as BJ sifted through some papers in her lap. "We noticed a new Amish bakery down the road. Did a lot of new businesses spring up after the devastating wildfire?"

"We should interview the baker, too," the cameraman said. "Since we're in the area."

There you go. Sic these Englisch television reporters on unsuspecting Naomi Kaiser. But Agnes had to answer this question, since Isaac seemed to be at a loss for words. He looked at her, one eyebrow raised.

"You already know about the construction company and the Amish market," Agnes began, remembering that Bishop Miah had mentioned Gabe Lapp and Gideon Kaiser's having also received letters from the television station. "There's the bakery, a Christmas tree farm, and a small engine repair shop that is trying to get started up." Hopefully, what she'd said made sense.

"Small engine shop?" BJ's voice held doubt. "But Amish don't use—"

"Stereotypical," Isaac replied. "Each district is different and some do use them. However, whether we do or whether we don't personally use them has nothing to do with our ability to fix broken machines."

At the conclusion of the interview, the cameraman took some more photos of the candy, including the recipe Agnes was testing, though the fudge needed more time to cool before it was ready for taste-testing. BJ bought two slabs of fudge weighing one pound each—a blessing—before the crew finally gathered their equipment and left to visit an unsuspecting Naomi at her bakery. Agnes wished she could warn her friend somehow. Naomi would likely kum over as soon as the news crew had left, at which point they could commiserate together about the surprise visit.

"I'm going to give the horses some water." Isaac disappeared out the door.

At least he'd kept his promise to be there when the reporters came. She hadn't expected he would really kum, especially when she hadn't known herself when it would be. Gott must have sent him right on time.

She returned the tables and chairs to their rightful positions, then glanced at the quiet kinner—ach, the girls' hair. What a mess. She shook her head. Thinking she might have a comb in the office, she hurried in that direction to look.

She stopped in the kitchen to check on the fudge. It had cooled, so she cut off a few small slices, divided one of the slices into three smaller ones, and went to deliver the samples to the kinner and Isaac.

As she entered the front room, Isaac came inside, his crooked half-smile in place. "The baker is chasing the TV reporters out of her shop and flapping a floury towel at them. That BJ woman is squawking like a hen and trying to run in those shoes at the same time." He chuckled.

Naomi had more courage than Agnes had thought. She always seemed like she would make the perfect Amish frau. Quiet. Submissive. It seemed still waters ran deep.

In fact, Naomi had more courage than Agnes, who'd counted on hiding behind the bishop's firm refusal—which he hadn't given.

Agnes handed each smiling child a tiny piece of the fudge she'd cut into thirds. Mary popped her piece into her mouth, while Martha squeezed hers in with the play dough. Agnes wrinkled her nose. She'd have to watch and make sure she didn't eat it later. She approached Isaac with a full-sized slice. "It's a new recipe. White chocolate with dried cranberries and pistachios."

"Danki." Isaac surveyed the piece for a moment before taking it from the paper napkin she'd placed it on. "I love the look. Almost Christmassy, with the combination of white, red, green, and brown."

She hadn't been going for Christmas, but that holiday was coming soon and people would want to order fudge for their holiday gatherings and parties. Maybe she should experiment with some peppermint recipes using crushed candy canes.

As Agnes prepared to taste the piece of fudge she'd cut for herself, the door whooshed open with a mad jingle of the sleigh bells and the redheaded baker swept in, her green eyes hard. "Really, Agnes, what were you thinking, sending those reporters to my shop? I have nein time for such foolishness and that poor girl I have helping me this summer is left sweeping up all the flour I flung when I grabbed the towel to chase them out."

Agnes blinked. "What?" *Wait.* Daed had always held Naomi up as an example of the perfect Amish girl. But it seemed Naomi was really a spitfire. So much for being quiet and submissive. Maybe speaking one's mind wasn't such a bad thing. Now that she knew the truth about Naomi, Agnes thought she could become friends with her.

Isaac's lips quirked. He pressed them together, then retreated several quiet steps toward the corner opposite the kinner and raised the fudge to his mouth to take a bite—or maybe to hide his laughter.

Agnes returned her attention to Naomi. "I didn't send them. They noticed your shop and decided to visit it themselves when they finished here. Bishop Miah gave permission for the interview."

"Hmph. Well, they have nein business bothering me. Not even having the courtesy of coming in as customers," Naomi snapped.

"I didn't really want to do the interview," Agnes admitted. "It was scary and I could hardly wait for them to leave so I could breathe again. But at least they bought some fudge. And with all the pictures they took, maybe I'll get some free advertising out of the ordeal." Agnes immediately cringed at her verbal vomit.

Naomi slumped. "I could've used the advertising. My parents are hoping that new man in town will want to court me, though, so I won't have to work. Have you met him? Ike Mast. Of course, you must've. His nieces and nephew are here." She waved a hand toward the kinner. "Are you babysitting for them still?"

"Not exactly. Sort of." Agnes frowned. She needed to distract this bold woman. "Here, try this. It's a new recipe."

"Danki." Naomi took the fudge but stopped before tasting it, apparently noticing Isaac lurking in the corner. Her face flamed a brilliant red, then faded to a pasty white. She backed up a step. "Who are you?" she squeaked.

Isaac's mouth still twitched. "Isaac Mast. Sam's brother."

Naomi gulped, then shook her head. "Katherine referred to you as 'Ike,' so that's what my parents called you. I'm supposed to bring a meal by for you and your nieces and nephew to-nacht to impress you with my baking skills." She waved her hands toward the three kinner. "I'm also supposed to impress you with how quiet and docile I am." She grimaced. "I made a chicken potpie. It'll be ready to bake when I bring it by."

Agnes bit back her jealousy at the realization that other girls were trying to impress him in an effort to steal him from her. If only she could cook for him every day and shoo the other girls away. But that aside, was it hard for Naomi to try to be quiet and docile when she really wasn't?

"Don't feel obligated to fall in love with me."

Isaac coughed. "Danki for taking me off the hook. And you can tell your parents I've never met a woman as quiet and docile as you."

Naomi snickered. "I'm sure you haven't." She took a bite of the fudge. "This is really gut, Agnes. What do you think, Ike?"

"I agree. One slice isn't enough." Isaac winked at Agnes.

Maybe it was okay for Agnes to just be herself. After all, Isaac was laughing with and teasing Naomi, clearly accepting her as herself. Maybe he'd been serious when he said he liked Agnes the way she was.

"You should put this type up for sale." Naomi finished her piece of fudge. "I need to get back to the shop before Paris wonders if those report-ers abducted me."

"Wait. Take a slice for Paris, too. Tell her I want to know what she thinks." Agnes hurried into the kitchen, then slowed once she was out of sight.

Who would've guessed Naomi wasn't who she seemed to be. That meant she had fooled Daed. And if Gott told Daed everything....

Agnes shook her head.

Nein question about it. Daed had been wrong. And if he'd made an error in judging Naomi's personality, maybe he was mistaken about Agnes's being forever unwanted.

⌒

Isaac watched Naomi leave with her second sample of fudge. Then he turned to Agnes with a smirk. "Are all the women in this district so outspoken?"

"All the women?" Pink rose in Agnes's cheeks as she busied herself wiping off the tables.

"You. Naomi. Sarah."

"That's only three." Agnes glanced at him. "And I had nein idea Naomi had it in her. Her daed and brother run the Amish salvage-grocery store, you know. And I thought someone was courting her, but maybe whoever it was left the area and has yet to return—if he does at all. Some people are still waiting to see if the community revives. It's been only six—almost seven—months since the fire."

Six months. Most of which Isaac had spent in blissful ignorance of the severity of his brother's injuries and his family's need. He still felt like a jerk for not knowing his twin was in trouble.

Agnes touched Mary's shoulder. "Let's put the play dough away for now. We'll wash up and then I'll teach you how to make rock candy." She smoothed her hand over Mary's still-messy hair. "I forgot to look for a comb."

"Can I help with the candy?" Timmy started gathering the multicolored farm animals.

"Absolutely. I couldn't do it without you. Even Onkel Ike can help, if he behaves himself."

"Isaac to you. Not Ike. Please."

Agnes whirled and stared at him, a hurt expression in her eyes. Her lips were slightly parted.

Too late, he realized how that sounded. He stepped closer and rubbed a small circle on her upper arm with his fingertip. "Englischers prefer Ike. I put up with some Amish calling me Ike, but those who are close to me know I prefer Isaac. And you, Agnes, are pretty close." He lowered his voice to help make his point.

Her expression eased. A smile flickered and grew. "Danki for that."

His hand tightened on her upper arm. "I didn't lie either. I'd love another slice of the fudge, if you don't mind." His lips brushed her ear. "Like your kisses, it's addicting."

She blushed and glanced at the kinner. "Go ahead and take Martha to the potty and make sure all three wash their hands. I'll cut a piece for you, then I'll get started on the rock candy."

Isaac frowned. "Do we need to worry about them getting burned?"

"Nein. I'll handle the hot stuff."

Isaac grinned. "You are hot stuff."

Her face flamed red. "You are, too."

He winked and looked at the kinner. "Remember, I'm gonna marry this girl someday."

17

Wednesday came too soon. Agnes stood on the front stoop of her shop, Martha in her arms, Mary and Timothy on either side, while Isaac loaded his suitcase and backpack into the rear of the white van that would take him to the bus stop.

Tears burned her eyes, blurring her vision.

The driver slammed the back door shut and Isaac hesitated, then bounded up the stone stairs to where they stood.

Timothy surged ahead, wrapping his arms around Isaac's neck when the tall man crouched to his level. "You'll kum back, ain't so?"

Isaac hugged him. "I'll be back, Timmy. You be gut for Aenti Agnes, okay?"

"I will. I'll take gut care of her." Timothy firmed his shoulders.

"Atta boy." Isaac hugged the two little girls. Both were crying, but Agnes didn't think Martha understood exactly what was happening; she was just mimicking her sister.

"Don't go." Mary flung herself at him, weeping. "I never see you, just like Daed."

A muscle jumped in his jaw. "Your daed will be back. I promise. He just needs to get well first. And I'll return. I wouldn't go now, but I need to work." He patted Mary's back and kissed her cheek, then did the same routine with Martha when she babbled something and patted his arm.

Finally, he straightened, meeting Agnes's stinging eyes. He'd probably be shocked if she wrapped her arms around him and hugged him tight in front of anyone who might be witnessing this moment, but she didn't exactly care. She set Martha down, then reached for Isaac, who took control. He grasped her shoulders, pulled her into his embrace, and kissed her cheeks. Both of them. Then he dropped a kiss on her lips.

She trembled and leaned into him. "You will return, jah?" Her voice broke.

"Jah, I will." He kissed her again. "Be brave. Will you take the kinner back to the bishop's while I'm gone? You'll have help there."

"We'll stay at Sam's." She stepped out of his arms. "I don't need help. Besides, Katherine is worn out. She needs a break. And then, when you return, I'll move into the extra room here."

He arched an eyebrow at her. "Here. With nein furniture and your bad back."

"I have chairs and tables. It's just the evil sink, really. But it's time."

"Here. With an unknown druggie attempting to rob the place with a loaded gun. What's going to stop the man from trying again?" His brow furrowed in a frown.

Agnes felt a flash of fear, but she suppressed the urge to shiver. "Here." Her voice cracked.

"You won't change your mind?"

"I'll be fine." Agnes firmed her shoulders. Though she would probably find herself continually reciting Bible verses about lying down in peace and sleeping.

"You are the most capable woman I know."

She doubted it. Most women were more capable. But it was a nice thing for him to say.

"Mamm always called the kitchen the 'heart of the home.'" A wistful expression crossed his face. "And while this isn't exactly a home, it is your kitchen."

Agnes grinned. "Then I'll be here where the heart is."

The van driver honked his horn.

"Be right there," Isaac called over his shoulder. Then he gathered Agnes into his arms again and hugged her tight. "I'll be in contact, Beautiful."

And with that lovely sentiment, he turned, ran down the stone steps, and climbed into the van. Three seconds later, he was gone.

Vanished in a blur of tears.

Agnes swallowed a hard lump, then crouched and gathered the whimpering kinner in her arms. Timothy's shoulders shook, but he'd managed to blink back the flood, like Agnes.

Her shattered heart speared shards into her. This hurt worse than she'd imagined. And they would be repeating this routine almost weekly for the time Isaac was here.

And then would kum his permanent departure. The one he wouldn't return from. At least, not for a long time. She should probably try to get used to this feeling of abandonment. For the sake of the kinner, she would be brave…and pray their daed and mamm came home soon.

She gulped at the stubborn lump.

She would manage. Had nein choice but to manage. Even if he didn't return. He'd said he would, but would he, really, once he'd gotten away from his family grindstone to the freedom his single life allowed? He'd accomplished his goal and found someone else—Agnes—to watch the kinner, even though her responsibilities were supposed to be only temporary, until his return. He'd won her heart, wrapped her around his little finger, before leaving.

He'd probably forgotten her already.

She brushed at a tear that had escaped the self-made barricade, then straightened. "Let's go see how much the rock candy grew over-nacht."

Timothy took her hand. "Do you think it'll be enough to eat some?"

Agnes shrugged. "Probably needs a few more days, but we'll see."

She turned around, opened the shop door, and herded the kinner inside, then flipped the lock. It wasn't time for her to open yet, and she needed to be alone to mourn.

Well, as alone as she could be under the circumstances.

Montana temperatures in late August seemed comparable to what Isaac had left behind in the Upper Peninsula of Michigan. According to the weather app on Isaac's phone, it was 76 degrees. He rubbed the sleep out of his eyes and wandered into the store/restaurant in this Amish community. Even though it was late in the afternoon, he needed a cup of koffee. Had needed one since yesterday, but none of the bus stops had anything palatable to offer. Nothing seemed palatable anymore, now that he'd tasted Agnes's koffee. Everything else reminded him of Katherine Brunstetter's.

Maybe Katherine's koffee wasn't all that bad, compared with anything but Agnes's. Perhaps the sugary scents of the candy shop somehow flavored Agnes's. Or maybe it was her sweet personality that made her koffee taste wunderbaar. He should've asked her to fill a thermos for him before he left. But even if he had, the stuff would've been long gone by now.

"Ike Mast?" A gravelly voice greeted him.

Isaac turned to the gray-haired man slumped over the checkerboard set up near the cold woodstove. The elderly gentleman seated next to him adjusted his glasses on his nose and peered up at Isaac. "We was waitin' for ya. Want to eat the evening meal first or after we head to the auction site for a look-see?"

Isaac put his bags down. He needed koffee more than food at this point. He tried to smother another yawn. Sleeping on buses or in bus depots was almost impossible, so he'd been mostly awake for over forty-eight hours—counting stops and layovers—during the long trip. It'd be a blessing to reach wherever he'd be staying to-nacht for a few hours of uninterrupted sleep before he attempted to talk to someone about bidding on some items that Agnes needed.

"Koffee any gut here?" He nodded toward the restaurant. "I can eat later but sure could use a shot of caffeine."

The elderly men chuckled. "Already ordered ya a big cup to go," the first one said, fingering his long beard. "Go git it for 'im, Sol."

The other man—Sol—grunted. "Lazy, Levi."

Levi chortled at the jab, reminding Isaac of Bishop Miah.

Sol slowly stood, hunched almost double, as he groped for the back of the chair to steady himself.

Isaac winced. "I can get the koffee myself. Don't want to put you to any trouble."

"Just takes a moment to get the kinks worked out. I'll be fine once I get my feet under me." Sol rubbed his lower back with one hand, released the chair with his other, and turned. "I'll be back in a jiffy." He shuffled off.

Levi looked after him. "Does him gut to walk. He's had several surgeries already." He shook his head. "Have a seat while you wait."

"Actually, I've been sitting a lot. I'd like to stretch my legs a while."

Levi chuckled. "I hear ya. When my frau and I went to Pinecraft, I thought my bottom was gonna fall off, it was so sore from sittin' all that way."

Isaac nodded. He'd felt the same and his age was just a fraction of this man's. He glanced around the store. "Nice place." A display of postcards and greeting cards caught his eye. He thought he should probably send something to the kinner. To Sam and Jenny. And especially to Agnes.

"Do they sell stamps here?"

"Jah."

Isaac grinned. "I'll be right back." He hurried over to the display and picked out two postcards featuring mountain scenes, as well as a card that showed a glass far filled with glittery paper hearts and read, "Thinking of You."

Printed inside was the phrase "There are so many reasons to love you."

Short. Sweet. To the point.

Just what Isaac needed.

Hopefully, it would brighten Agnes's day.

He paid for the cards and the postage, then made his way back to Levi. He leaned down to tuck the small plastic bag of his purchases into a zippered side pocket of his suitcase before standing straight again.

Sol shuffled back into the room carrying a large koffee.

Nobody had asked Isaac how he took the drink, but considering the efficiency of the Amish grapevine, it was likely every community knew— or at least knew whom to ask—when Isaac came around.

Kum to think of it, Agnes hadn't asked either.

He rubbed his hand across his jaw. Rather scary to think that virtual strangers knew so much about him.

Bishop Miah probably hadn't needed to do so much spying, after all. He'd probably heard much of his "insider information" through the grapevine.

Of course, the man probably still needed to keep his eyes on Isaac and Agnes. Daed had grumbled once that it was easier to keep track of a sack of fleas than a couple in love.

Isaac grinned at the thought. He had kept Bishop Miah chasing after them, even though he and Agnes hadn't been in love. Yet. But there was definitely something there. Strong attraction. Infatuation. Something. He aimed his grin at Sol as he accepted the koffee. "Danki. I needed this."

"Or maybe the koffee needs you more than you need it." Sol patted him on the arm.

What? That comment messed with Isaac's head. It was truly worthy of the bishop's repertoire. His smile faltered. He hid it by taking a sip.

This was definitely better than Katherine's koffee. Better than the koffee at most bus stops. He would survive here, knowing the koffee was gut.

But whatever Agnes did differently, hers was still the best.

⌒

Agnes wearily returned the youth Bible storybook to the bookcase. They'd survived the second day without Isaac. The first day, the kinner had trailed Agnes around, not leaving her side even when she'd gone to milk the cow and feed the animals. If they'd followed Isaac around, too, he'd probably had an easy time of it.

Keeping them safe, at least, if not an easier time getting things done. He hadn't done any laundry, so after the kinner had gone to bed the previous evening, Agnes had washed a load and hung it out to dry over-nacht. She'd gotten up earlier than usual to get the remaining laundry done and hung out before she started on whatever else needed doing Thursday. The candy shop, like most Amish businesses, was closed that day. Thursdays were reserved for weddings.

The first nacht, it was still a novelty for the kinner to have her around and she'd accomplished the bare necessities before falling into bed and dreaming of Isaac's kisses. But today had brought, in addition to the mountain of laundry and chores, plenty of squabbles among the upset, lonely kinner, along with mud pies and more messes. Now Agnes was completely exhausted and dreading the thought of trying to keep the kinner occupied tomorrow at the store. The rock candy had already lost its attraction.

After dinner, Agnes gave the kinner a bubble bath and washed their hair. Then she read a bedtime story to the girls while Timothy sounded out letters in a book of his own.

When she went to tuck Timothy in bed, she gave him a kiss on the forehead. "Gut-nacht, Timothy."

Timothy hugged her. "Can you call me Timmy, like Onkel Isaac does?"

His sad expression broke her heart. "Jah, I can do that."

"Do you think he'll really kum back?"

Agnes sighed. "He said he would." But she wasn't sure.

She hugged Timothy—Timmy—again, then left to clean the kitchen and the bathroom. She scrubbed the floors before going into the master bedroom, where Isaac must've slept, and crawled into a bed that held his spicy scent.

The mattress was soft and she imagined herself safely cocooned in his arms. Or in the arms of Someone.

Ach, if only it were *that* Someone's. If only He loved her with the kind of love the bishop sometimes described.

She shook her head, pushing that thought away as hot tears escaped her eyes. Her first real tears since the nacht her family died.

She buried her face into the masculine-scented pillow, trying to smother the tears. Just once, she'd like to know der Herr was on her side. Instead, He seemed to have it in for her. "Gott, why don't You care?"

The wail broke out of her at full volume, startling even herself.

She sucked in air. She would wake the kinner if she kept this up. This was not a safe place to do her "praying."

But the pond wasn't as safe as she'd thought it was. Bishop Miah had known about it. He'd sent Isaac there to find her. For what purpose?

She shut her eyes.

Ach. He'd wanted to quit.

He'd. Wanted. To. Quit.

And she'd talked him out of it. Had tried to comfort him and he'd taken advantage of her hug, had turned it around, and...and...had seduced her.

Sort of. She'd been a very willing participant.

Either way, he'd gotten her right where he wanted her. Enjoyed his flirty fling of fun, unloaded the kids into her willing lap, and left town on the next bus.

She drew in a shaky breath.

Whyever would he kum back?

18

Isaac slapped the back of the small moving van to signal the hired driver, then stepped back and watched him drive it off to park it out of the way. They'd leave for Michigan in a day or two, probably Tuesday, since it'd be late Monday when the auction would officially close and he'd get paid.

He hoped Agnes liked the few items he'd managed to buy for her. The crowds had been actively bidding on things and it had been debatable whether he'd get anything for the amounts he was prepared to pay.

He'd looked over the remaining items that would be up for bid and decided he had nein use for them. Some were valuable antiques that would sell for quite a bit of money. There were several pieces of original artwork by a painter whose name he'd heard only at auctions; they would bring a small fortune. But none of them was a necessity. Someone undoubtedly would buy them and there'd likely be several bidding wars; the parking lot overflowed with vehicles of all kinds. The most popular and most expensive items were generally saved for the end.

He loved his work, really; but, today, still exhausted from the long trip and little sleep, he was a bit irritable. It was his job to drive up the prices and keep the competitors civil; the crazy bidding and selfishness that emerged sometimes disgusted him. Trying to sleep on buses and drinking awful koffee...he was over that. The biggest redeeming point was spending time with the guys over a meal...which reminded him of his hope for new friendship with Gabe and Noah. The bishop. Gideon. So many others he'd met only briefly.

His stomach growled. He was supposed to meet Sol and Levi for the noon meal in—Isaac pulled out his cell phone and glanced at the time—about a half an hour. He would survive until then. He adjusted the brim of his straw hat against the glare of the sun and headed in the direction of the booth where Sol had said he wanted to eat. It was wedged in between two stands that sold corndogs and lemonade, and funnel cakes.

With stands selling fried fruit pies, hamburgers, slushes, sno-cones, and more, this was almost a carnie's paradise—except this wasn't a carnival or a fair; it was an auction to benefit a member of the community who'd been diagnosed with a brain tumor. Isaac couldn't remember if the tumor was cancerous or not. He lowered his head and rubbed his eyes. The man was a daed with seventeen kinner, some adults and some still very young. His frau and family would struggle—were struggling—yet claimed they were resigned to Gott's will, even though they'd chosen to fight the disease using medical intervention.

Death wasn't the will of der Herr. It was a by-product of sin.

And that was another fist to the chest. Because of Isaac's sin....

And not just his nephew but also his parents.

He blinked at the burn. And 1 John 1:9 came to his mind:

> If we confess our sins, He is faithful and just to forgive us our sins and
> to cleanse us from all unrighteousness.

He'd confessed one of his sins to Agnes. Had he ever confessed his sins to the Father? Even when he'd joined the church—still in competition with his brother for Jenny's hand at the time—it'd been more about winning the girl than about denying self and confessing sins.

His stomach knotted. Clenched. His mouth dried.

Gott....

He needed to pray. Needed to find a patch of holy ground where he could bow in the presence of the Almighty and pray the prayer he'd intended to pray the nacht he kissed Agnes—just before the bishop interrupted him with a well-deserved lecture that Isaac had only half-heard. Or maybe a different prayer altogether because the one he'd intended to pray that nacht was that he and the kinner would survive and he'd be a hero in someone's eyes.

Like Sam. Jenny.

Agnes.

His eyes stung. He needed to confess his sins. Ask Gott for forgiveness. And then maybe Gott would hear, answer, help…forgive.

Forgive.

And then maybe he could forgive himself.

⌒

Labor Day afternoon, Agnes locked the front door of Sweet Treats, Martha hanging on her skirts with one sticky hand and holding a broken blueberry-flavored piece of stick candy with the other. It'd be gut to get the kinner home and to rest a few minutes before putting dinner in the oven. Maybe she'd give Timmy a pass on reviewing his letters together, since school would start the very next day.

There'd been nein word from Isaac. Of course, he had nein way of reaching her unless he were to call the phone shanty outside Bishop Miah's barn.

Not that he would've called. He was too nice to call and gloat about his trickery.

Actually, Agnes wouldn't even need to cook dinner that nacht. The fire department was hosting a chili cook-off fund-raiser that evening.

And she'd promised to bring fudge.

She sighed as she glanced at the locked door. Would it be so terrible if she conveniently forgot about her promise? Right now, it seemed like too much effort to unlock the door, go back inside, and decide what type of fudge would be best to take. She glanced at Mary and Timmy, running up and down the sidewalk and around the planters, and wished she had a fraction of their energy.

Then again, she would have to kum back through town to go to the fire station. It'd be easy enough to pick up some fudge at that time.

That settled, she dropped the keys in her purse, picked up Martha, trudged down the steps, and trekked toward the buggy with the other two kinner trailing behind her. This made her appreciate Mamm even more. Maybe she should've asked Katherine for a little help instead of being so noble.

The newly called preacher, Gideon Kaiser, pulled his buggy to a stop along the raised sidewalk. "Agnes, a couple pieces of mail came for you. They're in the store. And something for the kinner came, too. You might want to stop by. Daed's there. He'll get your mail for you."

"Danki." Probably just bills for her. But Timmy had brightened at the prospect of mail. And with the bu still mourning his onkel Isaac's departure and dreading the unknowns of school, it might be gut to pick up whatever had kum for him.

Maybe she'd purchase something cold to drink while she was there. She wiped the sweat beading on her forehead. It was still plenty hot for early September. She should ask after Gideon's frau, heavy with child, due either late this month or early the next. And after his mamm, who was suffering from an undiagnosed illness for which she'd been undergoing tests. "How's Liz—"

"I'm in a bit of a rush, but thought you'd like to know." Then he clicked at his horse and drove off.

Timmy tugged on her arm. "Can we get the mail?"

"Jah. Get in the buggy. We'll drive." It was only a couple blocks, but it was on the way to the haus.

When they reached the store, Timmy climbed out on his own, while Agnes unloaded the two girls and then carried Martha inside. Gideon's daed, Ben, stood at the cash register.

Agnes set Martha on the counter. "Gideon told me I had some mail."

"Jah. Been here since Saturday. I know you usually pick up mail only once a month, but I thought you might like to get it sooner this time. Especially seeing as this youngster got a postcard." He leaned over and rustled Timmy's hair.

Timmy grinned. "Is it from my mamm and daed?"

Ben shook his head.

"Maybe Onkel Isaac?" Timmy's eyes widened.

"Sure is. I'll get the mail and some cold juice boxes for you and your sisters." He nodded at Agnes. "I'll be right back. Have something for you, too."

Jah. Bills. Agnes forced a smile. "Danki. Appreciate it." How on earth was she supposed to concentrate on paying bills and reconciling her accounts with the kinner underfoot causing frequent interruptions?

She shifted her weight and glanced at the displays of gum and candy conveniently located near the cash register. At least she wasn't tempted. Being around sweets all day effectively deterred her from wanting to consume sugary items elsewhere. Besides, she was already plump enough, especially compared with the scantily clothed cover models on the magazines she sometimes saw at the Englisch grocery store a few blocks away. Thankfully, the Amish salvage-grocery store didn't carry such "reading material."

Did Isaac think she was too fat? Had he ogled the cover models on the magazines when he'd gone to the Englisch grocery store for disposable diapers? Probably so. He was a man, after all. Men noticed those things. It was proof enough that he first kissed her when she wore nothing but a swimsuit, ain't so?

But even that covered more skin than what the magazine models wore.

And the kiss certainly hadn't happened as a result of physical attraction. He was only trying to seduce her into taking care of the kinner when he left—permanently.

She was so gullible.

"Sorry it took so long." Ben reached into the tote bag he carried, crouched down, and handed Timmy a postcard and an orange-flavored juice box. "Your onkel must really love you to send such a beautiful postcard. Have you ever seen the Rocky Mountains?"

Timmy and Mary both crowded in to look at the picture. "Pretty," Mary said.

Ben nodded. "It's addressed to all three of you, so you'll have to share it." He handed Mary a juice box, too, then straightened and opened the third box before giving it to Martha. Then he zipped the tote shut and handed it to Agnes.

She took it, surprised by the weight.

"You might want to open the bag when you get home. Isaac sent a letter to the store, the contents of which paid for what's in there. He gave detailed orders for what he wanted, too. Some of his instructions were rather surprising, but I daresay he had his reasons." Ben winked, as if the comment meant something special.

Her curiosity rose and a bit of energizing excitement seeped into her bones. Her "mail" didn't seem to be bills after all.

"Danki." Agnes eyed the bottles of pop beside the candy display. Could she justify buying herself something to drink? "How much do I owe for the juice boxes?" She reached for a bottle of water.

"Isaac sent the money for them. And something for you. It's in the bag, too."

Agnes's heart thumped. Isaac had bought her a drink? She returned the bottle of water to the case.

"The change is in an envelope in the bag, too. He said that I should give it to you."

Maybe she'd misread Isaac. Agnes swallowed. "Danki, again. I'll see you at the fund-raiser to-nacht."

Ben shrugged. "We'll at least pick something up to go. Not sure we'll be able to stay."

"How is Reba doing? And Lizzie?"

Another shrug. "It'd be nice to have a diagnosis for Reba. She's bed-bound some days. Just can't find the strength to get up."

"I'm praying." If only der Herr would listen.

"Appreciate it." Ben returned to his spot behind the counter.

Martha squeezed the juice box, then laughed as orange fluid spouted out and flowed over her.

Agnes slung the tote bag over her shoulder, picked up the now-wet-and-sticky Martha, and motioned to Timmy and Mary, who followed her outside.

Once settled in the buggy seat, she peeked inside the tote bag. A brand-new, still-in-the-packaging set of full-sized pink sheets. Why would he send that? There was also a bottle of dark-colored pop, chilled. And two envelopes—one pink, the other white.

She pulled them out and opened them.

The white envelope contained a check and an order for fudge—lots of fudge—from the television station. She smiled. Not "pay me" bills but dollar bills instead. *Danki, Lord, for this unexpected blessing.* Tears welled in her eyes.

The pink envelope held a card. With hearts.

There are so many reasons to love you.

—*Isaac*

She fought tears all the way to the Masts' haus, while sipping her pop. The chilled drink won her back to Isaac's side. Especially with the check from the TV station triggering memories of how he'd saved that interview on her behalf.

Could it be that Gott heard her prayers, after all?

~

Isaac got into town in the wee hours of Wednesday morgen. Riding in the moving van was almost more uncomfortable than the previous bus ride, but at least the van didn't stop as often, so the trip went faster.

The driver stopped at a motel long enough to pay for a room, then dropped Isaac off at his brother's farm. They made arrangements to meet at eight the following morgen at the candy shop and then Isaac watched the taillights disappear before he turned to go inside the dark haus, a feeble penlight helping him see. He figured Agnes had kept the kinner at the bishop's haus, even though she'd told him she wouldn't. Surely, the bishop wouldn't have wanted her staying here alone.

He rubbed his eyes, anxious to crawl into the big bed in his brother's room and fall asleep. At the bottom of the stairs, he dug around in his suitcase for his pajamas, then set the penlight down. It flickered off.

A lantern was burning in his brother's bedroom. Odd, at not quite two in the morgen. He left the pajamas where they lay and went down the hall to investigate. Maybe Agnes and the kinner had spent some time at the haus and had forgotten to extinguish the light.

Isaac almost gasped at the unexpected sight of Agnes lying in the bed, partially covered by the blankets, an open book on her chest. She appeared to be sound asleep, her breaths quiet and even.

Then Isaac smiled. She had stayed here. Careful not to touch her, he lifted the book, set it on the dresser, and turned back to take the lantern with him to check on the kinner before he went to bed—on the couch.

Agnes made a sound in her sleep and Isaac hesitated, studying her. Then she shifted, causing the thin, white nacht-gown to stretch tight across her chest, highlighting her curves. He started to reach for her until his brain caught up and stopped what he was about to do.

He stayed motionless and studied her once more. Her thick lashes, feathery against her cheeks. Her soft, pink lips, slightly parted. Her amazing hair, unbound, flowing loosely over the pillowcase.

It might be too soon, according to the bishop, but Isaac loved her. Really. She was one incredible woman. One he wanted to know better. To take care of. To grow old with.

He wanted to kiss her awake. But it would be too dangerous. And whose name would she whisper? His? Or St. Gabe's?

Better that he not know. His name would be his undoing, while St. Gabe's would break his heart—but would also jumpstart his attempts to make her forget Gabe. Two equally dangerous scenarios with a kiss-awakened, sexy woman, and a man who would be tempted to overstep his boundaries.

I think I love you. Her unmediated confession, brought about by banana splits, replayed.

Ach, Agnes. Isaac released a heavy breath, then snatched the lantern and carried it out of the room. He peeked in on Timmy—wow, he'd missed the hero-worship of this youngster following him around—then checked on the slumbering girls. It amazed him how mess-free they were while they slept. He needed to catch his rest while he could. He finally changed into his pajamas—pants only, since it was hot—opened the windows for circulation, and extinguished the flickering light. He lay on the couch in the living room, using the throw pillows to cushion his head.

And dreamed verboden dreams until screaming awakened him.

"Onkel Isaac!" He barely covered his face in time to protect it from the flying arms of the five-year-old bu.

"Oof." Isaac grunted when his breath was knocked out of him as Timmy attempted to hug him.

"Timmy, what in—" Agnes gasped sharply. "Isaac? When did you get back?"

Isaac sat up, while Timmy clambered onto the seat next to him and gave him another hug, chattering about something.

Agnes's eyes skimmed Isaac's bare chest. She blushed and looked away.

Isaac grinned. "Hi, honey. I'm home."

19

How could a man look so gut? Agnes snuck another peek at Isaac, even though he was now fully clothed, as they drove into town after dropping a crying Timmy off at school. Timmy had clung to his onkel until Isaac promised he'd pick him up right after school and would spend all evening with him.

Which, of course, was a given, but it'd seemed to pacify Timmy.

"You brought the sheets, ain't so?" Isaac angled a glance at Agnes.

She eyed the tote bag, the contents undisturbed, except for the bottle of pop she'd consumed the day before. She'd wanted to display Isaac's card in her kitchen—or future bedroom—and needed to deposit the check and get started on fulfilling the television station's order for fudge. "Jah, they're here. What're they for?"

"A bed" would be the obvious answer, but she didn't have one of those.

Isaac chuckled. Winked. "You'll see."

Had he found her a bed? Her heart rate increased. If so, she'd be alone to-nacht, sleeping in her new room. Her new home. Except there wasn't a stable or food for Wildfire. She'd need to stable him at Bishop Miah's until she figured out a place to do that in town. The Amish grocery store had a stable for those times when either Ben or Gideon stayed over taking inventory. She might be able to keep the horse there and walk the two blocks to her shop.

"Did you find a farm sink?" She twisted around to glance at the girls, each of them clutching a doll in her arms. Isaac had brought the toys home with him, as well as a small fire truck for Timmy.

Isaac frowned. "Nein. But I have another auction this weekend in Mio. I'll look there."

"Mio, Michigan? Both my sets of großeltern live there. And a host of aents, onkels, and cousins."

"Perhaps you'd like to go with me to visit them?" Isaac lifted an eyebrow.

Agnes coughed. "I'm pretty sure I forgot to tell them I survived the fire. They'd think they were seeing a ghost."

Isaac jerked his head her direction. "You're pretty sure...? You forgot...? How could you forget something like that?"

Her face heated. "At first, we were so busy trying to stay alive...and then I guess I got preoccupied with other things and it slipped my mind."

Isaac shook his head. "You're coming with me. We'll take the kinner, too."

"But—"

"Your family should know, Agnes. They'll want to see you. In fact, you should probably write a letter today so they can be somewhat prepared."

"Can anyone be prepared to see someone come back from the dead?" Agnes muttered.

Isaac snorted. "That's not what you're doing."

Agnes opened her mouth to argue the point, but she shut it again when she saw the moving van parked in front of her shop. Her eyes widened. "What...?"

Isaac chuckled. "You'll see. Grab the tote bag and unlock the shop door. I'll bring the girls in." He parked in front at the hitching post, next to Naomi's horse and buggy, and jumped out.

Agnes scrambled out after him, grabbed the tote bag and her purse, and speed-walked to the shop. What was Isaac up to?

A man climbed out of the truck's cab as she approached. "Agnes Zook?"

She managed a nod as she dug through her purse for her key ring.

"I'm Tom Sawyer. No relation to the literary character. Ike Mast said—"

"Hey, Tom!" Isaac came around the side of the building, Martha in his arms, and holding Mary's hand. Both girls still clung to their new baby dolls.

Agnes turned away, fumbling with the key in her haste. Finally, she unlocked the door and flung it open.

Isaac set Martha down. "Go on inside, girls. Agnes, make sure the doors to the other rooms are open."

"All?" Agnes asked. But Isaac had disappeared out the door. She shrugged and went to do as instructed.

Moments later, Isaac and Tom carried into the office an antique, wrought-iron bed frame. They set it up, went back outside, and returned with full-sized box springs, followed by a pillow-top mattress. "The mattress is new." He nodded to indicate the plastic wrapping he and Tom ripped off. "I got the bed frame for a song. I'm thinking it'll look great painted white, but that's up to you. If you want it painted, I'll take care of that tomorrow."

"Danki." Agnes pressed her hand against her chest. "I'd love it in white. You did this for me? How much do I owe you?"

"I said I would. Don't worry; you already paid for it with childcare. And fudge. Get the bed made. I have another surprise or two in the van." He winked.

At least the pink sheets made sense now. Agnes checked on the girls, who watched the men from the front window, and then made up the bed with the new sheets, just to see what it looked like.

Isaac returned with two fluffy pillows and a tumbling-block quilt in shades of pink. "The quilt was a gift, since it didn't sell. I guess nobody wanted a pink quilt. I figured you would. We have a dresser out there, too, but it needs refinishing. I'll take care of that for you. White, to match the bed?"

Tears burned her eyes. How was it that this man Agnes had known only a week had managed to provide her dream bedroom, when her parents had never managed it?

"Jah, danki."

Isaac touched her hand. "I'm still not convinced that living here is a gut idea. You don't even have a tub or a shower. But it would at least be gut for putting the girls down for naps. Or for staying the nacht if you get stranded during a heavy rain or a blizzard or something."

Agnes shook her head. "I need to move out of the bishop's haus for gut. He's getting too involved in my life."

Isaac frowned. "You say that like it's a bad thing. The way I see it, it's because he cares."

"You'd think differently if it were your life he was getting involved in."

He snorted. "He *is* getting involved in my life. Don't pretend differently."

Agnes glanced at him. "It doesn't bother you?"

"He cares, okay? The man is a born rescuer and he's determined to save us from our pasts and keep us on the straight and narrow. Besides, Gott probably has a tally marker going in heaven for Bishop Miah's brownie points."

Agnes blinked. "Brownie points?"

Isaac's lips quirked. He shrugged. "It's an Englisch term. I'm not sure what it means, exactly. I'd better go help Tom with the dresser. But consider this: I need to be able to protect you. I'm worried about your living alone. Especially here in town, where there are would-be thieves and other questionable strangers."

～

And with that not-so-pleasant thought, Isaac walked off, a coil of panic winding through him, wrapping around his heart, and squeezing. How could he keep her safe when she refused to be taken care of?

"Hi, Isaac. I have some sandwiches at my bakery for you and the kinner." Naomi grinned at him as she passed him on her way into the kitchen area. "Agnes?" he heard her say. "What's going on?"

Naomi probably thought she would get more information from the talkative Agnes. And she was right. He would've told her to speak to Agnes anyway.

He understood Agnes's need for privacy. Bishop Miah and Katherine seemed to have unofficially adopted Agnes, taking on the role of parents and supervising every area of her life. They'd likely been overly involved in the lives of their own kinner, which might explain why they still lived in their big farmhaus instead of a dawdi-haus attached to it.

"Familiarity breeds contempt." "Too many cooks spoil the broth." Or something like that. More sayings that Bishop Miah would likely spout if he were giving himself advice. Had the time spent with Sol and Levi rubbed off on Isaac?

Or maybe the reason none of the Brunstetters' kinner lived at the haus was simply because both Bishop Miah and Katherine were physically in gut shape. Their sons did perform the majority of the work on the family farm. Isaac had seen them working in the oat field, but he didn't know what they were doing. He knew nothing about growing oats. Only corn, which his parents had grown.

He didn't even know what Sam grew on his farm, but it seemed a moot point, since Sam was in a specialized burn unit and it was already September. A bit late for planting anything, as far as Isaac knew.

He shook off the thought.

Of course, Bishop Miah might've chosen to stay in the big haus for the sole reason that he was a caretaker—of everyone. Every homeless, injured, visiting, or orphaned person seemed to land on his doorstep and stay for a spell while Katherine and the bishop ministered to him or her. Bishop Miah was a true man of Gott.

Someone Isaac should emulate actually. If he had a haus to call a home.

Finally, the van was unloaded, except for Tom's Harley and his helmet. Tom was anxious to start back to Montana. After the two men consulted various apps on their smartphones over several cups of Agnes's koffee and a sample of fudge, Tom decided to return the same way they'd kum—across the Upper Peninsula and through Minnesota, North Dakota, and most of Montana. He'd hoped it was a shorter trip through Canada. It wasn't, especially once one factored in border patrol.

At twenty-eight hours' travel time, it was still shorter than the trip to Montana via bus. Isaac had to travel south through Michigan, then west to Chicago, and farther from there, hitting all the major city bus stations and, of course, enduring every delay and layover.

When Tom left to return the van and start for home, Isaac checked on the girls. They were in the kitchen, baby dolls forgotten. Martha sucked on a stick of purple-colored rock candy, while Mary helped Agnes organize the rest of the rock candy sticks into different jars so they could be set out for sale.

"Don't forget to write your family." Isaac caught Agnes's eye.

She wrinkled her nose. "I still don't think—"

"Trust me on this. They'll want to know. I'm going to go find something for us to have for lunch."

"Check at the bakery. Naomi just said something about making sandwiches for you and the kinner."

Isaac frowned. "She didn't mention you and I don't want to feed any unrealistic expectations."

"You're a gut man, Isaac, but…"

He sighed. "I'll stop there first, if you promise you'll have a letter written and in the mail today. Time is of the essence. We'll be there this weekend."

"That assumes the bishop agrees to permit the kinner and me to go with you."

Isaac gave her a level look. "You'll be visiting your family. It's a nonissue. Besides, I don't intend to ask for permission. You're going."

After enjoying a delicious sandwich from Naomi's shop, Agnes sat at the card-table desk in her office and tapped the end of the blue ink pen against the sheet of paper she'd laid on the table.

Dear Daadi and Mammi,…

She didn't know what to say. How did you word a long-overdue letter to relatives to let them know, "Ach, by the way, I'm alive"?

She couldn't think of an easy way to do it.

And six months—seven months, now—after the fact seemed a little late.

Despite Isaac's concerns, it might be better to just go to Mio, drop in, and announce, "I'm alive!"

Besides, maybe they did know she had survived and they simply didn't care. After all, the Amish grapevine did keep people informed of most things. They likely didn't want anything to do with the maidal who'd been left alone—orphaned—because they didn't want to take care of a spinster. Especially if they'd heard the rumors that she'd gone insane the nacht her family died.

A sob caught in her throat, threatening to choke her with its intensity at the memory of her grief…and guilt. Would they blame her for the loss of their loved ones?

Agnes pressed her fingers together between her eyes and massaged the upper bridge of her nose.

Maybe it'd be best to just throw it out there.

I survived the fire, and I'll be arriving in Mio sometime Friday...

She raised the pen. Stared at the words she'd written.

Would they worry that she was moving in? She'd be the unwanted guest who never left. And what about her business? Friday and Saturday were the busiest days for tourist business. Besides, she still had that big order from the television station to prepare. She glanced at the check—three digits in front of the decimal point!

It was pure foolishness to even consider going. She had candy to make.

She crumpled the letter. Threw it into the circular trashcan beside the door.

She'd get out the recipes for the fudge that was ordered and work on those.

Write them. They'll want to know.

Ugh! Bishop Miah would likely agree with Isaac. In fact, he'd probably wonder why she hadn't written before now.

In the other room, Isaac laughed at something. Probably teasing his nieces.

Agnes tore off another sheet of paper and laid it on the table.

Dear Daadi and Mammi,

Sorry I didn't write sooner. I should have. I have nein excuse, really. I hope I haven't caused undo distress.

Either by not telling them or by getting into contact at long last.

They wouldn't want her barging into their lives. She'd always had a gut relationship with them—or so she'd thought—but she wouldn't be welkum under these circumstances. Staying a week or two was different from moving in permanently.

She didn't want to move in with them.

I own and operate a candy shop, and I am happy.

Wait. Maybe that was wrong to say.

She crossed out the last three words.

Isaac appeared in the doorway. "We have ice cream left over. Would you care for some?"

Agnes brightened. "Jah, danki." She needed to escape the emotional mess, and a carton of ice cream would do the trick. Or, at least, as much ice cream as she could get. But the last time he served ice cream, she'd blurted out her feelings. She pushed the paper away.

Isaac evidently interpreted that as an invitation to peek. He picked up the paper, read it, and then put it down with a shake of his head. "You're overthinking it. Here, let me help." He dropped into the chair across from her, scribbled a few lines, and then slid the paper in her direction as he stood. "I'll dish out the ice cream."

Dear Family,

I'm sorry I didn't write sooner. I survived the fire, and I'll be in Mio this weekend to visit. I'll tell you what I've been up to then.

With love,
Agnes

Short. Sweet. To the point.

"I think I love you." She looked up at him with a smile she knew was a bit sappy.

Isaac chuckled. "I think I love you, too." And then he walked out.

Her face heated from his teasing, but the words she'd spoken were true this time.

His concern for her safety, and the furniture he'd brought her, were evidence of love in action. But did he feel the love he acted on?

20

Isaac opened the door to the candy shop, preparing to take the trash to the dumpster located alongside the building. He stopped, the bulging white kitchen bag dangling from his hand. "Bishop."

"Isaac." The older man moseyed up the steps. At the top, he removed his hat, swiped at the sweat beads on his forehead, and frowned. "I hear rumors you bought our girl some furniture."

Isaac resisted the urge to roll his eyes. "It's gut to know the grapevine is alive and well."

Bishop Miah's lips curved upward in a slight smile. "Do I need to ask your intentions?"

"I already told you my intentions. They haven't changed."

The bishop's smile widened a little. "Furniture, Isaac?"

Isaac set the trash bag down beside him. This conversation had the potential of being long and drawn-out. "She told me when I came home that she was moving into the shop. I didn't want her sleeping on the floor."

"And when did you get home? I've heard reports that it was late last nacht."

"Ach, now we're getting to the real reason for your visit." Isaac sighed. "Let me take this trash to the dumpster. You go on in, get a cup of koffee, and we'll have a discussion."

"So, it was late last nacht."

"You know it was." Isaac hefted the bag, carried it to the end of the row of shops and down the steps, and tossed it into the dumpster. Then he returned to the candy shop.

The bishop stood behind the counter, pouring himself a cup of koffee.

"I just dished out some ice cream. There's still a little left, if you'd like some." Isaac went through the swinging door to the kitchen without waiting for the bishop's reply.

Mary and Martha sat on the floor, wearing more ice cream on their faces than the amount they had eaten. Agnes stirred something on the stove. Isaac sniffed. Sweet and chocolaty. More fudge. He couldn't wait to taste-test.

"The bishop is here." Isaac took the container of ice cream out of the freezer and dished the rest into a bowl. "He wants to discuss some things with me."

Hopefully, the bishop wouldn't see the need to grill Agnes or impose unrealistic expectations on either one of them. But if he decided to order them to marry in order to quiet the already-wagging tongues, Isaac wouldn't object.

That wouldn't happen, though. It'd be too easy and too contradictory, considering Isaac had already stated his intentions and the bishop had declined to sanction them.

"What things?" Agnes turned from the stove, the wooden spoon dripping puddles of chocolate on the floor.

Isaac shrugged, hoping the gesture wouldn't translate into a lie. Then he cringed. "Some rumors."

Agnes grimaced. "The gossips love talking about me."

"It's a compliment, Agnes. You're colorful and you draw attention." But he knew as well as she did that drawing attention to oneself wasn't encouraged. Not among the Amish. "I'll handle it. Stay in here. You can give the girls a bath."

She glanced at the girls and did a double take. "You gave them too much ice cream."

"Impossible." Isaac winked, then grabbed a spoon and the bowl of ice cream he'd dished out for the bishop, as well as his own now-melting treat, and returned out front.

Bishop Miah had sat down at the table closest the front window and farthest from the kitchen. Gut. He didn't want to involve Agnes either.

Isaac delivered the bishop's dessert and then lowered himself into a chair, kicking his legs out into the aisle. Might as well get this over with. "Jah, I got back late last nacht. Or, rather, at two this morgen. Agnes was asleep. I went to bed on the couch. You can ask Timmy where he found me this morgen."

"Nein need. Timmy blabbed it to the whole school. Teacher Gwen was all of a dither when I stopped by to deliver a package that was left at my haus. And you know some of the scholars are going to tell their parents."

"So, if you know where I slept…?"

"Appearances, Isaac. Some members of the community are going to assume you were together, and…well. You could've slept in the barn."

Seriously? Isaac frowned. After traveling more than twenty-four hours in a moving van, he was supposed to be able to think straight enough to consider that option? "You know, I considered it. But the mice were unwilling to share the hayloft. Rather unkind of them, ain't so?"

Bishop Miah chuckled. "You could've kum to my haus."

"I could've woken Agnes and sent her home, too." But if he had awakened her, they would've kissed and he might not have had the strength to stop.

"That wouldn't have been a gut idea."

"Which is precisely why I didn't. And just so you know," Isaac added, "I asked Agnes to kum with me to Mio this weekend. She has family there and she never let them know she's alive. She needs to go. I'm aware the gossips will run wild with this when they see us leaving together on a trip."

"She never let them know?" Bishop Miah added a spoonful of vanilla ice cream to his koffee and stirred it. "Jah, she needs to go. For a visit, that is. Not to stay. She belongs here."

"That's her decision." Isaac took a spoonful of his almost-liquid ice cream.

"She has a business. Her daed never intended for her to go to their family in Mio if something happened to him. He intended for her to take care of herself until she married."

"Did he really believe she would marry?" Isaac raised an eyebrow. "Sounds to me like he thought she was destined to be an old maud."

The bishop sighed. "It doesn't matter what he believed. He tended to be a pessimist who gave up too quickly. Of course, she'll marry. She just needs to wait for the right man."

"What if he's in Mio?" The thought hurt. Isaac finished his ice-cream soup to ease the pain. Not that it helped.

"He's not." Bishop Miah speared him with a glance. "But he's yet to discover where he belongs. Not to mention a few other important details he needs to know."

⌒

Agnes gave the driver the address for Mamm's parents—her großeltern—and he entered it into some sort of device mounted to the dashboard that talked. "Proceed to the highlighted route," the voice said.

Rather scary, having a talking vehicle. Agnes was glad to be sitting in the backseat, far away from it.

Whenever she'd traveled with her family to Mio, Daed had usually wanted to stay at his own parents' haus. As far as Agnes was concerned, she was overdue for a change. Grossmammi Zook was judgmental and opinionated, whereas Grossmammi Schwartz loved feeding birds and watching them eat while she sat on her front porch shelling peas. Fond memories, there. Agnes would rather shell peas and watch overfed birds stuff themselves than be judged and found wanting. Grossmammi Zook would likely give her a lecture, scolding her for surviving the fire. Agnes beat herself up for it enough. She had sent her a letter, though.

Since she was minding kinner who weren't her own, it made more sense to take them to the haus where they wouldn't receive frequent scolding and criticism. Especially since Isaac had said something about needing to meet with the auction coordinators once she and the kinner had been dropped off.

Someday, she'd need to learn more about his job.

Even though she'd chosen the more laid-back home as their destination, Agnes's hand shook uncontrollably when they arrived. She struggled with the latch on the car seat where Martha was snugly buckled in beside her. The disagreeable mechanism wouldn't disengage.

Isaac opened the door beside her and, without a word, touched her trembling arm, then leaned over her and effortlessly pushed the little red square button, then released the restraint.

Agnes stared at his tanned skin, breathed in his piney scent, and struggled not to lean closer and nuzzle his neck. He probably would've done so if their positions had been reversed.

He lifted Martha out of her seat and over Agnes, and the pleasant piney scent was replaced by the unpleasant odor of someone in dire need of a diaper change.

"I'll stay long enough to see what your welkum is like before I go to meet with the Eichers." Isaac stepped back as Agnes struggled to get out of the car. "If your family acts like they don't want you here, I'll find another place for you and the girls. I'll keep Timmy with me at the Eichers' haus to-nacht."

Agnes's stomach hurt. Would her family reject her completely? She should've stayed home. The television interview, as scary as that was, had been less stressful. How nice of them to place such a big order for fudge. She'd sent it that very morgen, then had gotten caught up on her business bookkeeping and made a trip to the bank. The nacht before, she'd even enjoyed a quiet, but weird, evening alone at the shop after getting Wildfire set up in the stable at Ben and Gideon's store.

The haus seemed quiet as Agnes led the way to the back porch. She hesitated.

"Should I unload the luggage?" asked the driver from behind them.

"Not yet." Isaac glanced at him. He handed Martha to Agnes and crouched to pet a tabby cat that began winding its way around his ankles.

Agnes gave Isaac a frantic look. He appeared not to notice, so she firmed her shoulders, marched up the steps, and opened the screen door. "Mammi? Daadi?" She adjusted her grip on Martha, letting the girl ride lower on her hip, which jutted out to the side. Wow, the child stank. Agnes probably should've changed her diaper first.

Her back ached. She longed to stretch it out. She shifted again.

A young woman came into the dimly lit kitchen. Agnes narrowed her eyes, trying to identify her. The woman stopped in the doorway and stared hard at Agnes before her eyes darted to Martha, then to Isaac, and then lower, to the two kinner beside him. She said nothing.

"Hi, Cousin Priscilla," Agnes guessed aloud. Priscilla and her sisters bore a strong resemblance to one another. She shifted again. "It's me. Agnes."

"Priscilla, who's here?" asked a weak, shaky voice from the other room. *Mammi.* Agnes wanted to run to her.

"Some woman claiming to be my cousin. But she isn't." Priscilla pursed her lips and glared at Agnes.

Isaac stepped up behind Agnes, a source of silent support. She wanted to lean back against his chest and have him put his arms around her, holding her, protecting her, shielding her. She didn't have that option. "I'm Agnes Zook. I wrote a letter. It should've arrived by now."

"Jah, whatever. My cousin Agnes isn't a mamm." Priscilla's upper lip curled and her nose wrinkled as she looked at the toddler on Agnes's hip.

Agnes opened her mouth to explain, but Isaac touched her shoulder and said, "These are my nieces and nephew. She's the nanny."

Agnes's entire body jerked. She turned to stare at him. "The *nanny?*" Ouch. That hurt. With all his talk of marriage and his heated kisses, she'd imagined she was more. A lot more. But she wasn't. Especially since the bishop hadn't approved of his intentions. She'd do well to remember that. *The nanny. Just the nanny.*

He grimaced and mouthed "Sorry," but she ignored him and spun back around to face Priscilla. There'd be time enough to deal with Isaac later. First, she had to convince her cousin of her identity.

Priscilla tilted her head. "Who was courting me?"

Was? "Quil," Agnes said quietly. Priscilla had gloated about that. Quil's family owned a Christmas tree farm. "You whispered it to me the last time I saw you. Is he not courting you any longer?"

"Okay." Priscilla's lips relaxed. "You're Cousin Agnes. I'll tell you later."

A grunt came from the other room, then the sound of something metal tapping on the hardwood floor. A few seconds later, a walker appeared in the doorway, and then an elderly woman. *Mammi.* Agnes sucked in a breath. Her mamm's mamm had aged a lot since the fire.

"Agnes? Is it truly you? How is it that you lived and nobody else?" Grief lined the woman's face.

"I wasn't home that nacht," Agnes whispered, shame filling her voice.

"That's a blessing. One member of my only dochter's family survived." Tears trailed down the woman's face. "And you're working as a nanny?"

"Apparently so." Agnes moved backward, accidentally stepping on Isaac's toes. Or maybe not-so-accidentally. Served him right. It might even make him think she'd done it on purpose. To his credit, he didn't grunt. He wrapped a hand around her upper arm, steadying her. His touch sent delicious tingles through her. She stepped aside, dislodging his hand, because she was trying to stay mad at him over the "nanny" label.

"Will Agnes and my nieces be able to stay here, with you?" Isaac asked Agnes's mammi. "I'll take Timmy with me."

"Who are you?" the woman asked.

"Isaac Mast. The auctioneer. I need to go meet the organizers, but we'll unload their luggage now if they can stay here."

"Of course, they can," Mammi said.

Agnes sighed with relief.

"I'll have Priscilla ready a room. You'll join us for supper, ain't so?"

Agnes's heart did a traitorous leap of hope that she'd get to spend more time with him. That he'd get to know her family, at least a little bit.

Isaac frowned and then shrugged. "It depends on whether or not I'm expected somewhere else. But I will try to kum back later to tuck the girls into bed."

Ach. The girls. Not her.

"You're a gut onkel. Not married, are you?" Mammi got a speculating gleam in her eyes as she glanced from Isaac to Agnes and then to Priscilla. Probably discounting Agnes as a potential bride in favor of the beautiful Priscilla.

Agnes's stomach churned. Priscilla hurried from the room as if she wasn't interested. What was the story with Quil anyway?

Isaac chuckled. "Not married yet. And any possibility isn't open for discussion right now. Let's just say I'm seeing someone." His finger trailed down Agnes's spine and she shivered. "I'll help the driver bring in the luggage, and then Timmy and I will go."

"Timmy can stay here with us, if you want." Agnes turned to face Isaac.

"I promised he could kum with me, but he's playing with the cat. I'll see if he wants to stay. It'll give me another gut excuse to return, since he'll be with me over-nacht."

"Of course." Mammi inched nearer, step by wobbly step. "And we might be willing to keep an eye on the bu if you want to take a certain young lady on a walk."

Isaac grinned. "Now that is an offer I can't refuse. I'll definitely be back." He leaned forward, bent down, and kissed Mammi on the cheek. "Only if you think your ehemann won't mind."

Mammi giggled. "Go on with you."

Isaac winked at Agnes, then followed the driver out to the van.

"That one is a keeper, Agnes," Mammi said. She moved closer and wrapped Agnes in a hug, even though the stench of Martha's diaper was stronger than ever. "And I'm so glad you're alive and here now."

Later that evening, Isaac and Timmy strode up to the big farmhaus where they'd left Agnes and the girls. The two of them were staying only two farms away, within easy walking distance, at the farm owned by Elijah Eicher, the auction clerk. Elijah's dochter Bethel worked with her daed as the cashier. Their host family had served a satisfying dinner of barbequed pork sandwiches, homemade sweet-potato fries, and sweet corn, straight out of their garden. Juicy watermelon slices still on the rind had completed the meal. Timmy would need a bath before bed, but Isaac figured the dogs and cats at the home of Agnes's gro⊠eltern would play more with Timmy if he tasted gut. Besides, any licks the bu might receive would probably make the impending bath a bit quicker.

Which, in turn, might give Isaac more time to be alone with Agnes, once the two little girls were tucked into bed.

He arrived in time for baths and bedtime stories, the latter of which neither girl wanted to end. Isaac was surprised that Agnes's gro⊠eltern had so many storybooks to choose from. Granted, most of them were Bible stories or tales featuring farm animals. He read while Agnes helped with the supper dishes, and then he kissed the girls gut-nacht and went downstairs to check on Timmy.

Agnes's daadi had set up the game Candy Land.

"Do you want to play, Onkel Isaac?" Timmy bounced to his feet and ran over to him. "I chose the green person, but you can pick him if you'd rather."

"Ah, nein. I'd love to play, but I'm afraid all that candy will make my teeth ache." He cupped the left side of his face with his hand. "Ach, it hurts just thinking of it."

"It's not real candy, Onkel Isaac." Timmy went over to the board and ran his hand across it. "See? Just pictures."

The grossdaadi chuckled. "I might could scare up some real candy, but you'll not have any to-nacht, Timmy. Much too late for sugar. Your onkel won't appreciate it if I give you any."

Jah, it was much too late for candy. A lesson Isaac had already learned the hard way. Only once had he made the mistake of bribing the kinner to get ready for bed with promises of sugary treats. They had eventually fallen asleep, but not without making Isaac wish for a pair of earplugs and a locked door on the other side of the haus. Instead, he'd responded to innumerable pleas, taken away noisy toys, and had needed to carry them all back to bed multiple times.

"Besides, I think your onkel has his mind set on getting a different sort of sugar." The older man glanced up and winked.

Heat crawled up Isaac's neck. He swiped his hand over his jaw. "Now how am I supposed to answer that?"

Agnes's grossdaadi chortled. "That was the idea. There is a nice, well-chaperoned porch swing just outside that window." He nodded toward it.

Timmy looked at him. "Candy's bad for you, too?"

Isaac managed a self-conscious chuckle. "I think it's safe to say I won't get any sugar either."

21

Agnes hung the dishtowel on the rack as Priscilla carried the dishpan to the back door and poured the dirty dishwater over the rosebushes growing alongside the porch. None of the plants were still in bloom, since it was the second weekend in September, but old habits die hard.

Priscilla sighed as she hung the empty dishpan on a nail just inside the back door. "Since you're here to help Mammi get ready for bed, I'm going to take a walk. It'll be gut to have a break."

"Meeting someone special on the walk?" Agnes teased. "Quil, maybe."

Priscilla blushed. "Maybe not."

Agnes raised her eyebrows as a giggling Priscilla slipped her feet into a pair of dark blue garden clogs and darted outside.

After double-checking to make sure the kitchen was spotless, Agnes went into the other room. Hopefully, Isaac would want to slip out with her for a walk.

Mammi sat in a recliner, darning a sock in the glow of a gaslight. At the koffee table a few feet away, Daadi, Timmy, and Isaac moved colorful plastic people around an ancient-looking Candy Land board.

It was nice seeing Isaac interact so comfortably with her family.

"Onkel Isaac says he's gonna marry Aenti Agnes someday." Timmy moved his piece two spaces. "He said it twice. That means it's true, ain't so?"

Agnes froze in the doorway. She covered her mouth with her hand. Would her family get their hopes up? Or would Isaac deny it?

Isaac shifted. "You're not supposed to share everything you hear, Timmy. Agnes and I aren't published yet."

"But you will be. Then she will be truly my aenti."

"Is that so?" Daadi glanced up and met Agnes's eyes, then nudged Isaac's shoulder. "You know, Isaac, I think the porch swing is off-balance. Since you lost this game anyway, Timmy and I will play one more round while you check to see if you can level it."

"Maybe it could wait until tomorrow, Daadi. If he has time," Agnes suggested. She didn't want Daadi's fix-it list to monopolize any time they'd have to spend alone.

"Nein. It definitely must be done to-nacht," Daadi insisted. "And you can help."

Any excuse to spend time alone with Isaac was a gut one.

Isaac glanced toward the window as he rose to his feet. "Jah. It won't take but a minute, I'm sure."

Now Isaac was trying to foil their time alone? A minute wouldn't be nearly long enough.

"Might take a gut half hour." Daadi shuffled the color cards.

"A half hour." Isaac glanced at Agnes with a crooked grin.

"Or more." Daadi set the cards down. "If you want to do it right."

"It definitely needs to be done right." Isaac's gaze lowered to Agnes's mouth.

Her lips tingled in response. "But…it'd be easier to fix in the day-time," Agnes argued.

Isaac caught her hand and tugged her in the direction of the door. "We'll be back directly."

"Take your time."

Isaac shut the door firmly behind him.

"We don't have a lantern," Agnes pointed out. Hopefully, the swing would be a quick fix.

"We don't need one." Isaac led her down the porch steps. Away from the swing.

"But—"

"The swing's fine, Beautiful. Your daadi likes me. This is a moment alone. Enjoy it."

"Ach." Shivers worked up Agnes's spine. "But Priscilla is meeting someone."

Isaac nodded. "We noticed the flashlight bobbing toward the road. She left to meet her beau. And I've someplace else in mind to go."

He entwined his fingers with hers and slowed his steps. Too bad, really, because if he had in mind what she did, she wanted to hurry and get there.

"I didn't expect the opportunity to spend time alone with you." His voice was husky.

She swallowed. "Neither did I." But she was glad. Ever so glad.

"Your großeltern are sweet. I like them." He guided her behind the barn.

Right now, her großeltern ranked among her favorite people on earth.

He stopped and turned toward her. And just stood there, gazing down at her in the moonlight. "Ach, Agnes...."

She reached out, taking his face in both her hands, and kissed him full on the mouth.

Isaac chuckled, easing back a centimeter. "Anxious, are we?"

Shouldn't she be? She frowned. Had she misunderstood his intentions? He *had* just stood there. "I'm sorry." Her face heated.

"Don't be." His arms curved around her, slowly drawing her near. One hand rose to cradle her neck. The other flattened against her back.

Then his lips were on hers, with a slow, gentle, teasing kiss that drove her mad. She arced against him, her arms going around his neck, drawing him in, and kissed him the way she wanted to be kissed.

He growled, pressing her between himself and the barn, deepening the kiss.

What might've been fireworks lit inside her, coloring her world. She moaned, her hands sliding over his back. His touch setting her on fire.

Too soon—way too soon—he pulled away. "Ach, Agnes. You're dangerous. I'm thinking the bishop had better approve our marriage sooner rather than later. Maybe even this fall."

That sounded gut to her. Wunderbaar, in fact. She waited for him to say the three words she longed to hear for real and not teasing. To admit he felt the magic between them. A declaration of love would make their wedding plans more than a decision based on his desperate need for a frau and her similar desperation for an ehemann.

His finger trailed from the back of her neck and around to the side, up her neck with her pulse pounding inside, over her jaw, to her lips. He traced their shape, then stepped back. "I must go."

His voice held the right level of huskiness.

But those weren't the right words.

~

Isaac surveyed the crowd from the safety of the auctioneer booth. Beside him, Timmy stood on his tiptoes to see over the computer and the sound system. When it was time for the auction to start, Isaac and Timmy would leave the booth to the clerk and cashier, and join the chaos of the crowd. For now, though, it was a safe place to unwind with a cup of koffee—even if it wasn't as gut as Agnes's—and a funnel cake he shared with Timmy.

"I don't see Aenti Agnes or my sisters," Timmy said with his mouth full.

"They may not be coming." This was a social event that most Amish made an effort to attend, but Isaac hadn't stuck around long enough last nacht to confirm Agnes's plans. He'd been too tempted and had needed to walk away from Agnes before he dishonored her. And her großeltern.

Three or four boys about Timmy's age or slightly older ran through the crowd, jostling people as they raced by. One man, using a quad walking cane, stumbled and grabbed ahold of another person to steady himself.

Since Agnes's grossmammi used a walker—and seemed unsteady on her feet with the contraption—the family might have decided not to attend in order to avoid risking any falls. It'd be easier for Agnes to watch the two little girls in a haus instead of amid this crowd, too. However, Agnes's cousin Priscilla was there, walking alongside a vaguely familiar man with whom she spoke. They weren't touching, since it was daylight, but she clearly liked him. He glanced at her often, too, always with a smile. As if she alone made him happy.

Probably the way Isaac looked at Agnes.

When Gott had made her, He'd broken the mold, for sure.

Someone in the crowd waved a hand, drawing Isaac's attention. It was Agnes's daadi and he stood with two other men—one of them middle-aged, the other closer to Isaac's age. With the strong resemblance, the two were probably his sohn and his gross-sohn. Daadi Schwartz smiled when he caught Isaac's eye and waved again.

Another older couple approached him, sour expressions on their faces, and spoke to Daadi Schwartz. Likely Agnes's other set of großeltern, though Isaac couldn't be sure.

The female cashier, Bethel, poked her head into the booth. "Ike, Daed sent me to tell you that there's a farm sink, with the measurements you mentioned, included in a junk box. Daed needs to know if you want someone to bid on it."

"If it's in gut condition, jah. It's for a candy shop. Danki, Bethel."

"The color is sea-foam green. Will that matter?"

"Ach, nein." He grimaced. "Maybe. I was really hoping for either white or stainless steel." He pointed out the window to Agnes's gross-daadi. "Ask Elias Schwartz if Agnes is here. If she is, ask her. If not, then, if it's in gut condition, go ahead and have somebody bid on it."

Bethel nodded. "Daed's still looking through the late arrivals that were put out this morgen. If there's a white one or a stainless-steel one, we'll have someone bid on that instead. Daed will be here to record the sales and bidders in a few minutes." Then she shut the door. Moments later, Isaac saw her working her way through the crowd toward Daadi Schwartz. An older Amish man with a beard waylaid her en route and told her something. She skittered away, as if she were afraid of him. Odd.

Isaac finished his koffee, then looked for something to use to clean the sticky sugar off Timmy's face and hands. There was a packet of wet wipes in a desk drawer. Perfect. That job done, he took out his phone and checked the time. The auction would begin soon.

Bethel walked past the booth again, probably on her way to find her daed.

Fifteen minutes later, she returned with her daed—Elijah, the auctioneer clerk. "There is a stainless-steel farm sink that fits your measurements. We put that ahead of the junk box and we'll see if we get it," Bethel told Isaac as she settled into the chair Timmy had just vacated. "Agnes is here and she didn't act too excited about a sea-foam-green sink. She did say she would take it if nothing else was available."

Isaac tossed the used wet wipe and the paper plate from the funnel cake into the trash, then connected the portable, battery-operated microphone to his shirt. "It'd be better than what she has, for sure." He glanced at Timmy. "Do you want to stay in here or kum with me?"

"I'll kum." Timmy moved to the doorway. "It's hot in here."

It was warm outside, too, though the breeze was nice. "Stay right beside me the whole time. Promise?"

"I promise."

The crowd swelled as Isaac flipped the microphone on and started the auction. The first item was a beautiful Amish-made wedding-ring quilt in shades of blue. That seemed to be the favorite color of most people, Isaac included; quilts with blue themes always sold well.

Isaac scanned the crowd as he did his singsongy chant, but he didn't see Agnes anywhere in the sea of people. He paused now and again to make a personal comment or to verify amounts when bidding got serious between two women. The quilt finally sold for over a thousand dollars. A gut start to the sale. Isaac announced the winning ticket number to Elijah and the amount, then moved on to the next item.

Timmy stayed close to his side, a bottle of water in his hands, gazing up at Isaac in awe. This was his first time hearing Isaac chant like an auctioneer. It reminded Isaac of how enthralled he'd been, listing to his auctioneer grossdaadi when he was a bu and realizing he wanted to grow up and do the same thing. Daadi Mast had encouraged him, allowing Isaac to stand with him on the auctioneer block and letting him try his own occasional auction for practice.

Mid-morgen, one of the men nearby handed Isaac a bottle of ice-cold water. Isaac downed it and handed the empty bottle back to him. "Danki." He glanced around, this time noticing Agnes standing near the sour-faced couple who'd spoken with Daadi Schwartz earlier. She had somehow procured a double stroller, where Mary and Martha sat side by side.

Isaac winked and waved.

Agnes gave a tiny smile and a wave of her fingers, almost as if she didn't want the couple beside her to notice.

The man assisting Isaac held up the stainless-steel farm sink. Isaac looked it over and made a few comments about it, then glanced at Agnes with his eyebrows raised. She nodded with a bigger smile. Ach. She'd apparently been hoping she wouldn't get the sea-foam-green sink. Isaac looked at Elijah and tilted his head toward the sink. Elijah pointed his finger at someone in the crowd.

Isaac looked to see an acknowledgment. It came from Daadi Schwartz. It was gut to know someone in Agnes's family supported her business.

A short time later, they broke for lunch. Isaac paid for the stainless-steel farm sink, then he and Timmy headed to lunch with Bethel and Elijah.

Isaac sent Timmy to secure a picnic table for them. As he got into line at the food stand, he blinked in surprise to see Gideon from the Amish salvage-grocery store. "Hey. I didn't know you were coming today."

"I didn't know you were the auctioneer, or I would've asked you to bid," Gideon said. "My frau and I are having an addition...I came for boppli items. Daed told me to look for a wheelchair or a walker for my mamm, too. She's undergoing tests, but it's not looking gut."

"Congratulations on the boppli. There's a crib and a rocker coming up this afternoon. Haven't seen a wheelchair, but I wasn't looking for one." Isaac moved ahead a step. Of course, he hadn't been looking for boppli things either. He'd noticed them while searching for a desk for Agnes. But the only desk there today was an antique school desk.

He ordered two meal deals for himself and Timmy—a hamburger, a bag of nacho-flavored chips, and an ice-cold pop—then stepped aside to wait for their food.

"Onkel Daed!"

The welkum cry meant that Mary was near. And if Mary was near, then Agnes would be close by, too.

Isaac turned. Agnes was in line a few spaces behind him, gripping the handle of the double stroller. Beside her stood Daadi Schwartz and the sour-faced couple.

"Hi, Beautiful."

⌒

Her heart pounding, Agnes glanced at Isaac in time to catch his wink. Then she looked at her Zook großeltern. They scowled. She'd gotten the same questions from them about her survival of the wildfire as she had from the Schwartz großeltern, followed by the expected criticism for her not having been home with her family at the time of the tragedy. While the Zooks hadn't explicitly said they were glad she was alive, neither one of them had left her side since spotting her at the auction, so Agnes hoped that meant they were happy to see her. It was nice to feel wanted. Loved.

Earlier, Daadi Schwartz had invited them to supper that nacht. They'd accepted, adding to Agnes's pleasure, at least until Isaac spoke to her. Then the unspoken tension had flared again. Having dinner together would invite more questions. And more thinly veiled criticism, because, of course, her großeltern all knew Daed's doubts that she would ever marry, due to her outspoken and independent nature. They would probably accuse her of throwing herself at Isaac, just as Bishop Miah had done.

Both Daadi and Mammi Zook turned questioning eyes to Agnes as Isaac sauntered over.

"He's, uh, the girls' onkel. I told you I'm their nanny." Agnes gestured to Martha, who whammed her hands on the stroller tray, and to Mary, who'd somehow managed to escape the confines of the stroller's restraints and now wrapped her pudgy arms around Isaac's legs.

Isaac opened his mouth as if he wanted to say more, but then he shut it again. Pressed his lips flat. Maybe he liked that description of her as much as Agnes did. Not at all.

"As you know, he's also the auctioneer here this weekend. I traveled down with him and the kinner," Agnes added. "Isaac, these are my daed's parents, Wilbert and Agatha Zook."

"Agnes was sort of named after me." Mammi Zook stared at Isaac. "Her daed wanted her to be, but her mamm refused." She pursed her lips.

Agnes was glad Mamm had refused. Her name was close enough to that of her grossmammi. She used to long for a more traditional Amish girl name, like Carolyn or Marilyn, or even Deborah. Maybe she wouldn't have stood out in such a negative way if her name had been more normal.

"Your sohn must've thought awful highly of you to name his dochter after you." Isaac smiled at Mammi Zook. "And she is every bit as beautiful as you are. I hope you enjoy the auction."

Mammi Zook's expression softened. For a moment, she almost smiled. "I'll see you at supper to-nacht at the Schwartzes'?"

"I hope to, but I may have plans with my host family. We'll see."

"Ike Mast," called the Amish man behind the food booth.

Isaac turned, scooping up Mary as he did. "My food is ready. Join us at our table for lunch." His gaze fell on each of them in turn, ending with Agnes. His smile softened a smidgen.

Agnes watched Isaac stride toward a table where Timmy sat with an older man and a younger woman. Gut thing it was a big table.

"Nice young man you have there," Mammi Zook said.

Jah. Isaac was a flatterer for sure. How much of what he'd said was the truth? Agnes had a sense that much of it was meant to make the listener feel gut.

Wait. Mammi Zook's comment indicated approval of Agnes's having a beau. Did that mean maybe she wouldn't judge Agnes? And that maybe Agnes wouldn't get a lecture from her großeltern over Isaac's calling her "Beautiful" in public?

Agnes smiled as she ordered a meal for herself and another for the two little girls to share, then stepped aside to wait as her großeltern—three of them—ordered their own lunches. Agnes missed Mammi Schwartz, but the woman had understandably opted to stay home where it was quiet. While Agnes waited, she pushed the double stroller over to the picnic table where Isaac was seated.

Isaac looked up. "Agnes, this is the auctioneer clerk, Elijah Eicher, and his dochter Bethel, who is also the cashier. They're the ones who found the stainless-steel farm sink and asked Daadi Schwartz to bid on it for you. I paid for it right before lunch."

"We won it? I wasn't sure." Agnes smiled at the man and his dochter. "Really nice to meet you both. Danki so much." Then she turned to Isaac. "I'm going to leave Martha with you while I get our food."

Isaac nodded. "I'd get it for you, but—"

"Nein need." Mary was still perched on his lap and Timmy leaned against his shoulder. Isaac was truly a natural with the kinner. Agnes was glad it was working out so much better for him than he'd imagined it would.

"Agnes Zook," called the man behind the counter.

She turned and went to pick up the food. On her tray, in addition to the hamburgers, were two bags of chips, a bottled water for her, and juice boxes for the girls—which would likely lead to a sticky mess, but with the heat and humidity, they needed something cold to drink. She also picked up a plastic knife to cut one of the hamburgers in quarters for the girls.

Agnes turned to carry her tray to the table, then hesitated. Bethel sat across from Isaac with her chin propped in her palm, leaning toward Isaac and gazing dreamily at him. Isaac didn't seem to notice as he talked to her daed. But, still, he was staying at the Eichers' home. And Bethel suffered from an obvious crush. Was that the way Agnes had looked when she gazed at Gabe? She cringed. Nein wonder Gabe had run in the opposite direction.

Well, they were in town only until tomorrow. Then they'd return to the Upper Peninsula, leaving Bethel behind.

Agnes forced herself to approach the table. Pasted a smile on her face.

Isaac looked up as she neared. He nodded to the empty spot next to him. "Sit here, Beautiful."

He wouldn't call her that if he had any return interest in Bethel. He was as gut as publicly declaring that he and Agnes were a couple.

Agnes allowed herself to breathe and climbed over the bench to sit next to Isaac—as if she belonged there. And maybe she did.

If she dared to feed the dream.

22

I t felt gut to get into a routine. Two months had passed with auctions every weekend and when Isaac was home—when had this district turned into his home?—he took care of the three kinner and spent as much time as he could with Agnes at the candy shop. The better he got to know her, the more she fascinated him.

He couldn't wait to see her in just a few hours. It was mid-November, and Sam and Jenny were due back home any day. They'd been gone much longer than the expected eight weeks, as Sam had required additional therapy to recover from a serious infection he'd contracted after his last surgery. Isaac was glad Sam had finally recovered enough to kum home, but he realized he would miss spending so much time with the kinner. And miss his ready excuse to spend time with Agnes. He wasn't sure what Sam's return would mean for his own future. Would his brother still need help around the farm? Would their relationship be stilted and uncomfortable because of the past? And where would Isaac live?

Isaac shifted on the uncomfortable bus seat. He'd been trying to sleep—or at least rest—on the trip north from an auction in Florida, where the temperatures had been downright pleasant. Michigan's Upper Peninsula had turned bitterly cold, with occasional snow showers. Nein significant accumulation yet, but the Yoopers talked as if that it could happen at any time.

Interfering with his efforts to sleep was his rumbling stomach, thanks to the aroma of fried chicken permeating the air. A family had smuggled the meal onto the bus at the last stop. While fried chicken sounded gut, being in Florida had put Isaac in the mood for seafood like the kinds he'd enjoyed over the summer in Florida, when vacationers were there. A clam bake on the beach, lobster, shrimp…all you could eat of the delicious goodness. Food that wasn't available in the small-town grocery store. So, he'd called Gideon at the Amish salvage-grocery and asked him if he could order several types of seafood, plus some other items not typically carried by the small-town grocery. He had a special nacht planned for as soon as his brother returned, to celebrate his homecoming and also Isaac's resulting ability to take Agnes out to court her properly, rather than being chaperoned by three little people.

The bishop would probably still spy on them.

Or maybe not, if Isaac requested to become a member of the district and promised to look for a place he could call a permanent home. He wanted to settle in an area with such a godly and wise preacher as Gideon, with whom he'd had multiple discussions over the past several weeks. Also, Bishop Miah. Now, there was a man of Gott. Plus, he'd be close to his brother and the three kinner Isaac had grown to love. That is, if his brother had truly forgiven him.

A place where, if things proceeded as Isaac hoped, he would eventually carry Agnes across the threshold as his bride. It was an Englisch tradition but one he looked forward to observing. Except, the season of autumn had passed without the bishop's agreeing to publish their wedding plans. Now they might be looking at a winter wedding. Or possibly even one as late as next fall.

Isaac glanced out the window at the miles of woodlands they traveled through as they traveled Interstate 75 north of Saginaw. They were about forty miles from the bridge when the sky turned dark and stormy. The wind picked up. Thunder rumbled, some of the booms loud enough to cause a child on the bus to scream in terror. Then hail pounded the roof and slammed against the windows, and visibility reduced to virtually nothing.

Ahead of them, traffic came to a complete standstill as cars pulled off the road. Some drivers had parked beneath an overpass, blocking the highway completely. The bus was left unprotected about three or four cars shy of the overpass. The driver muttered a curse.

Nein point in trying to sleep now. Isaac yawned and stretched the tight muscles in his back as he prayed for protection.

He fidgeted in his seat as the hail pounded the vehicle in noisy thumps that made it sound as if rocks were hitting it. Hopefully, nein windows would break. He pulled out his cell phone to see if the Mackinac Bridge was closed. According to the latest update, it was still open.

Some of the Englisch kinner on the bus started to cry. One of the women shielded her baby on an aisle seat, while her husband or boyfriend muttered a string of words that would make a sailor blush with shame. If those had been Isaac's frau and kinner, he would have been shielding them from the threat of shattered glass and wrapping them tightly in his arms.

Stuck on a bus with nothing to do but watch the hail pound the windows, Isaac rummaged through his carry-on bag to find his Bible. That morgen, he'd read from the book of Isaiah. He now thumbed his way to the page he'd marked with the ripped-out corner of a Florida newspaper. There it was. Isaiah 55:7–9:

> *Let the wicked forsake his way, and the unrighteous man his thoughts; let him return to the* LORD, *and He will have mercy on him; and to our God, for He will abundantly pardon. "For My thoughts are not your thoughts, nor are your ways My ways," says the* LORD. *"For as the heavens are higher than the earth, so are My ways higher than your ways, and My thoughts than your thoughts."*

Isaac ran his fingers over the printed verses. Could Gott have mercy on him? Abundantly pardon him? Even though he'd started reading his Bible every day since that long-ago Montana trip, he still had difficulty believing the truth.

He pressed his lips together and closed his eyes, trying to ignore the cries, screams, and curses, as well as the continual pounding of hailstones hitting the bus from all sides. The sound reminded Isaac of that horrible Fourth of July celebration that turned into a nacht-mare when Titus drowned in the well.

Isaac had been the one to find Titus. He'd climbed into the well and dragged the bu's lifeless body out. Jenny was screaming, crying. Sam raged, cussing and weeping. Isaac had apologized, tears streaming down his face, but nobody listened. Daed came running from the barn and suffered a massive heart attack when he realized what had happened, dropping dead at their feet. Blaming himself for the double tragedy, Isaac had left everything behind but the clothes on his back and hit the road, turning into a wanderer.

Isaac heard through the grapevine that Mamm had died of a broken heart a month later. Nein wonder, after losing her gross-sohn, her ehemann, and a sohn on the same day.

If only Isaac could do that day over. He wouldn't have flirted with Jenny, would've realized Sam had left the cover off the well, and would've kept Titus far away from it. He would've tried to keep Daed quiet and calm, and he would've hugged Mamm and told her he loved her.

He needed to apologize to Sam, again, for sure, both for his actions and for abandoning his responsibilities and running away. Maybe it would heal their relationship a little if Isaac owned his mistakes. Though nothing specific had been said during their chance meeting three years ago, when Sam had actually treated Isaac cordially. The exchange had been polite, if not close, like that of two twin brothers should be. Probably because they hadn't been alone but rather in a crowd. There was safety in numbers and nein way to bring up the past. Isaac grimaced.

Snippets of conversations he'd had with Bishop Miah over the past two months came to mind.

"I can explain it to you, but I can't understand it for you."…"You're not alone."…"Gott is a Gott who won't let go."…"The Lord will help you when you kum to Him lacking strength and hope."…"Jesus never leaves the faithful to suffer alone. He heals the limping man's faith."

Isaac was definitely a limping man.

Lord, heal my faith. I'm weak. I need Your strength when I face my brother and his wife.

A gut start, but he needed to ask forgiveness, too. *If we confess our sins.…* Jah. That was a necessary step.

Gott, please forgive me. I didn't mean to kill my nephew or my parents. If there is any way I can make this right, please show me. Forgive all my sins and cleanse me from all unrighteousness.

That was in the Bible somewhere, but Isaac couldn't remember the reference.

I want to be Yours. To serve you, like Bishop Miah does. To put You first. Help me to be the man You created me to be.

Something fluttered to life inside him, and for the first time since Titus's death, Isaac felt free. Forgiven. Strengthened.

The bus lurched and Isaac opened his eyes. The wind still blew, the sky was still dark, but the rain and hail had stopped as suddenly as they had started.

Isaac shut his Bible and held it close to his chest.

Help me to forgive myself.

Would it be selfish to ask Gott to help his dreams kum true?

⌒

Agnes turned at the sound of sleigh bells ringing on the shop door. Business had boomed since the television interview had aired, with visitors to the Upper Peninsula coming by to check out the Amish-owned candy shop. She hadn't expected so many Englisch customers during the autumn, but it seemed deer hunters liked fudge, too. Who knew?

Isaac walked in and set his luggage down. "Hey, Beautiful." He sounded tired. There was a weary slump to his shoulders and the shadow of several days' growth of whiskers on his chin.

She tried to control a squeal but failed as she rushed toward him, into his open arms. "You're back!"

He picked her up and spun her around in a circle. She giggled and then wrapped her arms around his neck as his lips found hers with a kiss that made her forget everything else. Several heart-pounding minutes later, he set her down and looked around. "Where are the girls?"

"With Sam and Jenny. They returned yesterday evening, just as I was getting supper on the table." She'd driven her buggy back to town and spent the nacht in her shop, not even eating the meal she'd prepared at the Masts' haus. Jenny had made it clear she wanted to be alone with her little family and Agnes was an intruder. Agnes had taken one of Isaac's cans of chicken noodle soup to warm at the shop. The contents tasted nothing like the homemade version.

Isaac sobered. "How is Sam?"

Agnes frowned. "He looks like he survived a fire. His ears are mostly gone and there's some scarring on his face. The injuries to his ears and face won't be so noticeable once his hair grows back. I couldn't tell anything beyond that due to his long sleeves. He and Jenny seemed surprised to see me and asked where you were. I explained that you had gone to work an auction and they said they didn't know you were still working. Why didn't you tell them?"

Isaac shook his head. "I figured that was a given. Did they expect me to quit my job? I may be a wanderer with nein home, but I still have expenses."

He had nein home? How had Agnes missed that detail? He'd said he joined the church—but also that he lived in so many different communities, he didn't follow the rules of any one district. Somehow, it hadn't registered with her that he was homeless; that all his belongings were probably in that suitcase and carry-on bag sitting just inside the door.

She frowned. "Do you ever think about settling down?" Or, more specifically, did he think about settling down here?

He gathered her close. "More and more often. Every time I think of you." He gave her a quick kiss, then released her. "My brother...did he seem angry when he mentioned me?"

"Nein. Simply confused about why you weren't there. But I made it clear you would be back soon."

Isaac sighed. "Do you suppose the bishop will let me stay at his haus to-nacht?"

Agnes frowned again. "I'm sure he will. You don't want to stay with your brother?"

"You've been there, Beautiful. They don't have a spare room. And it might be wise to have a third party present when we meet again."

Ach. He would be worried about that.

"It's not your fault," Agnes reminded him. "Not totally. Sam shouldn't have left the cover off the well. He and Jenny should've been watching their sohn. Not you."

Isaac's jaw flexed. "I'm not sure they'd agree. Sam had made it very clear he blamed me for the deaths of both Titus and my daed. Probably my mamm, too."

"Your daed?"

"He died of a heart attack once he saw my nephew's dead body." Isaac's voice cracked.

Agnes sucked in a breath. "Ach, Isaac. They never said a word about it." But, of course, Agnes wasn't friends with them. They seemed years beyond her in age, maybe since they had three—technically four—kinner.

Jenny was almost thirty, which meant Sam, and Isaac, would be close to the same age.

Nein wonder Isaac seemed so mature. He was.

And she was his junior by maybe eight years.

Did that matter?

Then again, she'd grown up a lot since the wildfire. Starting her own business, taking care of the three Mast kinner, and helping Bishop Miah and Katherine…sometimes she felt years older than the girls she'd gone to school with. Even girls she knew to be her age.

"Close the store early." Isaac urged her back into his arms. "Kum with me to the salvage-grocery store to pick up a few things and then spend the evening with me." He punctuated every few words with a shower of kisses.

Would it be woefully irresponsible to say "Jah"? She had nein customers at the moment. Just a messy kitchen, dirty dishes, and cooling fudge.

She flipped the sign from "Open" to "Closed" and locked the door. "I'm all yours."

Isaac chuckled. "I like the way that sounds."

⌒

After the candy shop was clean and all the tasks were done, Isaac reluctantly dragged himself from the privacy of the store and followed Agnes out onto the busy main street of town. He left his luggage at the shop, as well as his hat, since the wind gusted hard enough to blow any unsecured items into next week.

He wasn't content walking even a foot away from Agnes. He'd missed her and he didn't care who might discover they were a couple. Tongues would wag, for sure, but he pulled her close and held her hand—fingers entwined—as they strolled the two blocks to the Amish salvage-grocery store.

She shivered, despite her coat, and leaned even closer to him. Her skirt whipped around her legs, probably showing glimpses of the sensible black stockings she wore with the not-so-sensible pink tennis shoes he'd bought her as a gift on one of his trips.

She'd cried when he presented them to her. Happy tears.

Katherine and Bishop Miah had shaken their heads at the sight of the colorful footwear but said not a word—at least in Isaac's hearing. Considering she still wore them in public, Isaac guessed nothing had been said privately either.

If Agnes traveled with him to auctions once they were married, he'd buy her a pink dress, too. While most districts frowned upon that shade in favor of darker, more serviceable colors, there were a few districts that embraced lighter, brighter hues. If Agnes were to give up being tied to a specific area, as he had done, then she'd get away with wearing whatever colors she wanted.

There'd be much to discuss when they talked seriously about their future together. Would Agnes give up the candy shop and embrace his nomadic lifestyle, or would she want to keep her business and live alone half the year while he traveled? Isaac supposed he could give up the more demanding schedule of his occupation, as it was, and start farming, or doing something else. A farmer, he wasn't. Though the skills might kum back to him if he studied up on them. With Agnes by his side, any sacrifice would be worth it.

Despite their slow pace, they eventually made it to the Amish salvage-grocery store and ducked inside, relishing the warmth of the building. Gideon's daed, Ben, stood behind the counter. He wore a rather somber expression, with his lips pressed flat and his eyes lacking their usual twinkle. Isaac didn't know him well enough to feel comfortable asking if something was wrong. Whatever it might be, it probably fell under the "none of his business" category.

"You just caught me," Ben told them. He scribbled something on a piece of paper, then bundled some cash in rubber bands before sliding the lot into a zippered bag that bore the bank's logo. "My sohn's frau was just taken to the hospital…." He sighed heavily.

"Ach, nein. The boppli?" Agnes apparently had nein qualms about inquiring after a subject that was not typically talked about in mixed company.

Ben nodded. "Gideon says there are complications, and the midwife thinks it'd be wise. I'll be going to the hospital as soon as I finish here, to keep Gid company while he waits." He closed the drawer and slipped the bank bag out of sight. "Is there anything I can help you find?"

Isaac nodded. "I asked Gideon to special order some items. Have they arrived?"

"Ach, jah. Someone will be feasting to-nacht. Is this in celebration of your brother's return?"

It seemed as gut a reason as any. "Part of it is. And part of it is for a different reason." He tilted his head toward Agnes.

"Young love." Ben smiled briefly. "Let me get your order. I'll be right back." He turned and speed-walked toward the back of the store. Minutes later, he returned, carrying a grocery bag. "Gid had it ready to go." He told Isaac the price.

Isaac handed him a cash payment. "I'll be praying for your dochter-in-law."

Ben nodded. "I've been praying since I heard. Nonstop. Bishop Miah was in here earlier and he reminded me that Gott hears even the silent prayers of a sincere heart."

Agnes's breath caught sharply.

Isaac glanced at her.

Tears welled in her eyes.

Ach. Isaac thought back to what the bishop had said when he told Isaac about Agnes's trips to the pond. *"She goes to pray—shouting, as if she believes Gott is hard of hearing."*

Too bad the bishop hadn't thought to share with Agnes the same proverb he'd told to Ben. Or maybe he didn't think she would truly hear, understand, or believe his words.

Ben didn't appear to notice. "Sometimes He says jah, sometimes He says nein, and sometimes He wants us to wait. I'm praying for a quick, positive response, but the will of der Herr, not mine, be done." His forehead wrinkled in a frown, forming two deep furrows.

"I'll let you finish closing so up you can get on your way," Isaac told him. "We'll be taking Agnes's horse and buggy out to see Bishop Miah and my—" Isaac sighed. "My brother."

Worry pressed in on him. Again. This meeting would be private— sort of. And the proverbial elephant in the room couldn't be avoided.

Let prayer be the key to the day and the bolt to the nacht.

23

Once the horse and buggy were hitched just outside the salvage-grocery store, Agnes gave Isaac control of the reins, glad there was someone else to drive the buggy in such high winds. They went straight to the candy shop to collect his luggage and hat, and also to drop off some of his grocery purchases. He refused to allow her so much as a peek. From there, they traveled to the Brunstetters' home.

As they stopped in the circular drive between the haus and the barn, Bishop Miah stepped out of the barn, one hand holding his hat in place to keep it from blowing away.

Isaac took off his own hat and climbed out of the buggy as the bishop approached.

"I'd wish you a happy *winds*-day, but it's not." The bishop didn't chuckle at his joke. "So you're back."

Isaac's expression matched the bishop's. Sober. Serious. "Jah, and I hear my brother is, too."

Bishop Miah nodded. "Agnes stopped by to tell me last nacht. I'm headed that way in a bit, then I need to go to the hospital—"

"Any updates?" Agnes poked her head out of the buggy. Not much time had passed since she'd heard about Katie from Ben, but it seemed the Amish grapevine spread news at an unsurpassed speed.

The bishop glanced at her. "Not yet."

Isaac cleared his throat. "Would you be willing to let me stay here to-nacht?"

"Nein need to ask. As soon as I heard you were in town, my frau got the bed made up. Want to follow me over to visit with Sam and Jenny?"

Isaac sagged. "Jah. Please."

Agnes wanted to comfort him but didn't know how. RESUME

"I won't be staying long. The driver's supposed to pick up Katherine and me in about an hour."

An hour should be long enough to determine the nature of Isaac's welkum, though Agnes doubted he would receive anything other than an outpouring of gratitude. Isaac had stepped up to the plate and even though he had been away more than he'd been in town, when he was around, he was very active with the kinner, taking full care of them. He'd more than proved he could handle them.

He climbed back into the buggy next to Agnes and sighed heavily as they waited for the bishop to finish hitching his horse and buggy.

Agnes reached for Isaac, wrapping her fingers around his. "It'll be okay." *Hopefully.*

His Adam's apple worked and a muscle jumped in his jaw. He nodded, a curt acknowledgment rather than a show of agreement.

She was scared, too—not that they'd turn him away, because why would they have entrusted three small kinner to him for so long if they blamed him for Titus's death? Nein, her fears came from a different quarter: What if they didn't like *her?* What if they thought she'd gone off in den kopf and was not suitable to be courted by Isaac? Not that the two of them *were* courting. Yet. She had high hopes, though. Had romantic daydreams about him asking to marry her, maybe even in the way her imagination had spelled out.

But that was unlikely. Because, even if he did begin to court her, he probably wouldn't ask her to marry him until next summer, when there'd be nein chance of hearing snow crunching pleasantly under her feet, near a Christmas tree, when he proposed.

She sighed. He probably didn't remember that conversation.

"I'll be okay," she said, thinking she should repeat herself, though more to convince herself than him.

"Of course, you will be." His glance showed confusion.

"What?"

"You said, 'I'll be okay.' You will be."

"'I'? I meant *it.* It'll be okay."

His chuckle held nein humor. Instead, his fingers white-knuckled the reins as they watched Bishop Miah drive his rig out of the buggy shed.

~

Isaac's head throbbed, the sure sign that a tension headache was starting. He dipped his chin a little. *Gott, help. I'm scared.*

It took longer to reach his brother's haus when driving along the road than it did to cut through the fields on foot. Even so, they seemed to travel at warp speed. They got there long before he was ready.

Isaac parked behind the bishop's rig.

Timmy came running out of the haus. "Onkel Isaac! My daed's home!" He threw his arms around Isaac's thighs.

"I heard." His voice sounded gruff. He cleared his throat and ruffled Timmy's hair, then looked up.

All his breath exited his lungs with a whoosh.

Sam, emerging from the haus, looked like a shell of his former self. Nein longer tanned from hours in the sun, the parts of his body that weren't concealed by his clothes were red, wrinkled, and scarred. Nein hair grew on his scalp or his chin, his ears were at least half the size they used to be, and his fingers had been reduced to mere stubs. His eyes...his eyes were filled with tears. Filled, overflowing, falling....

Isaac gulped as his emotions ran through a wide range. Soon tears dripped from his chin in rapid succession.

He took one hesitant step toward his brother, Timmy at his side. Then, something blurry flew toward him, launched into his arms, and clung. Sobbing.

Jenny.

Agnes made a strange whimpering sound.

Sam slapped Isaac on the back. Not hard, really—a mere whisper of his former strength—but it was still felt. Isaac set Jenny aside, stepped back, and went to give his brother a hug. But then he hesitated. The mandatory slaps on the back would probably knock Sam over. Isaac could still hug him though.

"It's gut to see you. Danki for all you did." Sam's voice was husky. Raw. Whether because of damage from the fire or due to his emotions, Isaac didn't know.

A hand came to rest gently on his back, giving several pats that gave way to a rubbing motion. Isaac's nerve endings sprang to life in response to the familiar touch and he glanced over at Agnes beside him. His beautiful Agnes, crying unabashedly.

She was not a pretty crier.

He reached out one arm, wrapped it around her waist, and drew her into the family circle of himself, Timmy, Sam, and Jenny. Unintelligible babbles rose from the vicinity of his knees, so he knew Martha was there, too. And if Martha was there, then Mary was, as well.

Finally, Jenny stepped away, breaking the circle. "It's been too long."

Isaac slid his hand across Agnes's back and then grasped her hand. "You know Agnes Zook."

"She's gonna be my aenti," Timmy blurted out.

Agnes coughed.

Jenny made an odd sound, then turned to Agnes and wrapped her in a hug. "Welkum to the family. Are you two published?"

Isaac looked up and met Bishop Miah's gaze. "Ah, nein." He'd forgotten the bishop was there. "We...uh...we haven't officially courted. Yet."

The bishop muttered something that sounded like "courted, schmorted," but that made nein sense.

Then again, much of what the man said didn't make immediate sense. It was in hindsight that Isaac understood his veiled comments.

Apparently just noticing the bishop's presence, Sam stepped toward him, hand outstretched.

"Welkum home, Sam." Bishop Miah shook his hand. "Sorry I can't stay. A church member is in crisis. I'll be back later. Be assured, the community will continue to step in to help with the livestock when Isaac is away."

Isaac frowned. "I plan to stay for a while—"

"Life is as uncertain as a grapefruit's squirt." The bishop glanced skyward for a moment, then turned and trudged back toward his buggy, clutching his hat. "Winds are shifting.... It's an ill wind that blows nein gut. Confounded citrus fruit."

Okay, then.

A chill worked through Agnes at Bishop Miah's strange comments. The last time he'd spoken in similar fashion, a wildfire had swept through the area soon after, killing her family. She tightened her grip on Isaac's hand.

Isaac stared after the bishop's buggy, frowning. Then he shook his head and turned toward Agnes's buggy. "I have some food and wanted to have a celebration, if it's okay. You're both home; the family is reunited. I'll cook."

"If you cook, it will be a celebration." Jenny grabbed hold of his arm and held on.

The action bothered Agnes. Jenny was married and Isaac had admitted to having had a crush on her years ago. Nein wonder. Now, even after four pregnancies, she was still beautiful and she had the easygoing, super-friendly personality men flocked to. Just like Agnes's cousin Priscilla.

Unlike Agnes. Her own sense of inferiority threatened. Her shoulders slumped. Tears burned her eyes.

Isaac shifted enough to dislodge Jenny's hand from his arm. "None of that, Jenny. You just cuddle with Sam and your kinner. Leave Agnes and me to heat up the kitchen." He glanced at Agnes and gave her a long, slow, exaggerated wink, accompanied by the crooked half-smile that always turned her insides to mush.

She shivered.

His grin widened.

Heating up the kitchen sounded like a wunderbaar-gut plan.

24

While Isaac steamed the lobster and crab legs, mixed up some garlic butter for dipping, and sautéed shrimp over the hot stove, Agnes chopped vegetables for a garden salad. In spite of her cool-temperature job, she somehow managed to heat him up. As he watched her slice and dice, she put her whole body into motion. Who knew slicing cucumbers or shredding carrots could be so sexy? Then again, he'd seen her mixing fudge ingredients and washing dishes with the same action...and been equally attracted just as strongly.

He couldn't wait to get her alone.

After he talked to Bishop Miah about his long-term plans, the bishop would surely agree that Isaac and Agnes should marry, sooner rather than later. Or so Isaac hoped. If not, then...then Isaac might go insane. That was all. Either that, or he'd talk Agnes into eloping and adopting his nomadic lifestyle.

He swallowed hard, forced his attention away from her, and went to call everyone in for supper as Agnes made a final swipe of the dishcloth over the table.

When he returned to the kitchen, she was setting the table with ceramic plates and silver eating utensils—not the disposable conveniences he'd insisted on using to make life easier when he was in charge.

"Agnes, you're amazing." He took a step toward her, intent on embracing her and maybe stealing a brief kiss before his family barreled into the room.

But he was too late. Mary flew into the room at full speed. Jenny was right behind her, arms outstretched, and headed directly for Isaac as if she intended to hug him. "It smells *amazing* in here, Ike. I had nein idea you could cook. I figured my kinner lived on peanut-butter-and-banana sandwiches the whole time we were gone."

Isaac smiled sheepishly as he stepped out of reach. He didn't want Jenny's hugs. She needed to save them for Sam and not try to win Isaac's affections again. He and Sam had enough troubles between them without her adding her flirtations back into the mix.

A gut reason *not* to settle here, kum to think of it.

Agnes bit her lower lip and watched with wide eyes. Isaac couldn't blame her. He'd had nein room to condemn her about St. Gabe. None. Her treatment of Gabe, at least that he'd seen, had been far more reserved than Jenny's right now.

Isaac grimaced. He would apologize later for judging her.

Sam hobbled into the room and sat at the head of the table. "Looks and smells wunderbaar, Agnes."

Agnes smiled. "Isaac cooked. I just made the salad." She cast an apologetic glance toward Isaac.

"You surprise me, Ike—Isaac." Sam's voice still sounded raw.

Isaac shrugged. "I learned to make these dishes in Florida. These are some of the best things they serve down there."

"I can't wait to try it." Sam grinned. "I can't remember the last time I had lobster. Jenny's been talking about wanting to cook shrimp. We tried it for the first time in Minnesota." Sam folded his hands. "I'm so glad you're here, Ike. Perhaps you'll marry and settle down in this area. Timmy and Mary can't stop talking about you."

"Ich liebe Onkel Isaac." Timmy bounced into his seat between Isaac and Sam. "When I grow up, I wanna do what he does."

"We all love Ike." Jenny sat down at the foot of the table and fluttered her eyelids.

Isaac tried not to cringe when he spotted Agnes scowling at Jenny. He would have to be even firmer with Jenny. She'd always had trouble taking a hint.

"I love your onkel Isaac, too. He does have a fine occupation." Sam smiled at Timmy. "Let's pray."

Isaac glanced across the table at Agnes, seated next to Mary. There'd be nein hand-holding during this meal.

Isaac bowed his head. *Gott, danki for the better-than-I-expected welkum from Sam and Jenny. Danki for this meal and for all You've done. Please make my pathway clear. Show me what You would have me do.*

"Amen," Sam said.

Jenny gave each of the kinner some salad and several pieces of shrimp. Since Isaac hadn't thought to order any of the special tools needed for eating lobster, he ended up cutting it and using a butter knife to poke the meat out of the shell.

"This is ser gut." Timmy scratched at his arm. "My arm's itching like crazy."

"Really?" Jenny looked at her sohn. "Your face is blotchy, too. You spent the afternoon roaming the woods." She looked at her ehemann. "Is poison ivy still poisonous in the late fall?"

"I don't know." Sam shrugged. "Don't scratch, Sohn." His gaze went to Isaac. "Do we have any allergy medicine in the haus?"

Isaac glanced at Agnes. He was glad Timmy's parents were home to deal with poison ivy.

"I never thought to check," Agnes told Jenny. "Want me to look?"

"I never buy it. None of us is allergic to anything." Jenny frowned at Timmy and reached over to still his hands. "I do have some Epsom salt, though. Maybe a soaking bath would help."

Sam shrugged. "Wouldn't hurt to try." He took another bite of food.

As Isaac studied his nephew, a distant memory surfaced. He certainly seemed to be having an allergic reaction to something, but poison ivy shouldn't spread that fast, even if the boy had rolled around in the leaves. Timmy was acting a lot like the guy Isaac had seen react to peanuts at a restaurant in Missouri.

Ach, nein. Was Timmy allergic to shellfish?

Timmy clutched his throat. His eyes rolled back in his head in an unholy manner and he slumped to the floor.

Isaac gasped and dropped to his knees beside Timmy, knocking over his chair in the process. "He's not breathing!" He yanked his smartphone out of his pocket and tossed it to Sam. "Call nine-one-one."

Jenny clutched at her chest, her eyes wide with terror.

Isaac glanced at Sam. He frowned at the phone. Unmoving.

Isaac stretched Timmy out and made sure his airways were clear. "Sam. You'll have to go out to the road to get a signal. Run!"

"There's a phone in the barn." Sam tossed the smartphone on the table as he jumped to his feet. Then he hobbled quickly from the haus, not bothering with a hat, coat, or shoes.

Gott, don't let him die, too. Isaac bent over the bu and started mouth-to-mouth resuscitation, breathing, listening, breathing.... *Gott, please.* If it was an allergic reaction to shellfish, it was Isaac's fault. He'd brought the food into the haus.

Sam ran back into the room. "There's an ambulance fifteen minutes out. First responders are on their way, too."

Isaac tried to ignore Jenny's piercing wails as he concentrated on counting breaths. Listening. Listening...and hearing nothing but his own guilty conscience screaming that this was his fault.

After several excruciating minutes, they heard the scatter of gravel in the driveway as a vehicle squealed to a stop. Seconds later, footsteps pounded up the porch stairs.

"First responders!" a voice yelled out. The door burst open and a man rushed into the room, a duffel bag slung over his shoulder. "What's going on?"

"Allergic reaction to shellfish, I'm guessing," Isaac said as he moved out of the way.

The man dropped to his knees beside Timmy. "Does he have an EpiPen?" He looked up from his kneeling position beside Timmy's motionless body.

"Nein...no." Isaac swallowed. He'd never anticipated that his nephew might need one.

He glanced at Sam, hugging his still-screaming frau. Sometime during the commotion, Agnes must have taken the two little girls from the room, for they were nein longer present.

The first responder leaned over Timmy. "The ambulance carries adrenaline, if it makes it in time."

"First responder!" the door opened again and another man entered.

Isaac pushed to his feet. Tears burning his eyes, he grabbed his phone from the table and shoved it into his pocket. He turned to Sam, who still held Jenny. "There's a phone in the barn?"

"In the back. Tack room." Sam didn't look at him. He was shaking.

Isaac swallowed. "I'll call a driver to take us to the hospital."

"We have a breath. It's thready, but he's breathing." The first man who'd showed up glanced at the second one to arrive. "Good thing he knew artificial respiration." He nodded at Isaac.

Breathing. *Danki, Gott.* Hopefully, Timmy hadn't been without oxygen long enough to cause damage to his brain.

"We'll probably still need to give him oxygen," the second man said.

An ambulance's siren wailed in the distance. Isaac rubbed his burning eyes and went to the barn. Three phone calls later, he'd found a driver. By the time he emerged from the barn, the ambulance was parked in the drive with its back doors open. Timmy lay pale on the stretcher as the EMTs carried him out of the haus.

Jenny followed them, still wailing. She stopped briefly to glare at Isaac before climbing into the ambulance with her sohn.

Isaac turned to Sam. "A driver is on his way. I'm sorry. I didn't know. I didn't mean—"

"I don't want to hear it." Sam flapped a hand at Isaac and turned toward the haus. "I'd better get what we need."

An Amish buggy pulled in and the driver jumped out. Isaac had seen him around, but didn't know his name. "What's going on?" he asked.

His frau exited the buggy behind him, a casserole dish in hand. "We brought supper."

Sam glanced at them. "We need to take Timothy to the hospital. Can you stay with the girls?"

Ouch. Isaac winced. He'd been watching the kinner for months— granted, he'd had Agnes's help—but there'd been nein mishaps. How was he supposed to know Timmy was allergic to shellfish? Especially since Timmy's own parents had dished out the food and served it to him?

He swallowed the stubborn lump in his throat, blinked back his tears, and went into the haus. He found Agnes in the girls' bedroom, reading them a story.

She glanced up, worry in her eyes.

He cleared his throat. "Another couple is going to stay with the girls. Do you want to kum to the hospital, or go home?" Not that the candy shop was her home.

"Hospital, please." She closed the book. "I'll just need my shoes and coat."

He nodded. Forced a smile at the two girls. If only he could tell them everything would be okay.

But it wouldn't be. Nein matter what happened, it seemed that his relationship with his brother and his brother's frau—and, consequently, with these kinner—was shredded beyond repair.

And it was his fault.

Again.

⁓

The hospital waiting room was crowded with Englisch and Amish alike. Everyone was quiet and subdued as they awaited updates on their loved ones. Sam was rushed back to the emergency room to join his frau and Timmy. Agnes followed Isaac to a quiet corner where he slumped in a chair, bowed his head, and stretched his legs out in front of him.

Would it do any gut to remind him that nobody had known Timmy was allergic to shellfish? The shrimp had tasted wunderbaar, what little of it she'd gotten to try. But it wouldn't do any gut to tell him that. Maybe someday.

She reached for his hand, in spite of the crowd of people around them. He latched on like a drowning man and clung.

Agnes lowered her head. *Gott, today, Ben mentioned that You hear even our silent prayers. If You can hear me, please, let Timmy live. Please, comfort Isaac. May his relationship with his family not be damaged further by this situation.*

Judging by Sam's apparent anger and Jenny's blatant dismissal of Isaac, some damage had already been done. Agnes wanted Isaac to get along with them and maybe settle here, with her. At the same time, Agnes could scarcely believe how Jenny had treated him upon reuniting with him. It was the way she treated men in general. She was a notorious flirt. And, for a married woman....

Agnes shook her head. Jenny was the type of woman who needed men to pay special attention to her. To desire her. That didn't necessarily mean she would be unfaithful to Sam, but it did speak volumes about her ehemann. He must have considerable faith in his frau not to stray. Either that, or he had resigned himself to the fact that he would never succeed in keeping Jenny's undivided attention. Especially now with all his visible scars.

Agnes glanced around. Bishop Miah paced the room, stopping now and again to gaze out the window. Praying, maybe. Katherine sat quietly nearby, crocheting a boppli blanket. Agnes didn't know for whom it was intended.

Ben Kaiser sat two seats away from him, his head bent—he might also be praying. The bishop's comments about the wind made a little more sense now.

Time stretched from minutes into hours. Agnes didn't know how long she'd been sitting there, holding Isaac's hand while thinking and praying, when, from somewhere in the recesses of the small hospital, a male voice roared a raw, guttural cry.

Ben lurched to his feet and stumbled across the hallway to the nurses' station.

Bishop Miah's shoulders slumped. Tears ran down his face and dripped off his chin.

Was it Lizzie and the boppli? Or Timmy?

Isaac tightened his grip on Agnes's hand.

"It's not Sam," she whispered. At least, she was fairly sure. With his hoarse voice, Sam didn't seem capable of making such a sound.

Isaac nodded. But he didn't relax his hold.

Ben returned to his seat. "They said a doctor would be out to talk to me. Sometime."

After another long wait, Sam came out to the waiting room, a smile on his face and tears in his eyes. "Timothy's awake and breathing. They want to keep him over-nacht to make sure he doesn't have something called a biphasic anaphylactic reaction, which can sometimes happen hours after the initial allergic reaction."

Isaac exhaled a long breath. "Thank Gott he's okay."

Agnes rubbed her free hand over Isaac's hand that still gripped hers, in celebration that at least some of her prayers had been answered.

"They're prescribing an EpiPen and recommending he avoid shellfish for now. We can have him tested as he gets older, to see if he outgrows the allergy." Sam turned away. "I'd best return to Jenny. They gave her something to calm her down, but she's refusing to leave Timothy's side. We'll both spend the nacht here with him."

Isaac released Agnes's hand. "We'll find the driver and head back to the haus." He swiveled to face Agnes. "You have a busy day tomorrow and it's late." He avoided her eyes.

Her day wouldn't be any busier than usual. In fact, it would be less busy, assuming she had nein childcare responsibilities.

"I'll go home, too." Katherine stood.

Bishop Miah paused his pacing. "I'll stay here a bit longer," he told his frau. "I need to be here for Gideon and Lizzie, too." He looked at Isaac. "Don't forget: Gott is a Gott who won't let go. He gives strength to the limping man."

Isaac pressed his lips together but said nothing. Instead, he reclaimed Agnes's hand and tugged her away from the stifling waiting room and outside, into the brisk mid-nacht air, where they would wait for their driver.

An hour later, when the driver stopped in front of the candy shop, Agnes wearily climbed out of the van. "I'll see you inside," Isaac said as he came out after her. He nodded at Katherine and told the driver to wait for him.

Once Agnes had unlocked the door to her shop, Isaac used his pocket penlight to survey the dark space. Deeming it safe, he shut the door behind them, moved away from the windows, and pulled Agnes into his arms. His lips claimed hers as his arms went around her, lifting her up and hugging her tight against him.

Her hands slid across his cheeks and around his head, tangling in his hair. "Isaac." His name came out as a groan.

He pressed her against the wall, his kisses deepening. Becoming more desperate. His hands trembled as they slid over her body, lighting her nerve endings on fire.

She whimpered, wanting more, all, everything. "Ich liebe dich, Isaac Mast."

"Agnes. Ach, Agnes." He moaned. And then, long before she was ready, he stepped away, striding toward the door. Opening it. "I've got to go. I'll return your horse and buggy in the morgen. Lock this door behind me, okay."

Jah, he had to go. The driver and Katherine were waiting. But Agnes wanted him to stay. She wanted to grab hold of him and hang on tight.

She wanted those three little words....

Instead, she locked the door, then watched him climb into the van and disappear into the nacht.

⌒

The next morgen, Isaac stepped outside a building in St. Ignace. Away from anyone who might be eavesdropping. Not that there were many people around. Just an Englisch man smoking a cigarette.

Isaac pulled out his phone and called the hospital. Even though he was family, he doubted he would get an update on Timmy. He wouldn't have been listed as an approved person on the forms Sam and Jenny would have had to fill out. Not when he was to blame for their sohn's hospitalization.

When a hospital phone operator picked up, he requested that the call be transferred to Timmy's room. Hopefully, Sam would answer.

The phone rang three or four times before Jenny answered.

"Jen—"

"Leave us alone, Ike. Don't call back." The phone went dead.

That was about what he'd expected. He rubbed his stinging eyes and redialed the hospital. This time, he asked to be transferred to the gift shop and he ordered a teddy bear to be sent to Timmy's room. He hoped Jenny wouldn't throw away the gift. Ideally, Sam would be in the room when it was delivered.

Should he order flowers for Jenny with a card expressing a heartfelt apology?

He shook his head. Best to leave things as they were. She wouldn't want to hear from him anyway. Not now. Maybe someday. Or maybe not. He should make an effort, at least.

His next call was to a local florist. Jenny's favorite flowers were roses, but there was nein way he'd send those. He ordered a bouquet of daisies and specified that the note should simply read, "I'm sorry." Nein excuses. He really didn't have any excuses. It'd been his intention to share some of his favorite food with the people he loved. He'd wanted it to be a special celebration to welkum Sam and Jenny home.

It'd turned into a nacht-mare.

So many regrets. So many broken promises.

So many dreams murdered before they became realities.

He swallowed the lump clogging his throat, blinked at the tears burning his eyes, and ordered a bouquet of red roses for Agnes.

And then he caught the first bus south.

25

Someone was pounding on the door to the candy shop. Not the front door but the back. Agnes glanced at the window. It was still dark outside. She rolled over in bed and squinted at the battery-operated clock. Six a.m. Most days, she was up by now, but she'd allowed herself the luxury of sleeping in since it'd been after one in the morgen when she'd gone to bed. After all, as long as she was up and had the store open by eight, who would know?

It was probably Naomi. She always started baking a lot earlier than this. And she hadn't been at the hospital last nacht.

The thumping sounded again as Agnes shrugged into her pink robe and stuck her feet into her slippers. She shuffled out of her bedroom and down the hallway to the back door, and peeked out the tiny window.

Bishop Miah stood there, holding his hat in place due to the high wind.

More bad news?

Agnes's stomach clenched as she opened the door. "Is Timmy all right?"

Frowning, the bishop thrust a note at her. There was a desperate look in his eyes. "He's gone. Found this on the table this morgen when I got home from the hospital."

"Timmy's...gone?" She reached for the wall to steady herself.

"Timmy's fine. He'll be released sometime today." The bishop's eyebrows drew together.

"Then…who's gone?" It was too early for this. Agnes blinked at him. Why couldn't he stop talking in riddles?

"Isaac. He left."

"Left?"

"Must you repeat everything I say?" Bishop Miah huffed. "Isaac. He packed his bags and left."

Ach. Pain sliced through her. "But…he just got back yesterday. Another auction? For how long?"

"Read the note." Bishop Miah started to turn. "I need to get back to the hospital. Keep Gideon Kaiser in your prayers. Lizzie died after giving birth. He has a *bu.*"

Agnes's heart broke for Gideon, but her sympathy was swallowed up in despair and hurt over Isaac's sudden disappearance. She unfolded the note the bishop had handed her.

I'd say do yourself a favor and forget about me, but I need your prayers. I'll never forget you or the community.

Isaac

What? Agnes reeled. What did this mean? Why couldn't Isaac have said those three little words she wanted to hear? Well, she supposed he wouldn't have written "Ich liebe dich" in a note to Bishop Miah.

Wait. "I'll never forget you"?

She opened the door and dashed outside. "He left?"

The bishop turned around halfway down the alley and gave her a look that clearly communicated he didn't think she was very bright in the *morgen.* "You might need some *koffee,* Agnes." Then he rounded the corner and disappeared.

She might need more than *koffee.* He was *gone?*

She went back inside, locked the door, and turned around, leaning against it. Then she slid slowly, inch by agonizing inch, to the floor. Buried her face in her hands. And wept.

She wasn't sure how much time had passed when she finally pushed herself to her feet. Her throat felt raw, her eyes burned, and she had a pounding headache. She needed ice cream. Too bad they'd finished all the ice cream the last time Isaac was home. After the family tragedy, the Amish salvage-grocery would be closed, but she didn't want Englischers seeing her in this condition.

For that matter, she didn't want the Amish to see her either. She could almost hear the gossip now. *Her daed always told her she'd never marry. Can you believe she actually fell in love? Of course, he left her. She's unlovable. Insane. She was so gullible to believe Isaac Mast.* The imaginary whispers ran through her mind.

Unlovable.

Somehow, her body summoned up more tears. She stumbled back to bed and cried herself numb.

Sometime later, someone pounded on the back door again. "Agnes, open up. I know you're in there." It sounded like Bridget.

"Go away." The words were a hoarse, sore, broken whisper. Agnes didn't have the strength to deal with anyone today. Not even her best friend.

Agnes buried her pounding head in her pillow.

Somehow, Bridget secured a key. Because she now sat beside Agnes on her bed, rubbing her back and praying aloud.

"Delivery." A man's voice this time. From the front door.

Delivery? She wasn't expecting anything, was she? Her grief-clouded mind couldn't remember. Better not risk missing out on whatever it was.

Despite her tear-stained face and her aching head, she went to the front of the shop. Bridget stood there, propping the door open for a man holding a bouquet of red roses.

"Oh, gut. You're up. I have a feeling this will make you feel better." Bridget's smile flickered.

Disbelieving, Agnes stared at the flowers. "Are they from you?" She glanced at Bridget.

"Not me."

"Agnes Zook?" the man said. "Sign here."

She penned a signature that nobody would ever recognize as hers, then reached for the clear vase holding six red roses and several clusters of baby's breath. It was lovely, but who...?

She reached for the card. It was pink, with a white heart on the front embossed with the word "Love" in an elegant script.

You are loved. Still holding out hope for the future.

Love,
Isaac

Still holding out hope....

Holding...hope.

Really? Then why had he left town without saying gut-bye? Unless his desperate kisses were meant as gut-bye. She sucked in a breath that sounded more like a snort, and shut the door.

Hope or nein hope, she had a business to run and she'd already spent most of the morgen in bed.

Hope.

You are loved.

Ach, Isaac.

She locked the door, then carried the flowers back to the kitchen, Bridget on her tail, and set them in the middle of the worktable. Next, she went to the bathroom and brushed her teeth before going to the bedroom to pull on a dress. She fixed her hair, pinned on her kapp, and returned to the kitchen to start her day...in the middle of the afternoon.

"Are you going to be okay? I need to go, but Naomi will be coming by to check on you in a bit." Bridget hugged her. "Praying for you. Hold on to that hope."

"Danki. Ich liebe dich, Bridget."

"Ich liebe dich, Agnes." With another flicker of a smile, Bridget went out the back door.

Agnes opened the refrigerator. And there, right where Isaac had left her mysterious packages the day before, was a box of heart-shaped cookies with pink icing from Naomi's bakery. And every one of them had the word "Love" written in italics with red frosting. And a pink Post-It note read, "From Isaac."

There was also a two-liter bottle of pop and the ingredients for home-made pizza. Another note: "From Isaac."

She wouldn't make a pizza for only herself. And who did she have to share it with? She'd save it for when Isaac returned back. Holding out hope...

She grabbed the package of pepperoni and moved it to the freezer.

And there she found an unopened carton of fudge ripple ice cream.

She caught her breath, pulled the carton out, and hugged it to her chest.

Ich liebe dich, Isaac Mast.

The jangle of Isaac's smartphone awakened Isaac from a restless sleep on the uncomfortable bus seat. He moved enough to pull his phone out of his pocket and glanced at the number displayed. He didn't recognize it. He sighed and pressed "Answer."

"Isaac Mast."

"Hello, Isaac. Bishop Miah here."

"Jah, I'm running away. What else could I do?" Isaac rolled his eyes. "How'd you get my number?"

"You left it on my answering machine when you called the first time. I don't clear my messages very often. Gut thing, ain't so?"

Isaac tried to stretch while still holding the phone to his ear. He smothered a yawn.

After another moment of silence, the bishop spoke again. "Running from your problems is a race you'll never win."

"Did you call to lecture me?" Isaac immediately cringed, realizing how rude he probably sounded. Still, the truth hit a little too close to home.

"Nein. Wanted to tell you that Timmy will live. And that your brother is aware that you saved Timmy's life."

Isaac chuckled bitterly. "I'm the one who bought the shellfish that threatened his life in the first place."

"You didn't know. Jenny insisted Timmy wasn't allergic to anything. Now we all know that he is."

Isaac shrugged. He was glad for Timmy's sake that the allergy had become known, but he couldn't shake his sense of guilt, or the certainty that Jenny and Sam would never again trust him with their kinner, even if the two of them were around to supervise. His heart broke at the thought of never being able to spend time with those three adorable kinner he'd kum to love.

"What about Agnes?" Bishop Miah asked.

"Will you finally let me marry her?" Isaac chewed his lip.

"Not if you're going to run away every time things go wrong."

"You make me sound like a coward."

Silence stretched for one beat. Two. Three.

Okay, Isaac got it. He was a coward. He shifted again.

"Gideon Kaiser's frau died yesterday," Bishop Miah said quietly.

Isaac frowned. "I'm sorry to hear that." He recalled the yell of agony he'd heard from the hospital waiting room. It must've been Gideon. His heart clenched in sympathy for man who'd lost the one he loved.

"Think on this: How will you feel when—not 'if'—Gideon realizes he desperately needs a frau and marries Agnes, not out of love but for convenience's sake?"

Isaac scratched his jaw. Whiskers poked the tips of his fingers. "You'd allow him to marry her for the sake of convenience and not me?" He didn't mean to sound so bitter, but he couldn't help it.

"If I'd allowed her to marry you, you would have used her, and then, as soon as your obligation to your family was over, you would've packed your bags and abandoned your frau."

Wow. That hurt. "You have an incredibly low opinion of me." But the bishop was probably right. At least, he was right in predicting how Isaac would have acted back then, before he'd gotten to know Agnes better. Before he'd fallen in love.

"Nein. I'm saving you from yourself. If I allowed you to marry her now, it wouldn't be for convenience's sake, would it?"

The bishop didn't fight fair, dangling Agnes in front of him like a much-desired treat, luring him home.

Home. It was true that home is where the heart is.

"Think about that," the bishop said quietly. "I'll talk to you later."

The skyscrapers of Chicago came into view as Isaac leaned to the side and slide his phone back into his pants' pocket.

It was hardly worth opening the candy shop during the day, considering how few customers had been coming in. Yet Agnes did have fudge to make, thanks to another large order from the television station and other orders that were placed via mail or voice-mail messages left on the answering machine at the bakery, where she shared a landline with Naomi.

She'd received a few packages from Isaac sent from various locations. One was a pink heart-shaped throw pillow with the word "Love" embroidered across the center, accompanied by a postcard from Chicago's Navy Pier on which he'd written, "Wish you were here. Love, Isaac."

Another was a glass Mason jar filled with sewn conversation hearts in different shades of pastel. "BE MINE." "KISS ME." "I LUV U." "MARRYME." "HOT STUFF." And more. They were sent in a box bearing a Tennessee postmark.

And a card that read "Miss You" on the front, postmarked in Florida, bore the handwritten message "I'll be back soon. Count on it."

It warmed her heart.

She woke up early the next day and started some koffee brewing. Some youngies embarking on a road trip to Niagara Falls, New York, were meeting in front of her shop to load their luggage into the back of a van. Agnes wasn't sure how many were going. Six, or maybe eight. They would want koffee for the trip. Or hot chocolate.

She listened to their excited chatter as she delivered steaming drinks in disposable cups to the travelers. Agnes would've liked to have gone on the once-in-a-lifetime trip, but she was holding on to hope. Maybe today would be the day of Isaac's return. As much as she loved receiving his unexpected gifts and notes, he couldn't continue this long-distance courtship forever. And she had nein way of reaching him because he seemed to be moving around at will. He might be in New York by now.

Ach. She sucked in a breath. Maybe he was in Niagara Falls.

With that faint hope, she ran out to wave the driver down and ask if she could go, too. But he drove away, paying her nein attention at all. One traveler in the van waved back.

Agnes sagged and returned inside her shop. She had a business to run and orders for Christmas fudge coming in every day. With Christmas only two weeks away, she really couldn't afford to spend any time away searching for Isaac.

He'd been gone for over a month. And for almost that much time, he'd been saying he was coming soon. Surely, he meant what he said. For now, however, he was keeping her dangling on the hook.

She was pushing through the swinging door to the kitchen when she heard sleigh bells ring. "Agnes?" called a quiet, masculine voice.

She spun around mid-push.

Gideon Kaiser stood there, his hat in his hands, with a hesitant, I-don't-want-to-do-this-but-I-must-get-it-over-with expression on his face.

Agnes smiled and stepped toward him. She should've provided a meal or something, but Gideon's sister and his parents lived with him; Naomi had assured her everything was being taken care of. Lizzie's mamm had also come to help out for a while. "How are you doing, Preacher Gideon? How's little Elam?"

He grinned wistfully. "Healthy and strong, praise be to Gott. He has Lizzie's smile."

"That's gut to hear. And how's your mamm?"

Gideon sighed. "That's why I'm here. She's been diagnosed with multiple sclerosis and can nein longer care for Elam while I work. Some days, she can't even get out of bed. Daed and Mamm suggested that you might be willing to marry me. I could court you this month, in hopes that Bishop Miah might let us wed in February. If you're willing."

She gaped at him. "Wed…? *This* February?"

Gideon frowned. "I know Isaac Mast was courting you, but Naomi said he's out of the picture now. It's been over a month. It doesn't matter to me if you still love him. I will always love Lizzie. You and I—we—could have a marriage of convenience. Daed needs a caregiver for Mamm and I need a nanny for Elam and…well, you're available."

Ach, jah. Those lovely words again. "Available." And "nanny."

Isaac had used the same words. *She was available.* Except, she was nein longer available.

She had the strongest urge to grab a pair of pot holders or a towel and flap it at Preacher Gideon while chasing him out of her shop, the way Naomi had done to the television reporters.

Instead, Agnes tried to think of a civil response. Isaac may have suggested they marry by citing her availability, but his recent actions showed that his motives had changed. And that four-letter word—the most important of the three-word phrase she longed to hear—kept showing up on cards, pillows, and other gifts that kept her holding onto hope. It was too soon to let go.

"Isaac is coming back." She hated the catch in her voice. "Soon, he said. Promised, in fact." There. She spoke with a little more conviction.

Preacher Gideon gave her a pitying look. "We could go for a sleigh ride Saturday. Naomi told me she would watch Elam. Think on it."

She said a silent prayer for courage. "Remember the Bible story of the brides waiting for their bridegroom? Some were prepared and others weren't. Isaac says he's coming back for me. I'm going to be ready for his return and I'm going to wait. As long as it takes."

Preacher Gideon gave her a wobbly smile. His eyes filled with something. Relief? He nodded, then turned on his heel and opened the door.

Another man entered. "Agnes Zook?" It was the florist with another bouquet of roses.

She took them with a smile, happiness flooding her. She resisted the urge to smirk at the preacher.

Preacher Gideon frowned. "He sends hot-haus flowers?"

26

A few days after another phone call from Bishop Miah, Isaac felt his phone vibrate in his pocket while he worked an auction at a small warehouse-type building in Florida. He ignored the incessant buzzing until his break, when he checked the call log and saw five consecutive missed calls from Bishop Miah.

He gulped as a multitude of worst-case scenarios played out briefly in his mind. Had something happened to Agnes? Or to someone in his brother's family? His heart thudded.

Whatever it was, he couldn't possibly be responsible, ain't so?

He hunted for a molecule of courage. Someone handed him a bottle of water as he walked outside for some privacy.

The phone buzzed in his hand. Bishop Miah. Again.

Something was definitely wrong.

"Isaac Mast. What's going on?"

There was a brief moment of silence. "Hello to you, too." Bishop Miah sounded amused.

Isaac huffed. The man wouldn't have called six times in a row if it wasn't important. "Hello. Hope you are well." The words grated. He wanted the purpose, not pleasantries.

"I've been better. I just got back from Niagara Falls."

Apparently, the bishop wanted pleasantries. Why on earth would he go to New York in the winter?

"I hope you had a gut vacation. I've got less than fifteen minutes before I need to be back to work." He strode toward a loading dock and sat down.

"You've got less than two months to get back here. Preacher Gideon asked Agnes to join him for a sleigh ride. His daed said they're looking for him to remarry in February."

Isaac's heart hurt. "Is that so? What'd Agnes say?"

"Gideon said she's holding on to hope you'll be back soon. Tell me it isn't false hope."

It wasn't false. "I'm trying to earn enough money for a down payment on some land. I heard her family's property was relisted for sale."

Silence. "I'm not sure she has many pleasant memories of that place."

"It's where she goes to talk to Gott." It was where they'd shared their first kiss. Kisses. She had pleasant memories. "I'm temporarily employed here until the regular auctioneer is cleared to kum back to work. He just had rotator-cuff surgery."

"And then?"

"Then I'll kum home."

Bishop Miah chuckled. "Home. I like the sound of that."

Isaac did, too. "I need to get back to work."

"Before you go, Sam asked how he could contact you. May I give him this number?"

A chill worked up Isaac's spine. *Nein.* He didn't want to deal with those emotions, the guilt, the condemnation. But if he intended to settle in that district, even on a part-time basis, he supposed he would need some sort of closure. "If you want to. Tell him to leave a message if I don't answer and I'll call him back." *Eventually.*

The bishop's sigh sounded like one of relief. "Hot-haus flowers, Isaac?"

Isaac chuckled. "I gotta court the girl somehow. Bye." He ended the call, then opened his water bottle and guzzled the contents on his way back inside.

During his lunch break, he would send Agnes another bouquet, whether Bishop Miah approved or not. On the card, he would include a Bible verse from the book of Jeremiah. *"I have loved you with an everlasting love."*

He'd nein sooner finished ordering the flowers when his phone rang again. Isaac glanced at the screen, then picked up with a sigh. "Isaac Mast."

"Ike, I'm so, so sorry," Jenny wailed. "I hope you aren't blaming yourself for what happened to Timothy. You saved his life and we never thanked you properly. You probably thought we were mad at you."

Isaac opened his mouth but closed it again at the sound of muffled shuffling and conversation coming across the line.

A second later, "Isaac, sorry. Sam, here. Jenny wanted to speak to you first. I'm sorry, too, for not reaching out sooner. We weren't aware of Timothy's allergies. The doctor said Timothy was lucky to have an onkel who knew what to do. We didn't tell you this, but Jenny was planning to make shrimp Alfredo like we enjoyed in Minnesota. She'd actually called the salvage-grocery store to order shrimp that morgen."

Isaac gasped. Jenny had been planning to feed her sohn the food he was allergic to. If Isaac hadn't prepared the meal that he had, Timmy would've eaten shrimp anyway, probably without Isaac's being there. Timmy easily could have died.

"We wouldn't have known what to do if we'd served shrimp and Timothy had reacted and stopped breathing. You saved his life, Isaac. Danki. Please forgive us for acting so coldly and seeming to hold you responsible. Won't you kum back home? Timothy's asking for his onkel Isaac. He carries the bear you gave him everywhere except to school."

Isaac stood taller as the heavy weight of guilt was lifted off his shoulders. "Danki, Sam. Tell Timmy I'll be home as soon as I can. I miss him, too."

"For Christmas?" Jenny must've grabbed the phone from her ehemann. Either that, or it was on speaker mode. "You *have* to be here for Christmas. For me."

"For us," Sam said firmly.

Isaac chuckled at Sam's attempt to rein in his frau. "Maybe not that soon. I have a job here and with travel time on a bus…nein. But as soon as I can."

⌒

January came with nein sign of Isaac. Maybe Agnes had been too hasty in rejecting Gideon, though he'd seemed immensely relieved by her decision. Not that she was offended by that. She couldn't imagine kissing any man other than Isaac, or loving another man with the same kind of intensity that he'd stirred in her heart, even though he had been gone more than he'd been around.

But midwinter's frigid temperatures and lack of sunshine seemed to freeze her hope, and now she fought despondency. She needed some sort of romantic light to brighten her future. Even her well-fingered cards and the frozen package of pepperoni weren't enough to lift her spirits.

Clearly, Isaac's definition of "soon" was much different from hers.

The shop door opened with a jingle of sleigh bells and Agnes emerged from the kitchen. She was surprised to see Jenny Mast standing there. Maybe she had news of Isaac. But the way she clung to him…. "Hi, Jenny. How may I help you?"

Isaac's sister-in-law smiled, though the expression appeared insincere. "How're you doing, Agnes? Any word from Ike?"

The question was like rubbing salt in an open wound. Agnes shrugged. "None to speak of." At least, none in the two weeks since she'd received the bouquet of flowers with a card that read "Everlasting Love."

Jenny's shoulders sagged. "I'd hoped…. Sam and I called him before Christmas and he said he'd be back soon and now Sam won't let me call him again. He says it's unseemly the way I 'fawn over' his brother."

He was right. Gut for Sam, putting his foot down.

"But he's like…a mirage, I guess. Something seen and so desperately wanted, but you just can't reach it."

Agnes frowned, puzzled. "I don't understand."

"He always held himself apart. Even when I played him and Sam against each other, Ike was distant. I couldn't figure him out and it seemed wiser to marry the more dependable, more steadfast man, you know? But something inside me still craves the excitement Ike provided and…well, I understand he'll never be mine and I did marry the better man. Sam almost died fighting to save us, you know? I love him. But I don't want you to keep reaching for the illusion of Ike. You'll never reach him. Nobody will."

Behind Jenny, the door opened again and Bishop Miah came in. Agnes smiled at him, glad for the reprieve.

Jenny didn't turn around. "Ike will never be yours. He's a wispy dream, fading from sight as soon as you try to grab hold. Find someone more dependable, like Preacher Gideon. He needs a frau."

"And I've heard I'm available." Agnes fought to keep her smile in place. Did Bishop Miah's presence mean he was agreeing with this assessment? *Hold onto hope….* She searched for her professional side. "Can I interest you in any fudge? Rock candy for the kinner?"

Jenny scanned the glass display cases. "Your candy is too expensive. You charge way too much."

"But it's worth it." Bishop Miah stepped up beside her and raised an eyebrow.

"I'll just have a cup of koffee. To go. It's free." Jenny flashed him a glance but otherwise ignored him.

Agnes wanted to shake the woman, but she wouldn't allow Jenny or the bishop to strong-arm her into giving up on Isaac. She poured the koffee and handed the cup across the counter. "Just so you know, I'm not available for free. I'm expensive but worth it. I'm not going to settle for someone I don't love."

"Well said." The bishop eyed the fudge on display. "Katherine and I really fell in love with the peppermint fudge you had for sale during the holidays. Can I place an order for some more? And give me a few sticks of the rock candy Jenny's kinner are so fond of. I'll bring them by the haus myself and tell them it's from Aenti Agnes."

Jenny snorted as she headed toward the door, free koffee in hand.

"Seems I need to have a talk with Sam about something," Bishop Miah said to her retreating back.

Jenny hesitated a moment but left the shop without a word.

At least she didn't slam the door.

Bishop Miah leaned closer to Agnes and lowered his voice. "Last I heard, Isaac was in Grand Rapids. He's on his way here. He asked that you plan on his company for dinner to-nacht."

Agnes couldn't keep from grinning. She knew exactly what was on the menu: pizza, salad, and pop. She smiled brighter as she looked into the bishop's twinkling eyes. "Pick out some fudge. It's on the haus. And then I need to close up so I can run to the store for something and clean the kitchen." Plus, she needed to make a deposit at the bank.

"You know what we like. But I insist on paying." Bishop Miah pulled out his wallet as she cut several slabs of their favorite candy. "You do so much. Katherine told me that you had meals waiting on us to defrost and bake when we got home from Niagara Falls a few weeks ago. I've been remiss in not mentioning our gratitude before. You've taken care of that woman's kinner for the better part of a year. Without pay. She should've considered that when she insulted your fudge. It's worth every penny you charge and more."

"Danki, Bishop Miah." Agnes blinked back happy tears at his support—emotional and financial—and the welkum message he'd delivered from Isaac, which implied his support of their courtship.

The bishop took the bag she handed him. "Danki. I'll turn the sign to 'Closed' for you. And tell Isaac that our door will be open for him, nein matter what time he gets in."

"I will." Agnes opened the cash drawer and slid the bishop's payment inside, then went to get a deposit slip and a zippered bank bag, her mind racing to plan out everything she needed to do before Isaac arrived.

Her steps were light as she hurried through her messy kitchen. She almost skipped on the way back to the front of the store. Isaac would *finally* be back in town!

She pushed the kitchen door open.

And stared into the barrel of a gun.

〜

Isaac had been hiking from the bus station toward town when a police officer pulled over and offered him a ride in the back of his squad car. Given the option of warmth and a quicker journey, Isaac had been glad to accept. Although, if any Amish saw him in the back of a police vehicle, tongues would surely wag.

Of course, tongues would really wag if he asked the police officer to cuff him and escort him into the candy shop, to present him as a prisoner of love. He grinned as he imagined how Agnes might react to such a scene.

The police officer drove into town, taking the bad roads slowly, and stopped in front of the steps leading up to the raised sidewalk in front of the candy shop. Then he got out and opened the door for Isaac. "Thanks for the ride," Isaac said. "I really appreciate it."

The candy shop door opened and a man stepped outside backward, a bulging bag in one hand, a gun in the other. The weapon waved as he shouted, "Count to sixty before you call the cops, or I'll kill you. Sixty. Got that? Out loud. One, two...."

"Take cover," the officer hissed at Isaac before leveling his gun at the thief. "Stop! Police!"

The crook wheeled around.

Isaac recognized him as the same guy who'd attempted to rob Agnes before. The time when Agnes had called Isaac her hero. He wanted nothing more than to be that hero for her again. But Gott was the true hero in this scenario. He'd somehow orchestrated the whole thing to have Isaac arriving with police escort just in time to catch the robber. He'd be her hero the way he planned for later this evening. Thankfully, the weather conditions were favorable.

Isaac wanted to run around the vehicle and up the stairs to rescue Agnes, but doing that would almost guarantee he'd get shot and possibly die. He got back into the squad car, next to his luggage. He felt like a coward, crouching behind his bag, but he'd rather not die today.

The man on the raised sidewalk opened fire, his gun still shaking. A bullet pinged the vehicle somewhere.

The officer returned fire and the robber stumbled, clutching his arm. He dropped his weapon and the bag, both of which tumbled down the steps.

Moments later, the officer had secured the man's wrists with handcuffs.

Isaac clambered out of the vehicle, grabbed his bags, and ran up the stairs.

And there was his Agnes, huddled on the floor in front of the glass candy case. Shaking, crying. But alive. And seemingly uninjured.

He dropped beside her. Reached for her. "It's okay. I'm here. The police are here. Everything will be okay."

"Ach, Isaac." Her tears fell harder.

"Shh." He pulled her nearer and whispered, "I am that hero."

27

Agnes sank into Isaac's embrace and let the magic of his touch glue her tired, broken pieces back together. She and Isaac had first met under similar circumstances, surrounded by broken glass and bullets and money floating around. Except, this time, the robber had gotten all the money into the bag...and had taken the bag with him.

She wasn't worried about the money. In fact, she was almost certain the police would return the cash to her, after they'd done whatever they needed to do with it. But, right now....

Right now, Isaac traced his hand over her back, rubbing it as he might a newborn boppli. He kept saying "Shh," and she realized that she was whimpering. But who wouldn't be? She'd been robbed at gunpoint.

And Isaac had somehow arrived in the nick of time. With a police officer, nein less. Amazing.

Only Gott could've arranged for such perfect timing.

I am the Gott who sees you. The Gott who hears prayers before they are uttered. Who hears silent prayers...

The Gott who loved her.

Isaac was back.

Isaac was back.

Agnes pulled away from him enough to free her hands, then pressed her palms against either side of his face. "Ach, Isaac." She looked deep into his blue eyes and leaned in close. Her lips brushed his.

"Ahem."

She pulled away, her face heating. A police officer stood just inside the doorway. Behind him were Naomi Kaiser and a few Englisch people who must've been in town at the time of the robbery. Couldn't they have waited until Isaac had kissed her?

Isaac stood up. "Later," he mouthed as he pulled her to her feet.

"I need you to tell me what happened, miss." The officer pulled a notepad and a pen from his pocket.

There wasn't much to tell. The robber had waved the gun at her and she'd said nothing. Just watched him through burning eyes as he stuffed the money from her cash register into his backpack. All her work, for naught. A silent prayer—*Gott, where are You?*—and then he'd backed out of the shop, his gun trained on her, ordering her to wait sixty seconds before calling the cops.

"The amazing thing was, Gott was right there. Watching. Working behind the scenes to make sure help was here when I needed it." She couldn't keep from smiling as she said those words at the end of her summary, Isaac standing beside her the whole time, his hand on her back in a show of support.

The officer slid his pad back into his pocket. "Thank you, miss. We're taking him into the station now. We'll return the money as soon as we process it and take some pictures."

"*We*"? She glanced outside. Multiple police cars blocked the street, their strobe lights flashing.

Naomi pushed past the officer as he exited. "Are you okay?" she asked Agnes. Then her gaze shot to Isaac. "You came back?"

He smiled briefly at her, then immediately returned his attention to Agnes. "But of course. I said I would."

And Agnes had believed him...most days.

"I'm fine." Agnes's hands were still shaking and she wished for something to warm them, maybe a mug of hot koffee to wrap them around. She went behind the counter and checked the carafe. It was almost full. She wanted to tell Naomi to get lost so she could wrap her arms around Isaac, but that would be rude. She needed to be polite. "Does anybody else want a cup of koffee?"

Isaac chuckled. "Who could pass up a cup of your koffee? It's the best."

"I doubt that." Agnes glanced at him, noticing his tanned skin, the glint in his beautiful eyes....

She shivered, wishing even more now that Naomi would hurry up and leave.

"Trust me. I've sampled a lot of koffee in my travels."

Naomi nodded. "Your koffee's just like your fudge. It can't be beat." She accepted the cup Agnes handed her. "Welkum back, Isaac. I'll take this with me and return the mug later. I'm sure you two would like some time alone. Bye." She glanced over her shoulder on her way out the door, a smile stretching across her face.

Isaac shrugged off his coat, draped it over the back of a chair, and picked up the cup Agnes had slid across the counter in his direction. "I noticed the sign said 'Closed.' Are you?"

"I was just closing up. The bishop said you were on your way and I wanted to go to the store for some things." Agnes poured herself a cup of koffee to keep from rushing around the counter and kissing him. She shouldn't appear too eager. Besides, he hadn't said those three little words yet. "And I needed to clean the kitchen before I made supper."

"I'll clean the kitchen. You can run your errands if you're feeling up to it. If you aren't, I'll go with you. I'm not in a big hurry to see Gideon, since I hear he asked you out." A muscle jerked in his jaw.

"I'm fine going alone. You heard about Gideon?" Who'd told him?

Isaac chuckled. "The bishop kept me well-informed. As soon as the shopping's done, I want to take you somewhere."

Agnes raised her eyebrows. "And where might that be?"

He chuckled again. "Go on. You'll see. Ach, and bring your horse and buggy back. We'll need transportation."

Anticipation shot through Agnes. She put her untouched cup of koffee down on the counter, grabbed her coat off the rack, and rushed out the door.

Wherever it was that he wanted to take her, she couldn't wait.

Besides, she hadn't gotten a kiss yet.

Left alone in the shop, Isaac peeked into Agnes's bedroom and smiled to see all the cards he'd sent her tacked to the wall, all the gifts he'd sent on display. He was glad he'd been able to do those things for her.

He went to the kitchen and opened the refrigerator to check for pizza ingredients. The pepperoni was defrosting on the top shelf. It hurt to realize she'd frozen it, but sweet of her for wanting to save it to share with him.

He had just finished cleaning the kitchen when Agnes returned. He wiped off the counter beside the now-empty sink and hung the washcloth on the edge as she neared.

"I still love the farm sink, Isaac. Danki so much for getting it for me." She opened the refrigerator and unloaded her groceries.

Isaac peeked and noticed salad ingredients, pop, and ice cream. Hopefully to go with the pizza he'd planned.

She smoothed out the sides of the canvas grocery tote bag and folded it, then turned to Isaac with a huge smile on her beautiful face. "I'm ready when you are."

"Let's go, then. I need to talk to you about something." He deliberately chose the same words he'd used months ago, hoping she'd pick up on the theme for the nacht. Words he'd spoken back before he knew her. Before he fell in love. Back when he was only looking for an escape route.

Her features fell with a look of disappointment. "Ach."

He fought to keep his grin under control. He couldn't wait to show her what he'd planned. Hopefully, she would be surprised and pleasantly so. It'd stung to find out Gideon wanted to court her—well, marry her—just because he needed someone and she was available.

But Isaac had done the same thing.

Jah, he was nervous. Would she reject him and send him on his way?

Maybe he should soften her up with a kiss. He eyed her lips.

Nein. He'd waited this long. He would survive another half hour.

He sucked in a deep breath, sent up a silent prayer, and reached for her hand. "Kum, Beautiful."

Agnes locked the candy shop door and hurried down the steps to the place she'd ground-tethered Wildfire.

"I'll drive, if you don't mind." Isaac climbed in, bent down to adjust the heater, then took the reins from Agnes. "I have a specific destination in mind."

"A specific destination?" She hated that her voice squeaked. "Are you taking me to see Sam and Jenny?" Hopefully not. She'd seen more than enough of Jenny already that day. "Because—"

"Later. Maybe tomorrow. I'm leaving my bags at your shop until I go to the bishop's after dinner. This evening, I want to concentrate on us. I really missed you." He took one hand off the reins and reached over to squeeze hers.

Us. What a lovely word.

Isaac whistled as he drove out of town on the familiar roads that led to the ruins of her old home. The lane had been plowed recently and at least two feet of snow was piled up on either side of the path.

Agnes's heart pounded. She didn't want to poke around in those memories to-nacht. *Nein, nein, nein.* But he drove past the gutted shell, following the tracks the plow had made, around the pond that she loved, and stopped. Someone had laid a foundation. Or at least had started to. Building supplies were stacked up, covered in tarps.

Someone was building here? In her special sanctuary? Someone else would enjoy the pond she loved? She'd wanted to live on this side of the pond.

She shook her head. At least she had someone who loved her.

Isaac climbed out of the buggy, then turned to help her do the same. But once she reached the ground, he didn't release her hand. The snow that remained wasn't deep enough to reach the tops of her pink tennis shoes and it crunched as she took a step. She smiled. She'd always loved the sound of crunchy snow. "What are we doing here? Whose land is it now? Won't they mind that we're trespassing?"

Why had he picked this particular place?

"Patience, Beautiful." He winked and then tapped her nose.

Agnes tried to be patient as they strolled through even more crunchy snow. But she wanted to hurry this along. To get to the gut part sooner.

"When I was in Florida, I worked for an auction haus. I wanted to earn enough money for a down payment on some land."

"And?" Was this land his? Hope surged. She bounced with anticipation.

"And…." He tugged her a little farther, nearer to the woods and the pond where she yelled at Gott. Where she'd had her first kiss. With Isaac.

Her heart was pounding out of control. *Jah, jah, jah…ach, Isaac!*

Then he stopped. "We're here."

She looked around. The pond on one side. A forest of trees on the other.

Pine trees. The Christmas trees that Gott Himself decorated every winter.

The setting of her dreams.

Her breath caught in her throat.

Isaac dropped to one knee in the snow in front of her. "The day we met, you said, 'Nein drop-dead-gorgeous, clean-cut hero is going to kum rescue me near a live Christmas tree while the snow crunches pleasantly under my feet.'"

Tears burned her eyes. He'd remembered that? He *was* proposing! Was this future haus theirs? "Is—"

"And I told you, 'I am that hero.' Ich liebe dich, Agnes Zook. Will you marry me and let me be your hero for the rest of our lives?"

She pulled him to his feet and wrapped her arms around him. She'd dreamed of this moment, but the reality was far better than what she'd imagined. Emotion choked her voice and all she could do was grab hold of her future. After all, she'd been waiting for him for months.

"Agnes. Ach, Agnes." Her name came out as a groan. "I'm going to kiss you."

His lips feathered across hers, tentatively, then he pulled back. His fingers trembled against her waist. His gaze caught hers, searching for something. Whatever it was, he must've found it, because with a soft moan, he was back in her arms.

Exploring. Demanding. Taking. But giving.

There was nothing and nobody in the world but Isaac and the magic he was working.

He started to pull away, but she whimpered and tried to tug him back.

He resisted.

Ach, Isaac.

"Is that a jah?" His half-smile quirked.

"Jah, jah, a million times, jah. Ich liebe dich, Isaac Mast."

"Gut. Because I got permission to marry you in February."

And then she was back in his arms, his sweet, addicting kisses inspiring all sorts of delicious new flavors for her fudge.

RECIPES FOR FUDGE AND ROCK CANDY
À LA AGNES ZOOK

Basic Fudge Recipe
Courtesy of Marilyn Ridgway

2 cups granulated sugar
2/3 cup evaporated milk
1/3 cup clear corn syrup
1/2 teaspoon salt
2 tablespoons butter
1 teaspoon vanilla extract

Optional mix-ins:
+ 1/4 cup cocoa powder plus 1 cup chopped nuts
+ 1/2 cup creamy peanut butter
+ 1/2 cup coconut flakes

In a heavy saucepan, mix sugar, evaporated milk, corn syrup and salt through butter and cook till it reaches the "soft ball" stage.
Remove from heat and allow to cool 5 minutes.
Add desired mix-in, along with vanilla extract.
Beat until creamy, then pour into buttered pan and allow to set before cutting into bite-sized pieces.
Store in the refrigerator.

Chunky Peanut Butter Fudge
Courtesy of Marilyn Ridgway

    1 7-ounce jar marshmallow cream
    1 cup chunky peanut butter
    1 teaspoon vanilla
    2 cups granulated sugar
    2/3 cup milk
    Pat of butter

Butter a 9 x 9 square pan.

In a large, warm mixing bowl, combine marshmallow cream, peanut butter and vanilla.

In a heavy saucepan, cook sugar and milk to the "soft ball" stage.

Pour sugar and milk mixture over peanut-butter mixture.

Stir until well mixed, then spread in buttered pan.

Allow to cool before cutting into pieces and serving.

Store in the refrigerator.

Peppermint Fudge
Courtesy of Laura V. Hilton

2 packages (12 ounces each) white chocolate chips
1 can sweetened condensed milk
1/2 teaspoon peppermint extract
1 1/2 cups crushed candy canes
Dash of red or green food coloring
Pat of butter

Line an 8-inch square baking pan with aluminum foil and butter the foil. In a saucepan over medium heat, combine the white chocolate chips and sweetened condensed milk. Stir frequently until almost melted, then remove from heat and continue stirring until smooth. When the chips are completely melted, stir in the peppermint extract, food coloring, and crushed candy canes.

Spread evenly in the bottom of the prepared pan. Chill for 2 hours, then cut into squares.

Reese's Peanut Butter Cup Fudge
Courtesy of Laura V. Hilton

> 1 bag (12 ounces) milk chocolate chips
> 1 bag (10 ounces) peanut butter chips
> 2 cans sweetened condensed milk, divided
> 6 tablespoons butter, divided
> 20 to 30 miniature Reese's Peanut Butter Cups or six regular-size ones broken into four or five pieces each

For the chocolate layer: Line a greased 8-by-11.5-inch baking dish with parchment paper.

In a double boiler or metal bowl over a saucepan of simmering water, combine milk chocolate chips, 1 can sweetened condensed milk, and 4 tablespoons butter. Stir until melted and smooth.

Pour into prepared baking dish and allow to cool to room temperature, then move to the refrigerator while preparing next layer.

For the peanut butter layer: In a double boiler or metal bowl over a saucepan of simmering water, combine peanut butter chips, 1 can sweetened condensed milk, and 2 tablespoons butter. Stir until melted and smooth. Pour on to the milk chocolate fudge layer and press pieces of Reese's Peanut Butter Cups into the surface. If desired, group candy pieces in a grid-like fashion for easier cutting later.

Allow to cool to room temperature, then refrigerate overnight or until set. Remove from refrigerator, lift out of the pan by the edges of the parchment paper, and cut into squares, with roughly one miniature peanut butter cup or piece of a cup per square.

Store in the refrigerator.

Homemade Rock Candy
Courtesy of Laura V. Hilton

1 cup water
3 cups granulated sugar, divided, plus a bit to sprinkle on a plate
Assorted flavors of powdered drink mix in small envelopes (to provide flavor and color)
Five or six craft sticks

In a saucepan, bring water to a boil, then add 1 cup sugar and stir until dissolved.
Once the sugar has dissolved, reheat the water and stir in a second cup of sugar until dissolved. Repeat once more with the third cup of sugar.
Set aside syrup to cool.
Put a small amount of sugar on a plate. Dip half a craft stick in water, then roll in sugar. Repeat and allow to dry.
Pour a small amount of each drink mix flavor you'd like to use into a separate glass. Fill each glass with some of the hot sugar water, divided evenly. Stir to combine.
Lower sugar-coated craft sticks into the glasses and allow to "grow" for seven days.

ABOUT THE AUTHOR

A member of the American Christian Fiction Writers, Laura V. Hilton has authored more than two dozen books. She is also a professional book reviewer for the Christian market, with more than a thousand reviews published on the Internet.

The Amish Candymaker is Laura's second book in the Amish of Mackinac County series; the first was *Firestorm*. Her last series, The Amish of Jamesport, included *The Snow Globe*, *The Postcard*, and *The Birdhouse*. Although not part of that series, her novels *Love by the Numbers*, *The Amish Wanderer*, *The Christmas Admirer*, and *The Amish Firefighter* also take place in Jamesport.

Laura's first series with Whitaker House, The Amish of Seymour County, consists of *Patchwork Dreams*, *A Harvest of Hearts*, and *Promised to Another*. In 2012, *A Harvest of Hearts* received a Laurel Award, placing first in the Amish Genre Clash. Her second series, The Amish of Webster County, includes *Healing Love*, *Surrendered Love*, *Awakened Love*, and *A White Christmas in Webster County*.

Laura and her pastor-husband, Steve, have five children and make their home in Arkansas. To learn more about Laura, read her reviews, and find out about her upcoming releases, readers may visit:

lighthouse-academy.blogspot.com

booksbylaura.blogspot.com

www.familyfiction.com/authors/laura-v-hilton

www.amazon.com/Laura-V.-Hilton/e/B004IRSM5Q

Welcome to Our House!

We Have a Special Gift for You ...

It is our privilege and pleasure to share in your love of Christian fiction by publishing books that enrich your life and encourage your faith.

To show our appreciation, we invite you to sign up to receive a specially selected **Reader Appreciation Gift**, with our compliments. Just go to the Web address at the bottom of this page.

God bless you as you seek a deeper walk with Him!

WE HAVE A GIFT FOR YOU. VISIT:

whpub.me/fictionthx

WHITAKER
HOUSE